New Fiction

France and an
Award. His boo
He is married
Tipperary.

Books by Mark O...

My Dad is Ten Years Old

MARK O'SULLIVAN

MY DAD IS TEN YEARS OLD

PENGUIN

PENGUIN BOOKS

Published by the Penguin Group
Penguin Books Ltd, 80 Strand, London WC2R ORL, England
Penguin Group (USA) Inc., 375 Hudson Street, New York, New York 10014, USA
Penguin Group (Canada), 90 Eglinton Avenue East, Suite 700, Toronto, Ontario, Canada M4P 2Y3
(a division of Pearson Penguin Canada Inc.)
Penguin Ireland, 25 St Stephen's Green, Dublin 2, Ireland (a division of Penguin Books Ltd)
Penguin Group (Australia), 250 Camberwell Road, Camberwell, Victoria 3124, Australia
(a division of Pearson Australia Group Pty Ltd)
Penguin Books India Pvt Ltd, 11 Community Centre, Panchsheel Park, New Delhi – 110 017, India
Penguin Group (NZ), 67 Apollo Drive, Rosedale, Auckland 0632, New Zealand
(a division of Pearson New Zealand Ltd)
Penguin Books (South Africa) (Pty) Ltd, 24 Sturdee Avenue, Rosebank, Johannesburg 2196, South Africa

Penguin Books Ltd, Registered Offices: 80 Strand, London WC2R ORL, England

penguin.com

First published 2011
001 – 10 9 8 7 6 5 4 3 2 1

Copyright © Mark O'Sullivan, 2011
All rights reserved

The moral right of the author has been asserted

Set in 10.5/15.5pt Sabon LT Std
Typeset by Palimpsest Book Production Limited, Falkirk, Stirlingshire
Printed in Great Britain by Clays Ltd, St Ives plc

British Library Cataloguing in Publication Data
A CIP catalogue record for this book is available from the British Library

ISBN: 978-0-141-33246-8

www.greenpenguin.co.uk

MIX
Paper from
responsible sources
FSC
www.fsc.org
FSC™ C018179

Penguin Books is committed to a sustainable
future for our business, our readers and our
planet. This book is made from paper certified
by the Forest Stewardship Council.

For Joan, Jane and Ruth – and in memory of Della

1

My dad is ten years old.

One evening last year when he was forty-two, he went jogging along our street. A quiet street leading down towards the river that passes through town. I used to like it here. Old three-storey houses, steep banks of steps up to the front doors. And lots of trees. And in the autumn, wet and deadly leaves. 'Worse than black ice,' the Guard said that evening, 'those leaves'.

So, he's running, my dad. He's wearing blue retro tracksuit bottoms. He's over six feet tall so they don't look too baggy on him. And one of his Zinedine Zidane jerseys. He has a collection of them. The club jerseys. The black and white stripes of Juventus. Real Madrid's white. An assortment of blue French national jerseys. That October evening, he was wearing his World Cup 1998 French jersey. His lucky jersey.

So, he's running. And he's listening to his MP3 player. His jogging music. The Undertones, a Derry punk band from the late seventies. Loud, catchy guitar riffs, a tearaway beat. And not angry Sex Pistols punk but, as he used to say, *joie-de-vivre* punk. Happy to be alive punk. Sometimes I wonder which track he was listening to when it happened. Like it matters. 'You've Got My Number' or 'Teenage Kicks' or his anthem, 'Jimmy, Jimmy'? We'll never know now because his MP3 player was lost in the chaos after the accident.

In my mind it's always 'Jimmy, Jimmy' that's playing when I think of that terrible day. His name is Jimmy. They told us not to call him Dad any more. It might freak him out. More than he's already freaked out, if that's possible.

So, he's forty-two and running. Clearing his head after another day in his workroom. Coming back from school, I'd look up at the first-floor window on the left where he sat when he worked and that smile would be there to greet me. It was like the sun breaking through on a cloudy day or a street light on a misty winter's evening. It was like he sat there all day waiting for his little girl to come home.

So. Running. On the return leg of his five-kilometre run out the Borris Road and along by the River Walk and back. Dad loved the river. When we were small, he used to take me and my older brother Sean for walks down there. We'd feed the ducks, big busy families of them squabbling over the bits of bread, but still floating away in convoy after the squabbling was done. We'd watch the swans drifting gracefully along the water. He'd get us to look below the surface to where their webbed feet paddled like mad. 'Looking cool is hard work,' he'd say.

He's zipping back through Cathedral Street now. It's getting dark and the cathedral clock is lit up like a yellow moon high above. Twenty to seven, give or take a few minutes. He crosses Blackcastle Bridge and jogs through the Town Square. Most of the shops have closed for the day and there's not many people about. He turns into the Long

Mall, passes the charity clothes shop, the rows of redbrick houses and, among them, our favourite sweet shop where he used to take me and Sean for treats.

It's one of those cool, old-style kind of shops. All dark timber and high shelves and old Mrs Casey, who happens to be our slightly peculiar next-door neighbour, shrinking a little more behind the counter every day. It's our kid brother's favourite sweet shop now. Except it's Mam who takes him for treats.

Tom, our two-year old. Also known as 'The Surprise Addition' shortened to Saddo by Sean. Also known as Snot – Sean's idea again, needless to say. Also known briefly as Zizou – Zidane's nickname – but only by Dad and not any more. Mam used to say Tom would end up with multiple-personality disorder, but she doesn't joke about stuff like that any more either. I wonder what we would have called the baby Mam lost a month after the accident?

What's Dad thinking about as he jogs by the shop? Some new angle for the series of books he was working on back then? That's what he did. Illustrated his own and other people's books for young kids. Like early readers, five- to seven-year-olds kind of thing. And he did freelance graphics for ad agencies. Logos for companies and organizations and such. When we were younger, he worked on animated films. We watched *All Dogs Go to Heaven* and *The Land Before Time* a hundred times to see his name come up on the credits, and he still did some work on cartoon shorts and other bits and pieces.

Or maybe he was thinking about some of the future projects he sometimes mentioned? A graphic novel, that set of books for kids with disabilities, some kids' books without texts he'd always wanted to try. That was Dad all over. Always wanting to move on to the next thing, always wanting to try something different to what had gone before. So, who knows what's on his mind as the junction into our street comes into view?

It's pure weird to think that I saw the kid on the bicycle maybe thirty seconds before our world exploded. I was in my bedroom directly above Dad's workroom. It was the last night of our school show and I was a bundle of nerves. Every year the final performance is filmed and released on DVD for parents who want to show off their little darlings – it's a joint production with the boys' school my brother goes to – or for those particularly sad little darlings who like to show themselves off. And I had another reason to feel nervous. Mam and Dad were coming that night. They'd wanted to come earlier and more often, but I wouldn't let them. I'm sorry now I didn't.

I can't remember why I looked down at the street at that moment. It was dark and the street lights were on. The kid on the bike was racing and looking back over his shoulder. There's a speed bump below our front gate that was put in after some joyrider crashed into the River Walk wall at the end of our street a few years ago. I knew the kid on the bike was going to hit the bump hard. He did. Then he went sailing over the handlebars.

At first, I thought he'd been racing some other kid, but the panicky way he scrambled back on the bike, his head snapping in the direction he'd come from, convinced me that someone was chasing him. Then he was gone. I waited a few seconds to see who followed him, but I heard the screech of car brakes in the distance and I thought, because there was no loud bang, he's just about missed getting wiped out.

I told Mick Dunphy about this after the accident. Sometimes I wish I hadn't. Like it matters why this kid, Clem Healy, was cycling so fast and recklessly? Now, I have to give evidence at the court case in October. Sean got right thick when he heard me tell the detective sergeant what I saw. Or what I thought I saw.

'Great,' he goes. 'Now the little bastard can blame someone else and he's off the hook.'

Dunphy calmed him down. He knows Sean pretty well. His son, Brian, and Sean are best drinking and, I suspect, hash-smoking buddies. Well, he knows about the buddies bit anyway. He dresses like a character from a seventies cop show, which is how he got the nickname Starsky. Leather bomber jacket, shirt opened down a few buttons, white sneakers and, worse again, white socks. He hasn't changed his hairstyle since about 1975.

Clem Healy has always denied anyone chased him that evening. So, I imagined it? Or he's too afraid of whoever was following him to say? The story around town is it had something to do with drugs. His father, Trigger Healy, is a well-known pusher and they say he used his fourteen-year-old son to move stuff sometimes. Still does, probably. He did the same thing with his older son, Sham, who ended up doing time in juvenile detention for handling ecstasy tabs. Some father.

So, running, thinking, listening. Dad's close enough now

to see the name plate of our street. He'd have seen the cars revving up at the junction to take off as soon as they got the green, but not the kid cycling like crazy on our footpath to avoid the speed bumps. 'Jimmy, Jimmy' or 'You've Got My Number' or 'Teenage Kicks'? Each song louder and faster than the last so it didn't matter which one was playing. Dad wouldn't have heard the slam and whine of brakes as the lights before the kid turned red, or the bicycle tyres screaming like a bag of cats to find a grip on the wet leaves along the path.

Then Dad turns the corner into our street and gets the flying missile of a fourteen-year-old kid, complete with hard helmet, into the forehead. He's thrown back and his head slams into the pebble-dashed gable end of the corner house, splitting his skull open. And he falls through the years like he was spinning down some sick time machine.

A few minutes passed, I don't know how many, before the whine of the ambulance siren reached me. I can't honestly say I knew straight off that Dad was in trouble. I heard the crunch of gravel on our drive and looked down. It wasn't Dad coming in. It was Mam going out. When she got to the footpath, she broke into a run. That was when I knew. I raced downstairs and out. Up ahead on the footpath, I saw some stranger kneeling and holding Dad's head like it might come apart if she let go. My memory blanks out after that. Dad's too. Except his never came back.

When he woke in the hospital he had a mental age of ten with no clear recall of anything that had ever happened to him. So far as the doctors and psychiatrists can tell, his memory is a broken jigsaw, the pieces scattered, too many of them lost forever. Much of the time, as Dr Reid at the rehab centre explained it, he's constantly bothered by the kind of dread you feel when you wake from a nightmare, but can't remember the details. He still doesn't know who we really are. Not Mam. Not any of us. He doesn't know who he was or is. And today Mam's bringing him home.

Sean's out and up to no good with Brian Dunphy as usual these evenings. Scooping pints of cider and playing pool in the backroom of Brady's Bar, no doubt. The Surprise Addition is asleep on my bed and snuggling up to his green plastic tractor. His fair hair's wringing with sweat after a couple of hours of jumping mad around the house. Some kids have mad half-hours. Tom has mad half-days. I don't mind. The thing is with little kids, you're so caught up in minding them, laughing with them, even getting thick with them, that you can forget what's bothering you. For a while anyway.

In the calm after Hurricane Tom, I'm at my window, but I'm not looking down at the street. I'm looking at my reflection in the glass. This pure loopy wig of orange-red curls on my head from last year's school show. And I'm humming 'Tomorrow'. I put on the wig every now and then to give Tom a giggle. Sometimes, it's the only way to make him laugh these days.

There's a car moving along the street outside. I don't see it but hear its slowing-down sigh and I know the car is ours. How weird is it that you get to recognize the sound of a car like the way you recognized your tiny brother's cry in a roomful of babies at the maternity hospital?

The car pulls into our short pebbled drive. I take off the

dumb wig and put on a smile. The kind you're never fully dressed without. I pick up Tom and he doesn't even wake. For a moment, I think how lucky he is to be so young and innocent. But, of course, he's not lucky. At least I had Dad for sixteen years. That's something to be thankful for.

Isn't it?

2

Dad's afraid. He stands with his hands hanging by his side in the hallway. His shoulders are hunched. He has on one of his blue French jerseys under the khaki green parka he always loved. Not the lucky 1998 jersey. They'd had to cut that off him after the accident. He's like a kid waiting outside the school principal's office for a ticking-off. For as long as I can remember, he's kept his head shaved, but over the last few weeks, he's let his hair grow again. The glossy black straggle of curls is dusted with grey and doesn't hide the long scar above his right temple. Nor does it hide the bald patch on top. His Zidane tonsure, he used to call it.

'Jimmy's here,' Mam says. I can see she's as gutted as I am that the house hasn't sparked some light of recognition in him. 'Isn't he looking well?'

She winces and I know why. It's so easy to slip into talking to him like he's a kid. But you can't exactly talk to him like he's forty-two either. So it's like trying to invent some new language in between.

'Hi, Jimmy,' I say and already I'm stuck for words.

'Awright?' His sweet cockney greeting stabs into my heart.

His voice is timid and shaky. Tom's forehead rests on my neck and I don't know if the perspiration is his or mine.

'I'll get the rest of the bags from the car,' Mam says. 'Is Sean here?'

'He's on his way,' I lie and silently curse him.

'Sean,' Jimmy says and brightens up some more.

Ever since we mentioned Sean, Dad's been asking when he can meet him. He knows nothing much about Sean except that he's tall and good at football and is into computer games and stuff. Mam thinks he's built up this big picture in his mind of some perfect pal. She's warned Sean about this and I swear I'll tear him to pieces if he doesn't play his part. I change the subject.

'Tom's tired out from jumping around all evening,' I say. 'He's getting to be a real handful.'

'Will he wake up soon?' Jimmy asks in a whisper. 'Can he talk yet?'

At the rehab centre Tom never made a sound. We didn't bring him often. The visits unsettled him too much, so he hasn't seen Dad for maybe two months.

'Talk? He never stops,' I say and then I suddenly realize I haven't kissed Dad like I did every time we visited him.

For me, everything was easier in there. The greeting kiss, the talking, even playing the games of matching shapes that helped him get back some of his hand-eye coordination or the child-like wordplay that got him speaking again. Our visits lasted only a few hours and not every day at that. It was like you always knew there was an escape hatch. I feel bad for thinking I needed one, but that's how it was. Now there's no escape for any of us. Except for Sean.

I kiss Dad on the cheek, but it's Jimmy I link with my free hand into the kitchen. I wish I could be the two-year-old sleeping through all this. Jimmy doesn't walk like he used to. He'll take a few steps that seem perfect. Then he drags the toe of his shoe along the ground for one step. Hemiplegia they called it at the rehab centre. The weird thing is that there's something really familiar about that walk and I can't figure out what it is.

'Are you hungry, Jimmy?' I ask.

'Yeah,' he says and I can see that the kitchen is yet another strange new world to him in spite of all the meals he's cooked here over the years in that 'Housewife of the Year' apron he designed and got printed for himself. It's got this drawing above the slogan. A bleary-eyed woman, her hair in curlers, a cigarette dangling from her lips. Nowadays, I wear it.

'What do you fancy eating?'

'Wha'ever,' he says but hardly pauses before he asks, 'you got any chocolate biscuits? And milk?'

'I'm sure we have. But not too many biscuits, OK?'

Damn. Now I'm at it. The kiddie talk. He lowers his head. He's hurt. The thing is Dad has put on a lot of weight. Before the accident, all the jogging and the five-a-side football he played twice a week kept him in shape. Now his stomach stretches the blue football jersey to its seams.

'Take off your coat, Jimmy,' I say. 'And make yourself at home.'

He gazes open-mouthed around the kitchen, and in my head I'm screaming. *Surely you remember something here? The cream-coloured Aga you baked brown bread in, the wine shelves you put up over by the door, the fridge magnets you were always buying*: 'You don't have to be crazy to work here – but it helps!' *and* 'Never do today what you can do tomorrow'*!*

'There you go, Jimmy. We're nearly out of biscuits.'

He's disappointed with the two chocolate rings on the plate before him. Mam sweeps in like it's another normal day coming towards an end. Putting the messages away, filling the kettle, talking for the sake of talking.

'. . . And the traffic wasn't bad until we got to Abbeyleix . . . but the petrol light was coming on and we had to leave the motorway and go into Urlingford . . . there's a nice new Italian restaurant there now, I never knew about . . .'

I don't know how she keeps it up. Dad follows her every word as though she's telling us something of vital importance.

People think Mam is cold, that she's too rational about what's happened. I've seen it in their eyes. But she was never the touchy-feely type. I prefer it that way, no matter what people might think of her. We never had to put up with that awful smothering-mother crack. She had her own life and didn't need to live every minute of ours. Her job as a social worker. Her passion for the choral group she sang with. Granny Rogan was the same. Practical, independent, busy.

Granny Rogan died when I was eight. I didn't know her very well. She'd moved to New York years before when her husband passed away. I saw her maybe three or four times in my life. Mam went over to New York a few times, but didn't like the man her mother lived with. He was way too loud and right wing for Mam's liking. She and her mother agreed to disagree. Granny Rogan got on with her life and Mam got on with hers. That's Mam all over.

But I watch her move around the kitchen and I see the change in her. She never did anything fancy with her long blonde hair and was never one for pots of make-up or expensive clothes. She didn't need them. Now, though, it's like the skin is so tight on her cheekbones and forehead you'd swear she'd had botox treatment or something. She doesn't look real any more. Her face looks like mine feels. Stiff and sore from pretending to smile.

I remember she told me once about the November day they got married and how bitterly cold it was when they went out to have the wedding photos taken in some hotel garden and how her face was frozen in this mad smile all through the reception. And Dad chips in, 'To tell you the truth, Eala, I thought I'd married one of the witches from *Macbeth*!'

'I'm finished,' Dad says. 'I'm still hungry.'

'How many biscuits did you have?' Mam asks him. She brushes a few crumbs from the corner of his mouth and pulls her hand away quickly when she realizes what she's done.

'Just the one,' he says, dead serious.

I don't know whether to laugh or cry. He's a kid who wants another biscuit, I tell myself, not my father telling a lie. There's a funny side to everything. Isn't there?

'You're a chancer, Jimmy,' I tell him. 'You had two.'

'Maybe it was two small ones,' he says quietly.

His head goes down again. He's doing the wristwatch thing. I know from the rehab centre that it's a sign he's getting agitated and he'll have to be popped up with more drugs to settle him down. The oversized digital watch he timed his runs with was about the only thing that survived the accident. Now he won't take it off day or night. When he's stressed he starts beeping the little buttons and looking at the watch like he's late for an appointment or waiting for someone to arrive. He's got this hangdog look on his face, his gaze flitting from the watch to the biscuit tin on the table.

'Take another then, Jimmy,' I say.

Suddenly he pops up from his crouched position, spreads his elbows deliberately wide and sends the biscuit tin crashing to the floor. I'm still holding Tom so I can't stop it from falling and all hell breaks loose. The bang of the tin on the hard ceramic tiles wakes Tom. He takes one look at Jimmy and starts screaming. He clings to me so tight, he's strangling me. Tom's screams startle Jimmy. He stands up and begins to back away.

'It's only D–' The word almost slips out. 'It's only Jimmy.'

'I didn't mean to,' Jimmy says. We've seen him throw wobblers in the rehab centre but this is different. This is home. This is where we have to live.

Tom's head comes up from my shoulder again and looks at Jimmy. He's recognized the voice, I'm sure of it. He looks up at me like I can make sense of all this. I can't. I hold him as tight as I can without hurting him.

Mam puts her arm round Jimmy's waist and gives him a squeeze and turns him away from the table. Her face is grey. Maybe all our faces are grey. That's what it feels like. We're the ghosts of the family who used to live here before the accident.

'Tom got a fright when the box fell is all,' she says and

steers him towards the door. 'Why don't we go sort your room?'

He looks back over his shoulder at Tom and me.

'They don't like me,' he says.

'Course they do, Jimmy,' Mam tells him, and they're gone.

3

Tom's sleeping again, at last. I lie beside him, my mind turning and turning as I listen out for Sean, ready to spring up as soon as I hear the back door creaking open. I had to read the same book three times for Tom. Not one of Dad's. I can't bring myself to look at Dad's books, never mind read them aloud. I doubt I ever will. Anyway, all of his books are in the workroom on the first floor and none of us goes in there any more.

All his stuff is exactly as he left it. The shelves of books. The antique wooden mannequin he bought in a junk shop in Waterford. The reams of drawings stacked on the floor. The architect's drawing board he worked on. The big ceramic beer mug he kept his pens and memory sticks and stuff in. A motto encircles it. *What goes around, comes around*. The high swivel chair that was like a carnival ride for me when I was a kid. His last, unfinished drawing is still pinned to the board. Terry the Tank.

Terry's an army tank who doesn't want to go to war any more. He wants to go play with the elephants instead. So he pretends to be an elephant. In the earlier books, he'd pretended to be a giraffe, a teapot, an ostrich. In each book he gets sussed out and rejected. The message being, of course, that he has to learn to be himself. Dad's having to learn that all over again too. He's come a long way.

At first, they told us he might never come out of the coma. After two weeks, we began to believe them. And terrible as it was to see him lying there in Intensive Care, hooked up to all kinds of monitors and drips, it was still him. Still our dad. Still forty-two years old. When you saw the flicker of his eyelids every now and then, you could believe that he was still in there, dreaming up new ideas. Then they told us that if he did wake he might be brain-damaged. We didn't believe them. Or only Sean did. Sean was tearing himself apart and we knew why. Like we don't all have regrets, Sean?

Long before the accident, I was well over the little girlie thing of believing in the perfect father. Secretly, though, I liked the fact that Dad was different. He didn't have some run-of-the-mill job for one thing. In looks and colouring he was different too. Dark-eyed and sallow-skinned, it was easy to believe as he did that his roots lay in North Africa. And he was so laid-back with that breezy *Eastenders* accent we'd tease him about while he mimicked our flat Tipperary accent and the phrases we use – 'fair lousy' and 'pure gutted' – that he found so hilarious. Sometimes he seemed more like an older brother than a father.

He told me once that he wrote those books of his because, inside, he was still too much of a kid to write anything else. When I think of that now, I so wish I'd asked him more about his childhood. It wasn't exactly a no-go area. He'd tell me funny stuff that happened to him, but there was never a mention of unhappiness and there must have been a lot of that. Never knowing who his father was, having little or no memory of his mother, who died when he was five years old, living in foster care and, at sixteen, making his own way in the world with no one to help him. Why didn't I dig deeper? Maybe I didn't want to risk losing that jokey, easy-going relationship we had. I knew I was lucky.

'I wish my dad would loosen up,' my friend Jill said once. 'And be more like yours.' In fairness she had good reason. Her dad's a religious nut and a bit of a tyrant.

'We fight too, believe me,' I said.

And we did, though I never had one real stand-up row with him. Just the usual stuff. Like me looking to get a picture phone when they first came out because someone in my class had one, or wanting to go to the over-sixteen night club when I was fourteen. Or the teasing he got up to. He was always at it. In the weeks coming up to last year's school show he drove me demented singing 'Tomorrow' at me, lisping the s's and rolling the r's. I'd get so thick but I'd never totally lose it. I knew he was messing and not sneering. Sean didn't have my patience. The night before the accident he exploded. And for the dumbest reason you could imagine that had nothing at all to do with Dad. Unrequited love.

Somehow, the Surprise Addition had managed to get hold of Sean's mobile in the kitchen and took it under the table with him. Sean and me were in the sitting room watching a Champions League match on TV with Dad. So Tom had a good chew on the mobile, mashed up the keys and cracked the screen before dumping it on the ground and toddling off to wreck something else. When Sean eventually found the phone and recognized the little teeth-marks, he went ballistic.

First he blamed Mam for letting Tom take the mobile. Patient as ever, she promised to get Sean a new mobile, but he was shouting by now.

'But I can't get any texts tonight. And I can't send any. And all my numbers might be wiped.'

'We'll get the new one tomorrow, OK?' Mam said.

'That little snot can do what he wants around here.'

'Why don't we lock him up in the garden shed for the night, Sean,' I said. 'Would that ease your pain?'

'Mind your own business, Eala.'

Tom wasn't helping the situation. He looked out from his hiding place behind Mam and grinned from ear to ear. Then, as Dad came into the kitchen to see what was up, Sean whacked Tom across the face. And I mean whacked. Tom had only recently started to walk and I don't know how he stayed on his feet, the slap was so hard. We were used to the pushing and shoving that most brothers and sisters get up to now and again, but this was way out of line. There was a stunned silence like everyone was waiting for Tom's screams to convince us we hadn't imagined what Sean had done. Then he started.

Sean tried to escape from the kitchen but Dad blocked the doorway. Mam picked up Tom. His cries turned to gagging and then coughing and I knew he was going to make himself sick if he didn't calm down.

'Let me pass,' Sean grunted. 'I'm going upstairs to finish my homework, right?'

'Do you feel better now, Sean?' Dad said.

'What?' Sean said.

'Now you've hit a small child, do you feel more like a man?'

Sean tried to get by but Dad wasn't ready to move yet.

'Did I ever hit you, Sean?' Dad said.

'Maybe you did . . . when I was a little fart like him . . . maybe I don't remember.'

'You reckon you'd forget somethin' like that?'

'Let me out, will you?'

'No one gets so angry about a mobile phone, Sean,' Dad said. 'What's all this about?'

'Nothing.'

But I knew and I punished him with it. Fair lousy of me, I know, but the school show had me all uptight that evening too.

'There's this girl he fancies,' I announced. The girl in question being my best friend Jill. 'And today he discovered she's going out with his best pal. How dumb are you, Sean?'

He fired off a couple of obscenities at me, found a gap between the doorframe and Dad, and made his escape.

'I can't believe he could do something like that,' Mam said. She's always had this major thing about violence and aggression. I mean most people do but Mam's seen the damage upfront all her working life ever since her first job as a social worker in a refuge for battered wives.

'I'll talk to him,' Dad said.

Which he did. We'd all gone to bed before they'd finished talking up in Sean's bedroom. Or before Dad finished talking, more like. He's never said, but I get the feeling Sean didn't take the dressing-down too well. Next morning, the morning of the accident, he'd already left for school when I got up and before Dad drifted downstairs. That's really getting to Sean now.

Over the last few months Mam's tried to get him to talk about that incident but he refuses. She worries about his dark moods, his late nights, the fact that he's even packed in the football, which was his main interest in life before the accident. Whole days go by when he doesn't stir from his room and he's up there reading those dumb fantasy books of his and the collection of 2000 AD and *Judge Dredd* comics Dad passed on to him. He's never come to the hospital or the rehab centre since Dad woke up. So he hasn't watched Dad struggle to get his speech back. Or witnessed those faltering attempts to get a fully laden fork to his mouth. Or seen that pride on his face when he showed us for the first time how he could walk without a Zimmer frame.

'I'm doing good, in' I, Judy?' he said to Mam.

That's who we are to him now. Judy and Eala, his big sisters or something totally weird like that. And all this time we've acted out our parts. Always good-humoured. Always praising and encouraging him even when he turned narky on us in his frustration. Always making excuses for him on those days when he wouldn't talk to us or, sometimes, even look at us. But on those hour-long drives down the motorway from Dublin we'd blank out. We'd look straight ahead and hardly exchange a word, no matter how well or badly the visit had gone. Only once did we ever cry and that was the evening Mam told me about her miscarriage.

'You probably noticed the morning sickness,' she said.

I nodded but the truth was that I hadn't. *You're nearly*

forty, Mam, I was thinking. *What were you doing getting pregnant again, for God's sake?*

'I felt I shouldn't keep you in the dark about it any longer, Eala, leave you wondering.'

Two months gone she was when she miscarried at work the previous week. At the hospital they'd wanted to keep her in overnight, but instead she came home and carried on as normal. While she spoke in the darkened capsule of our car, the steadiness of her driving never faltered.

'It would've been too much to cope with anyway,' she said. 'We'll have our hands full when Jimmy comes home.'

The car sucked us forward into the night like we had no choice in the matter. I knew I'd lie awake later and, as I always did after these drives, feel I was still moving.

'I'm glad you told me,' I said. Which was about half true. Glad, yes, to release some of the tears that had been welling up in me for so long. But sad, pure heartbroken. And uneasy too because the miscarriage felt like a bad omen.

Dad's steady progress got me through the long winter months that followed. There was less of that awkward waywardness in his walk and his speech gradually became less slurred and hesitant. Mentally he was catching up too. Because words came more easily to him, he lost his temper less often with himself and with us. I started hoping again. In spite of Miss Understanding.

Mam likes Fiona Sheedy. I don't. She's around Mam's age but looks older. They both went to Trinity College at around the same time though they didn't know one another back then. She's a psychologist at the health centre where Mam works. Maybe it's because she's had to listen to so many lousy life stories, but there's a weariness about her and she dresses drably in lumpy jumpers and washed-out leggings, which I know shouldn't matter, but somehow it does. Since the accident, she and Mam seem to have become soulmates.

'She's trying to help is all,' Mam said when I let slip the nickname I'd given her friend. Miss Understanding. 'Trying to keep our feet on the ground so we don't, you know, expect too much too soon from Dad. And the reality is there's so little help out there, we're lucky to have her fighting our corner.'

But Fiona Sheedy smiles too much. She talks too softly. She listens too sweetly. Her head a little to the side, a wide-eyed gaze, her lips parted a fraction. A face that seems to say, *I understand what you're going through*. I feel like hitting her sometimes.

A text message comes in on my mobile. Tom stirs at the message alert but settles down again once his hand finds the green tractor that goes everywhere with him. I don't check to see who the message is from. Jill, I suppose. She was here earlier and I came close to losing it with her. What happened between Dad and Sean isn't her fault, of course. She knows nothing about the row that's made a bad situation even worse, but hers is another of the faces I want to slap these days. It doesn't help that, for her, life is a game of *Snap*. I used to find it funny. I'd get a cold and she'd get flu symptoms. I'd get indigestion and she'd get suspected appendicitis. Now she's got a big tragedy of her own to rival mine. Her nineteen-year-old sister Win has had a baby and her parents are not happy campers. Like I'm supposed to care?

Another text rings in. Maybe it's Sean, I'm thinking. It's not. It's Jill again. I don't open her messages. I check the time. Nine o'clock and still no sign of him. Maybe he's out there somewhere, wearing a flowing cape and Y-fronts over a pair of tights like one of his comic-book heroes, saving the universe from destruction. The Boy Wonder. Wondering where he's going.

4

Half past ten. I head back downstairs. Mam and Dad are talking in the basement room below. I don't hear what they're saying. I close my eyes and try to pretend it's a normal, adult conversation, but I can't. All I can hear is the echo of Jimmy saying, 'They don't like me.' *Only a kid*, I tell myself, *and kids forget these things quickly, don't they?* Especially after they discover all the joys of a new room. The TV, the Xbox, the CD player, the treadmill exercise machine and all the rest.

It's a half-basement, really. Some of it below ground, the rest above. So, it's not like a dungeon or anything. Still, we hated the idea at first. The occupational therapist who came to give advice on Dad's 'living arrangements' reckoned it was the biggest space available and it is.

Our house looks big from the outside but the rooms are actually small and it's all a bit of a jumble with little stairs all over the place. The basement is one big open-plan space with windows to the front and back, and a door out to the garden. It's actually the brightest room in the house and was more or less ready for use before the accident. And how weird is this? Dad fixed up the room himself.

'I'm going stale in that workroom up there. I need a change of scene,' he announced one day last summer. 'So it's either the basement or Paris!'

'I'll book you a flight on the Internet,' I said.

'And I'll buy you a guidebook,' Mam added.

'Ha, ha. We're all very witty, aren't we?'

For three months Dad spent every spare minute down there. He knocked out a partition wall and dry-lined the outer walls. He put in a small shower room in the corner. Sean helped with the heavy work and I did some of the painting. Then we spent a few sometimes frustrating, sometimes hilarious days putting together the flat-pack shelving, and the new workroom was ready. But Dad wasn't.

He kept saying he'd move to the basement when he'd finished the Terry the Tank series he was working on. Usually he'd dream up a character, work up five or six ideas and be done with it after a few months. There were times when he'd slow down and I'd know he was struggling to keep the work flowing. He wouldn't exactly brood, but I'd notice him staring into the flames in the sitting-room fireplace for minutes on end. When I'd ask what he was thinking about, he'd put on his joky French accent and answer, '*Ah, les profunditées de l'existence!*'

But the problem with finishing Terry the Tank was down to a whole series of distractions. A couple of advert commissions came in that he couldn't afford to pass up and the deadline for a pretty major book he'd been contracted to illustrate was brought forward. Then everything got totally complicated when his computer crashed and burned. Luckily he'd backed up most of his work, but it took ages to get sorted again on the new laptop. So, the Terry the Tank series will never be finished. Even if he remembered the book existed, he can't draw any more.

I start tidying up the kitchen. Below the chair Jimmy sat on, there's a layer of crumbs on the tiles. On the table his glass has left a pattern of milky rings like a wonky Olympic logo. I know it's pure stupid, but I'm irritated by the mess. After the accident, I went from being carelessly untidy to this freaky 'Housewife of the Year' – complete with Dad's apron. I can't sit still in a room if it's not spick and span.

Mam told me once about a client of hers who was obsessed with cleaning. She lived in a terraced house in Davitt Street that opened directly on to the public footpath. At least once a week, this woman would scrub the footpath like it was a floor inside her house. As soon as she did, of course, some young fellows would come and plaster it with mud or whatever. Sometimes at night, they even peed on it, but she couldn't make herself stop cleaning it again. Now I know how that woman feels.

Mrs Casey's German shepherd, Argos, starts up one of his howling fits next door. From outside the back door come hushed voices and scuffling noises. Sean and his boozing buddy, no doubt. I swing open the door and it's Brian I see first. He's tall, sleep-eyed and knows he's good-looking. His early-Bob-Dylan-style mop of hair is always carefully tossed. In the school show back in that other life, he played the part of my adoptive father. He looks worried. In the shadows behind him Sean is wavering from side to side and taking a leak against the back wall. I smell the cider.

'He hasn't had much, Eala,' Brian says. He's staring at my front and I realize I'm wearing the mad apron. How sad am I?

'Yeah right.'

Sean staggers over and falls against his best pal. The best pal who swooped on Jill while he was still thinking about it. Who's dumped Jill and gone through a few more dumb bimbos in the meantime.

'You're totally right, man,' Sean tells Brian. 'I have to roll the sleeves up and . . . and . . .'

'You're not coming in here until you sober up, Sean,' I insist, but he pushes me out of the way.

'I'm all right, man,' he says.

This 'man' stuff is always a sure sign he's pure twisted. Brian puts his hand on my shoulder like he thinks he's my new daddy in the school show again. Sometimes I hate being so small. I've had as much as I can take tonight. I take a swing at his face, but he catches my wrist before I make contact. He thinks he's hurting me and I let him think it for a few seconds more.

'Sorry,' he says and as he releases me, my bracelet catches in his finger and breaks.

It's a cheap string of blue beads, but I made it myself and I'm fair thick. He makes to stoop down and retrieve it, but I cut him off.

'Get lost,' I tell him and I slam the door in his face. Sean's dodgy on his feet. He holds on to the table. 'You're such a loser, Sean. Make some coffee for yourself. And brush your teeth. Your breath stinks.'

'What you go trying to hit Brian for?' he says. 'If it wasn't for him I wouldn't be here, man. We talked it all out. I know what I have to do. Where are they?'

His head is slack on his shoulders until he hears their voices and it's like someone's thrown a bucket of water in his face and sobered him up. His eyes are half crazed. He makes for the kitchen door and I follow, trying to hold him back. He's too strong for me. His voice is mild now, mellowed with hash.

'It's all right, Eala,' he says. 'I'm ready for him.'

'Is that you, Sean?' Mam calls from below as we scuffle down along the stairs to the basement.

'You're going to break Mam's heart,' I whisper fiercely.

'No way, man,' he mutters. 'I'm going to make her proud of me.'

A few steps from the open basement door, Sean starts singing out loud.

'*Jimmy, Jimmy!*' Then he does the da-na na-na-na of the Undertones' guitar riff and shouts again. '*Jimmy! Jimmy!*'

'Sean?' I hear the trepidation in Mam's voice and my stomach sinks.

We're in the basement room. Jimmy's gaping at Sean, his eyes filled with wonder and worry. Mam gives Sean a dagger look, but he doesn't notice. He goes over to Jimmy and wraps his arms round him.

'*Jimmy, Jimmy!*' he sings. His eyes are closed. It seems like Jimmy's holding Sean up now and feeling pure freaked. I give him a reassuring smile like this is perfectly normal and he has nothing to be afraid of. Sean releases him from the bear hug. 'Hey, why don't we play some *Premiership* on the Xbox, Jimmy?'

'Yeah,' Jimmy says. '*Premiership*?'

'Football, Jimmy, remember?' Sean says and then realizes we're not supposed to upset him by asking if he remembers stuff. 'It's this new game. I'll show you how to play. Bet you'll demolish me.'

Jimmy chuckles. He's found his pal.

'One game, OK?' Mam says and it's like her face is some kind of ceramic mask and it's going to crumble any minute into dust or sand or whatever. 'It's getting late.'

So we leave them to it. I don't believe in this new Sean and neither does Mam. We climb the stairs and it seems to take forever. We've had handrails put along each wall to help Dad climb. We need them now.

'I can't believe Sean's gone and got tanked up,' I say. 'Tonight of all nights.'

'I'll have his life for this,' Mam says.

She's shaking. She holds on to the banister of the stairs with both hands. She presses her forehead against the timber so hard it must hurt.

'At least he's cheered Jimmy up,' she says. 'That's more than I've managed to do.'

She lets go of the trembling banisters and pulls in a big breath.

'We're going to make this work, Eala. We have to make this work.'

Down in the basement, Sean and Jimmy are laughing their heads off. And I feel so stupidly jealous of Sean, I wonder if I should have tried the cider too.

5

When Dad was forty-two, he had lots of friends. His five-a-side football buds and people he'd worked with over the years. Mostly men. And sometimes I wonder if that's why all but one of them dropped out of sight during his months in hospital and rehab. Maybe if hospitals served beer the men might have done better, Mam said. Pub-talk is easier to hide behind than bedside chat.

Ten, maybe, twelve of them called to see him. A few couldn't bring themselves to visit a second time. Others stuck it out a little longer but eventually fell from the radar. I was there for some of these visits. It was pure torture. For everyone involved.

One guy's voice seized up as soon as he saw Dad and, when he went outside, he completely fell apart. Pat Dillon, a big, broad-shouldered builder with muscle-packed arms, thought he was speaking normally, but what came out was a whisper none of us could hear. The ones who could speak usually talked about football and when that didn't work, which was often, they were stumped. The fact that Dad had forgotten a lot of stuff about football didn't help. He couldn't remember the names of even the most famous players. Not even his hero, Zidane's.

'If they're my jerseys,' he'd asked us early on at the rehab centre, 'why's his name on them?'

Club names escaped him too. Real Madrid, Liverpool, Man U. Past games, who won what trophy in what year, and the complications of 4-4-2 and 4-3-3 and 4-5-1 or whatever, were a total mystery to him. But the real problem, when his old friends came, went deeper. Their visits left him in a sweat. Miss Understanding said it was probably 'the effort of recollection, the sense of failure and confusion that got to him'. But I felt sure there was more to it than that. In their presence, he was nervous, even suspicious of them. After each one left he'd clam up for ages. And it was an uneasy silence. If he heard footsteps in the corridor outside, he'd watch the door, full of apprehension.

'Why do those men have to come here, Judy?' he asked one day.

'They're your friends,' Mam said in her patient, this-is-not-too-weird-to-be-true tone. 'They miss having you around.'

'I don't want them to come any more,' he told her. 'Especially Martin.'

We couldn't figure this out. We still can't. Martin Davis had been the closest of all these people to Dad. In a way, he was sort of a crossover friend. He'd known Mam since their school days. When Mam and Dad started going out together, Martin was one of the gang they hung out with when they came here from Dublin for weekends. After they moved down permanently, Martin brought Dad along to the football club he played with and they teamed up alongside one another in central defence. People used to think they were brothers. They had the same sallow skin and black hair. After Dad's other so-called friends deserted him, Martin was the only one who stuck it out.

Mam must have felt fair lousy explaining the situation to Martin. It hit him hard. He drives around in a Mercedes and owns a pile of property but, as Mam said, you lose your best friend, you're a kid again. He called to the hospital less often after that. When he did call, he never stayed for long. He hasn't been to the house since Dad came home two weeks ago. Last night, Mam told me he's coming over this evening.

'Do you think Martin and Kathleen might have stayed together if Angie hadn't died?' I asked her.

'Who knows?' she said. 'He never got over Angie, that's for sure. Threw himself into his work so he wouldn't crack up. He was trying to forget the trauma of losing Angie, but maybe he forgot about Kathleen too.'

Angie Davis was born the same month and year as me. She died of leukaemia two weeks after her second birthday. I've no memory of her or of asking Mam and Dad where she'd gone to, which apparently I did over and over again. When other kids had invisible friends, I had Angie. Sometimes when I'd get into trouble over doing stuff I shouldn't, I'd blame her. I'd tell Mam it was Angie who told me to draw on the walls or bring worms in from the garden to swim in the sink or whatever. She tried to get me to invent a different invisible friend, but I refused.

For some reason, Angie has come back to me since Dad's return. I've actually built up a picture of her in my mind. She looks a bit like me, dark-haired but prettier – and taller, which wouldn't be hard. And smarter in every way. And wilder, more streetwise. I imagine her telling me to loosen up, lighten up, grow up. I'm sure she'd have told me not to go into something so uncool as a school show and definitely not to wear that mad curly wig in public. I see her eating up guys like Brian and spitting them out when she's had enough of them.

But Angie can't distract me now, I feel so wired up about this evening. It's like this is another test for Dad. Will he overcome his strange suspicion of Martin and of men in general? If it wasn't for the strides Dad's been making since he came home, I couldn't even begin to hope that he might. But, to be honest, I'm wired up because of his progress too. The thing is I've had little or no part in it. For months I've been imagining all I'd do for Dad, all I'd do with him, how I'd devote myself completely to him. Instead, Sean's doing all the work. And Brian, which really bugs me.

Every afternoon Sean's buddie comes in by the door at the end of the garden and heads straight to Jimmy's room. Which saves me having to avoid him. They play games on the Xbox and it's definitely making a difference to Dad's hand-eye coordination and his reaction speeds. We see it at the dinner table. Dad's still hesitant when he picks up a glass and stuff, but he doesn't spill or drop things so much.

And they don't sit in front of the screen all day either. For an hour or so most days all you can hear from Jimmy's room are grunts, groans, thuds and the whirr of the treadmill machine. They're working Dad back into shape. He's lost five pounds in two weeks. It doesn't show so much yet except that his face is less puffy and his eyes are more alert somehow.

Nothing I've heard about Brian Dunphy prepared me for

this. Not that I trust gossip. But when all the stories are more or less in agreement, you have to believe there's some truth in them. Because his father is a detective sergeant, it's like Brian has a licence to do what he wants and never has to worry about the consequences. Cider, hash, whatever you're having yourself. He's done his Leaving Cert. and doesn't have a summer job, but he's always flush. He also happens to be a notorious two-timer with only one thing on his mind and it isn't love.

When Jill came over to watch a DVD the other night, I told her about his being here so often. I don't know why I did. Maybe I needed a break from hearing about her sister's baby and how her parents, being so religious and stuffy, can't get their heads around the whole business.

'Watch your back, Eala,' Jill goes, looking up from painting her fingernails. She's no airhead, but she's so into pink and all the frills that go with it. 'He's on the loose again. He'll be sniffing.'

'Do I look like a moron?' I said and turned the DVD back on to cover up the blush that swept across my cheeks for no reason I could think of.

'I'm only saying. He hasn't gone out with anyone for a few months,' Jill said. 'Not that anyone knows of anyway. Then again, he's good at keeping secrets. I learned that the hard way.'

'Maybe everyone's copped on to him,' I said.

'I'm serious, Eala,' she said. 'You don't want to get involved with that guy.'

This is Jill at her most annoying. The drama queen. You'd think she was a thirty-five-year-old on her third divorce. I should be at the cinema with her tonight. We always went on Friday nights. Used to. It's a while since I've gone. She keeps asking and I keep making excuses and Mam keeps wondering why. 'Do you fancy sitting through some dumb romcom for two hours?' I ask her.

The truth is I never want to leave the house these days. It's like I have to hang around twenty-four/seven so I can snatch even a few minutes with Dad. Besides spending all his waking hours with Sean and Brian, he insists on Sean sleeping in the room with him. He doesn't like to be alone at night. I shouldn't blame Sean, but I have to blame someone.

'Do you feel angry about what's happened?' Fiona Sheedy asked me a few days before Dad came home.

We were in the sitting room and I was pretending to do a sudoku puzzle while she and Mam talked. It was one of those pure obvious set-ups where Mam is there one minute and then she's gone to check on Tom, even though I know he's fast asleep. I was thick at her, but I stayed put. Unlike Sean, who makes himself scarce every time Miss Understanding arrives.

'No,' I said. 'Why should I be angry?'

'You have every right to be, Eala,' she says, all sweet sympathy. 'Your dad is, well, in many ways . . . for the present at least, very much a young boy and you've had to deal with stuff that no fifteen-year-old should . . .'

'Sixteen-year-old.'

'Who do you blame, Eala? Who do you want to punish?'

'No one.'

'Not even Clem Healy?'

'He's some kind of special needs case,' I said. 'So Mam tells me anyway.'

This is another thing people don't get about Mam. How understanding she is – even of that little creep. She's told me that Clem is one of these slow kids with all kinds of learning problems. She's seen his file at the health centre. I don't care what's on his file. He ruined our lives. There's no excuse for that.

'Are you angry with Judy?' the psycho goes.

'No.'

'Do you feel angry with yourself?'

'Why should I be? I did nothing wrong.'

But I do. I do feel angry with myself. And with Mam. And with Sean. And Jill. And Brian. And almost everyone who crosses my path. These days, like Dad used to say about one of the guys he played five-a-side with, I'd start a fight in an empty room. But Miss U couldn't drop it. She had to go and ask one last lousy question.

'Are you angry with Jimmy?'

I got up and walked out of the sitting room.

6

Martin's been here three-quarters of an hour and Dad still hasn't made an appearance. Not a sound reaches us from the room below. Here in the sitting room, it's getting harder to keep the conversation going. Mam tries to look interested as Martin finds another memory of Dad to fight off the silence with. This whole happy-memory thing bothers her. She's told me so. For Dad's sake we have to look to the future and not get stuck in the past, is how she sees it.

I don't agree with her. I want to hear every last story about Dad. I disagree with her a lot of late, but keep it to myself. Whole conversations go on in my head where I'm defending Mam while Angie, the invisible friend of my childhood, is going, *How come she never cries any more, Eala?* or *How come she spends so little time with him?* I'll have to stop doing all that Angie stuff. It's too weird. Especially when her father's sitting here in front of me.

Martin's short and wiry and one of those people who's always got a foot tapping or a finger drumming or a cramp in his neck to stretch out.

'We were playing Clonmel Town in the last game of the season and we needed a draw to win the League,' he says.

'We're a goal down and Jimmy calls me over and . . .'

Mam's having trouble hiding her impatience with the fond recollections and I can see the silence from downstairs is getting to her. Martin gets the message.

'Sorry, Judy, I'm talking nonsense,' he says. He cracks a knuckle and it hurts him into more talk. 'We never had a cross word, Jimmy and me. All these years. No, we had. Once. But we put it behind us.'

Mam's high cheekbones dust over with crimson. It's hard to tell whether she's annoyed or embarrassed. This is fair awkward. The three of us sitting here trying to think of something to say that won't fall flat. Martin tries again.

'It's bloody shameful how little there is for Jimmy in the way of services,' he says. 'How's he supposed to get better without more rehabilitation and treatment and –'

'He's doing very well here,' Mam tells him.

Sometimes she has this look that's so, like, superior. 'Judy's *hauteur*', Dad used to call it. She's aiming it at Martin now and he doesn't know why.

'But if there's anything I can do,' he says. 'You know, maybe get people in. Therapists, whatever. I can cover that, no problem.'

'It's not a question of money,' Mam says. I don't get why she has to be so sharp with him. Martin has stopped twitching. 'Eala, can you see if Dad's ready to come up?'

Martin looks at me as if to ask what he's done wrong. I can't help him. I get up and head for Jimmy's room. As I go down the narrow stairs, I can almost feel the hushed quiet thickening below. I see the flicker of the TV under the door. It must be on mute. It's hard to believe I'm creeping around our own house like I'm afraid what I'll find next. I knock lightly on the door and go inside.

Dad smiles like he's glad to see me. I feel this surge of pleasure. *But hold on*, I'm thinking, *he's just relieved it's not Martin*. Brian, halfway out of his armchair, is like a thief caught in the act. Sean is so pale, he's actually a light shade of green.

'Awright, Eala?' Dad says. He's whispering. 'Is the Man gone?'

Sean's head goes down in his hands.

'The man is your friend, Jimmy,' Brian says and I cut him a mind-your-own-business glare.

'He'd like to see your new set-up here,' I try.

Dad thinks about it. He's fingering his watch. A little beep goes off, catching him by surprise. He stands up suddenly and all three of us are startled.

'I've got to use the bog,' he says.

He goes over to the shower room with that odd walk of his, the drag of his foot every few steps. At least he can't lock himself in. There's no bolt or key because he still gets confused, sometimes over the simplest things like unlocking a door. Once he's inside, Sean starts up.

'Every night he's going, "The Man is in the house." I ask him who the Man is and he says he can't remember. Is it Martin? "I don't know," he says. I ask him where the Man is, which room? "Upstairs." That's all he ever says. "Upstairs somewhere".'

Now that I think of it, Dad hasn't gone further up into the house than the ground floor since he came home. I can feel Brian gaping at my side-face and it's making me even more uneasy.

'Are you moving in here full-time or what?' I ask him.

I've never seen him blush before. I didn't think he did blushes, but he does do quick recoveries.

'Only if you want me to,' he says and instantly regrets it. His blush is gone to puce. He can't look at me and the Angie in me wishes that he would, wishes that he'd raise those brown eyes and see someone other than this hyper sixteen-year-old midget, someone he'd fancy.

'I'm helping Sean out is all,' he says. 'And Jimmy.'

From the shower room comes the sound of the toilet flushing. Dad's head appears from behind the shower-room door, a daft grin on his face.

'My bleedin' zip's stuck,' he says. ' I nearly caught my –'

'OK, Jimmy, we get the picture,' Sean says and goes over to sort Dad out.

The TV remote is on the floor halfway between me and Brian. I stare at it while Sean fumbles with Dad's zip. From the corner of my eye, I can see that Brian stares at the remote too.

'Has he left, Eala? The Man?' Dad asks when Sean's done.

'He'll be going soon,' I say. 'You don't have to meet him. Maybe next time?'

Dad shrugs. I move towards the door and Sean follows me out. He closes the door behind him. Down here at the foot of the basement stairs, it feels like we're at the bottom of a dry well. He's standing there, avoiding my eyes.

'What?'

'Will you sleep down here tonight?' he asks. 'I need a break. I'm knackered.'

'You mean you need to go out and get hammered. You and Brian.'

He leans back against the wall and it's true, he is knackered.

'It takes hours for him to get to sleep and that dog next door is driving me spare, barking half the night.'

'OK,' I say like it's a problem for me, but it isn't. 'Don't get twisted, Sean. Please.'

'No way. I promised Mam. Thanks, Eala.'

When was the last time he thanked me for anything? Did he ever? I can't remember.

'We're going to get Dad right again. One hundred per cent right,' he says. 'We have to.' There's this intense, scary edge to his voice that freaks me a bit.

'Like any of us is ever going to be one hundred per cent again?' I say, which surprises me as much as it does him. Sean thinks about answering, but decides not to risk his big night out on the town. He heads up the stairs and I follow.

'I'll go and check in with Mam before we head,' he says.

Near the top of the stairs he stops dead. We both do. The sitting-room door is a few feet away and the door's open a fraction. We can hear Mam.

'Life doesn't stop,' she's saying. 'We have to move on beyond the bloody blame game.'

Martin's voice is too low for us to hear. Whatever it is he says doesn't please Mam. There's a rawness in the air that cuts into my stomach when I breathe it in. Sean slips back down by me. Thanks, Sean.

'The court case?' Mam's a decibel away from shouting now. 'What difference will the court case make to any of us? None. None at all. They're going to send some messed-up kid to jail for something like that? I don't think so. And if they did, what good would that do?'

From the bottom of the stairs, Sean looks up at me. I'm thinking, *If that kid gets off scot-free, Sean's going to lose it*. I reach the sitting-room door as it swings open and Mam's shouting,

'Eala!'

Then she sees me. She pulls me to her and it's like falling against a wall, she's so rigid. In the sitting room behind her Martin stands helpless, his shoulders hunched. He looks like he might have done in the first shock of losing Angie all those years ago. A question carved on his face that no one can answer.

7

'Eala? You awake?'

I check the time on my mobile. Ten minutes past two. Sean's not home yet. Mrs Casey's dog is barking again. A hollow kind of bark with a whiny complaint at the end of it. Dad's been tossing and turning since we turned off the light at half eleven. And talking. Not exactly non-stop, but in little unexpected bursts whenever I'm about to drop off to sleep.

'Yeah, are you OK?'

'Why does Argos bark all night? Does he think someone's about?'

'No.' Three messages on the phone and I haven't opened any of them. Tomorrow. 'No. He's too big a dog to be living in a small garden like that. He should be on a farm or somewhere out the country anyway. He's like a prisoner in Mrs Casey's.'

'She's a nutter,' he says. 'Did you ever see such a mad head on a woman in all your life?'

'That's not a nice thing to say about anyone.'

'Even if it's true?'

'Especially if it's true,' I joke and wish I hadn't. Dad chuckles.

Mrs Casey's an odd fish. Mam grew up in this house and the old woman lived next door all that time and long before. Yet she treats Mam like a passing stranger. Her family used to have a big grain business in town and she's never lost what Mam calls her 'notions of grandeur', even though all that's left of the family fortune is the sweet shop. Her husband, Raymond, died shortly after she married back in the late forties and, to this day, she still wears black.

She's well into her eighties, dyes her hair the maddest of colours – jet-black or red or lavender – and piles on the make-up like there's no tomorrow. Because she's so thin, she can still fit into the clothes she wore as a young woman in the 1940s. Square-shouldered jackets and coats, frilly blouses buttoned at the neck, a little hat perched on her feathery hair.

Dad, the old Dad, had always kept an eye out for Mrs Casey. He was the only person she'd allow inside her house. If he heard a loud thud in the night he'd check, first thing in the morning, that she hadn't had a fall. He worried too about the electrical wiring in her house, but couldn't persuade her that it might be a fire hazard. He changed light bulbs for her, fixed her kettle when it got clogged up with lime.

When, as often happened, she'd close the sweet shop and not stir out of her house for a week and more, Dad would be especially concerned. Some kid from the Centra supermarket would leave a bag of groceries at her front door every few days and she'd take it in under cover of night. Dad couldn't rest easy until she emerged again and unlocked the shop.

Once in a while she offered some reward for his efforts. He'd come back to our house in fits of laughter with a little paper bag of chocolate sweets gone dusty grey with age or a bag of bruised and wrinkled apples. I used to be amused at her antics too, but not any more. Never once has she asked after Dad's state of health since the accident. So maybe his calling her a nutter isn't all that surprising.

The brush and sweep of his duvet as he moves seems weirdly loud in the quiet of the night. At least he's not as agitated as he was earlier when he found out Sean wasn't going to be sleeping in his room tonight. He wanted to know why Sean was going out and where he was going and when he'd be back. Mam tried to explain, but he wouldn't listen.

This was up in the kitchen. Supper time, we used to call it. We still do. In my mind, I've a different name for it now. Pill-popping time. And with every pill we get him to pop, it feels like we're slowly poisoning him.

So, pill-popping time, and I was already in my dressing gown and slippers. Tom was there too, sitting on Mam's lap. He's still wary of Dad but, at least, he doesn't lose it every time he sees him. In the space of a few weeks, my baby brother has morphed from a screeching, wrecking machine into a silent, apprehensive little boy. His usual sleeping routine has gone out the window. He won't let Mam out of his sight. When she does finally get him to sleep during the day, he'll wake as soon as she leaves the room and start to bawl. Not exactly bawl. It's a stranger sound than that, like he wants to bawl, but is half afraid to. What comes out is a high-pitched whine with no volume or spirit to it.

So. We're at the kitchen table. Dad refuses his usual glass of milk. He looks at the biscuits on his plate like he really wants to eat them, but is working hard not to let himself. Then he says,

'Has Sean gone off me too like the rest of you?'

'Course he hasn't,' Mam says. Tom's arm is round her neck as it always is when Dad's nearby. 'I mean none of us has.'

'Will you sleep down in my room tonight then, Judy?' Dad asks.

I try to pretend this is normal. You know, like listening in on your parents' private conversations is normal? I do a frozen wedding-day smile. A nutter smile.

'It's Eala's turn tonight, Jimmy,' Mam tells him.

He doesn't answer, doesn't look at me. Tom's forehead slams into Mam's cheekbone. I can see from the brief flash of anger in her eyes that it hurts.

'You'll be sleeping on your own soon like in the hospital,' Mam says. Her sharpness, that almost casual tossing back of her hair, bothers me even yet.

'Why do I have to sleep alone?'

'Because . . . because the doctor said.'

'Fecking doctor,' Dad had muttered and we couldn't help laughing. He'd always been a big *Father Ted* fan and loved annoying us with his fecking this and fecking that until we'd be screaming at him to give us a break.

'Stop laughing at me.'

'But you were doing that Father Jack thing,' I said. 'Remember? In –'

I stopped myself. But he wasn't bothered at all. He laughed.

'*Father Ted*,' he said. 'Will we watch *Father Ted*?'

'Tomorrow, Jimmy,' Mam said. 'It's pretty late.'

She was right, of course, because we can't let him get hyped up before he goes to bed. Dad wasn't happy. The best part of an hour passed before we got him to take all of his tablets.

'Eala?' He's off again. It's going to be a long night down here.

'Yeah?'

'Why did the kid crash into me? D'ye reckon the Man told him to?'

'The kid didn't mean to hit you. It was an accident.' I hate this. Him sounding so weird. This obsession with *the Man*. My tongue sticks to the roof of my mouth it's so dry. I need a drink of water, but if I get out of bed, he'll be up too and we'll never get to sleep.

'Why do I have to be like this, Eala?'

'Like what?'

I can sense him grasping hopelessly for the words to describe what it's like to be inside his head. A child trying to catch soapy, rainbow-swirling bubbles without breaking them. His long sigh is like the breeze whisking the bubbles further from his reach. *The words will come*, I tell myself. *Maybe not tonight but . . .*

'There's more than one of me,' he says.

He sniffles and I'm thinking, *Please don't start crying because if you do we'll never stop.*

'This bed is very small,' he says.

I sink back on to the camp bed. I close my eyes, which makes the room oddly brighter. I'm so tired. Argos is still barking and he sounds weary too. It's easy to forgive Sean for staying out half the night.

'Who's with Judy?' Dad asks and I don't like where this is going.

'Tom.'

'What if the Man goes into Judy's room?'

'We have a good alarm system, Jimmy,' I tell him. 'No one can get into the house. Can we go to sleep now?'

It was maybe three weeks before Dad came home that the bed was delivered. We were down here and some guys hauled in the flat-pack and the special orthopaedic mattress Dad needs these days. The delivery men were very friendly and helpful. It wasn't their job, but they put the bed together, unwrapped the mattress from its plastic covering and put it in place. I waited until they'd left before I said anything. I was blushing like hell. The sweat was ticklish under my arms.

'It's a single bed,' I said.

Mam sort of rocked back on her heels like I'd slapped her in the face.

'Eala, this is difficult to explain,' she said. 'I've talked about this with Fiona Sheedy and her advice is –'

'I'm sick of that woman interfering in our lives,' I said and left her there. If she wanted him in a single bed, she could fix it up herself, I was thinking. Pure childish, I know. But how could I even begin to say what was really on my mind?

Before Dad came home, I'd spent a lot of time googling Acquired Brain Injury. ABI for short. It almost sounds like something you have a choice in. Oh, yeah, and I'll have two euro worth of that ABI over there? I don't google it any more. Not after I chanced upon the statistics for marriage break-ups in these situations. I was shocked, horrified. Forty per cent of marriages broke up, according to one survey. Anything up to fifty-four per cent, another concluded. One site even suggested that seven out of nine couples split up in the longer term. I couldn't get my head around it. I still can't. How could you abandon someone when they needed you most?

So much for love. Here today, gone tomorrow. Better never to fall in love as far as I can see. Better maybe never to love anyone at all. Not even your mother and father. That way you have nothing to lose if they disappear or leave or go all weird on you. Maybe Dad was lucky to have had no memories of his parents. He was a happy man after all, wasn't he?

8

The sun changes everything and today is a scorcher. I was awake at eight and even though I'd only slept for three or four hours, I knew it would be the best of days. And I wasn't wrong.

We watched four episodes of *Father Ted* back to back. Dad was on a high and it's like his excitement set off fireworks in his brain. At first, he imitated the characters like he used to in the past. Father Ted, Father Jack and Dougal and Mrs Doyle. Then the fireworks started off in my own brain. He began to predict lines of dialogue before they were spoken. I called Mam from the kitchen. Tom was doing his pet monkey thing as usual, hanging from her neck. As she watched Dad, I know she was thinking the same thing as me. *This is the closest we've come to finding the man we knew.*

Soon Sean appeared, his green tracksuit soaked in sweat. He'd been out running. Not a trace of a hangover on him. It was beginning to feel like a proper Welcome Home party. And like every good party, the surprises kept coming.

When I saw Tom climbing down from Mam's lap with his green tractor in tow, I didn't give it a second thought. I was too busy planning ahead. Thinking, *We should try the music next*. The Undertones. 'Jimmy, Jimmy'. 'Teenage Kicks'. Then the books he wrote. Terry the Tank. Frosty the Fireman. The Flutterbyes and all the others. All the while, I was glancing over at Dad. He sat on the edge of his seat. Sunlight streamed through the tall bay windows of the sitting room and most of it seemed to fall on him.

Then I saw that Tom had moved his green tractor within a few feet of Dad. He gazed up at him. Remembering? Dad never took his eyes off the TV. Tom went closer. A few more minutes passed. Mam and me swapped disbelieving looks. Tom's hand touched Dad's and rested there. Dad didn't turn from the TV, but he began to stroke the tiny hand absent-mindedly.

Tom didn't stay long there with Dad. It was like he knew in his own way not to rush things. He wandered over to me and it was more like me hanging out of him than him hanging out of me, I was so grateful. The last episode of *Father Ted* on the first series DVD was coming to an end.

Tom went back over to Mam. He was getting hungry and bored. Dad wasn't chuckling so much now. He still watched the screen, but I could tell that his attention was drifting. The big watch on his wrist that he'd begun to fiddle with, seemed to be counting down the seconds on this happy morning. Then with perfect timing, Brian came to the rescue. He'd let himself in by the open front door and hadn't bothered to ring the bell. Which annoyed me, but not for long. He stood in the doorway, posing in his red Che Guevara T-shirt, a white plastic football under his arm. He seemed to look at everyone but me.

'Howzit goin'?' he said.

Dad was on his feet straight away.

'Awright, Brian? Are we playing football today?' he asked and I was thinking, *Don't let this perfect day go wrong.*

'A kick-around is all, Mam,' Sean said. 'No rough stuff, I promise.'

'Yeah,' Dad chipped in. 'No rough stuff.'

I could see Mam didn't want to be the party-pooper. Or not the only one. She caught my eye and I knew she was asking me to be her ally. I pretended not to understand.

'No tackling,' I said. 'And no pushing and shoving.'

'No sweat,' Dad said, surprising us again with an old phrase of his.

'Be very careful then,' Mam said. 'I mean extra careful, right?'

So, for the first time since the accident, Dad stepped out on to the Bernabéu. That's what we used to call the back garden. The Bernabéu, Real Madrid's home ground. And today, we could actually be in Spain, it's so warm. 'Other people have flower gardens,' Mam used to complain sometimes. 'We have a football pitch.' But she wasn't really into gardens and never had much time to spend out there anyway.

I'm taking a rest from the kick-about, sitting in the shade of the high wall at the end of the garden. I haven't felt so good in such a long time. Hot but not bothered, the warm breeze stroking my closed eyelids. I hear the creak of the garden door opening. I open my eyes and the first thing I see is Brian watching me from the other side of the garden. He looks away and calls for a pass from Sean and touches the football nice and handy towards Dad. A pram appears at the garden door, followed by a gushing Jill. She's making baby noises and gazing rapturously into the pram. Jill is forever asking me to call over to the house to see Win's baby, but I haven't done yet. I don't know why.

'Well, Jill,' I say like I'm glad to see her. 'You brought Richard.'

She looks up. She hasn't spotted Brian and Sean until now. She reverses the pram back out the door and I follow. To be honest, I'm relieved she's not coming in. Outside in the lane-way, she waits for me.

'You should've warned me Brian was here,' Jill says.

'I didn't know you were coming over.'

'I texted. Why do you never answer?'

'My battery's dead is all,' I say.

I know I should be admiring the baby, but I can't even make myself look at him. Jill hasn't noticed yet. She's forgotten about Brian already and is billing and cooing at little Richard again.

'Isn't he only gorgeous?' she says. 'Aren't you only gorgeous, Richard?'

'Yeah,' I say, but still I don't look.

'Do you want to hold him?' Jill asks.

'No.' I don't mean to be so abrupt. Jill stares at me. I look at the baby so as to avoid her eyes.

My cold heart melts. My knees go all wobbly. Worse again, my eyes fill up with tears and I'm thinking, *What's this about? Why does the sight of this lovely little fellow make me want to wail?* He's so tiny, so perfect, his little fingers moving excitedly, the lashes above his wide eyes so long and beautiful. I'm too choked up to say anything. It seems unbelievable to me that Jill's parents will have nothing to do with the baby.

'I'll miss him so much when Win takes him back to Dublin,' Jill says. She reaches in and tickles his nose, and his mouth chases her finger. 'It'll be so hard for her going to college and trying to mind him at the same time.'

'Maybe Win should've thought of that before she –'

'Eala?' she says, but I can see she's spotted my stupidly watery eyes. 'What's wrong?'

I stop myself from telling her what a dumb question that is. Instead I say, 'Nothing. Nothing.' And before I can shut myself up, 'Everything.'

She moves towards me and I back off. She gets the message.

'Things'll get better, Eala. They really will,' she says. 'I thought Mum and Dad would never come around to accepting Richard, but I can see them changing. Mum actually held him for the first time yesterday and I swear she's been smiling ever since. Win says this little fellow is going to bring us closer together than we ever were.'

She's annoying me now. *Maybe she should see Miss Understanding*, I'm thinking, *and get real about her expectations*. That's one of the psycho's favourite words. Usually preceded by unrealistic or unreasonable. The baby gurgles sweetly, sings a happy cry and his legs kick under the blanket.

The garden door behind me swings open. It's Dad. He's pure fascinated by the pram.

'Is that your baby?' he asks Jill and she reddens up.

'My sister's baby. My sister Win, remember?' she says, all flustered. 'His name is Richard.'

Dad comes round to the side of the pram. He reaches and tickles the baby's chin. I catch a glimpse of Jill. It occurs to me that this is the first time she's seen Dad since he came home. Pity and panic mark her expression and I'm thinking, *This is how everyone looks at him now.* I'm furious but, to be honest, I'm wary of what Dad might say or do next. I'm trying to think of some way to get him back inside the Bernabéu when suddenly he swoops in and picks up the baby in his arms.

'Mr Summerton, please . . .' Jill murmurs.

'Call me Jimmy.' He's mesmerized by the baby's busy hands and feet. 'He's a lively little fellow, in' he?'

Jill is on the verge of tears. She catches my arm and I want to shake her off, but little Richard begins to cry and Dad places him carefully back in the pram. He's disappointed with himself.

'I didn't mean to upset him,' he says.

'Oh, he's just tired, Jimmy,' Jill says, skittery with relief as she inches the pram back from beside us. 'He wants to be on the move all the time.'

But Dad's not convinced and he retreats by the door to the Bernabéu without a word of goodbye to Jill.

'I'm taking him for a walk up to the town park,' she says. 'Do you want to come?'

'No,' I say. I don't really feel like giving her an excuse, but I do anyway. 'I've to help Mam tidy up inside.'

'Tomorrow, maybe?'

'Yeah, tomorrow. Maybe.'

I slip back inside the door to the garden. Dad, Sean and Brian are passing the ball from one to the other. He's cheered up again. He glances over at me when he kicks the ball like he wants to see if I'm impressed and I give him the thumbs up. Sean kicks the ball back to him and he tries a step-over trick with it, but gets his feet in a tangle. My heart skips. Luckily, Brian is close enough to steady him before he falls. I change my mind about joining the kick-about again. Next door, Argos launches into another howl. There's something empty about that howl like he knows no one cares much about his predicament.

Inside the house is quiet. Not silent because I can hear the thud and bounce of the football from the Bernabéu, cars bumping over the speed ramps on the street out front, the clothes dryer speeding up and then winding down. I think of Angie. I imagine I'm Angie's ghost. Not some lost, uneasy spirit, but one that feels no pain, feels nothing any more, not even pity. I could stand here forever.

I hear Mam. She's on the phone in the kitchen. The hush in her voice is too deliberate. Hiding something. I get as close as I can to the half-open door without being seen.

'This is too much,' she's saying. 'I can't take it in. You're telling me what? That Jimmy . . .?'

It's the hospital, I'm thinking. *It's not good news.* I sneak a look inside. Mam's holding a letter in front of her. It's shaking. I can't see her face. Her voice goes dead flat.

'So he lied to me?'

The wall holds me up. I'm seeing stars.

'Look, Martin,' she says. 'I don't want to talk about this right now. I can't. I'll call you later.'

She ends the call and I scoot up along the stairs as noiselessly as possible. I go by Dad's workroom. It's still locked in case he overcomes his fear of coming upstairs and finds his way in there. Too much of his past to deal with all at once. Wreck his head it might. Like mine's wrecked now.

I close my bedroom door. I go to the wardrobe and take out the curly red wig and put it on. I sit on the floor in front of the full-length mirror that's inside the wardrobe door. I'm not singing. *Look at the nutter*, I'm thinking. A text message comes in on the mobile. Probably Jill, but I check it anyway for something to do besides call myself names. I'm right. But there's an earlier message that makes me climb to my knees. I don't know the number. I open it.

CAN WE TALK? SOON? BRIAN

There's a carpet on the stairs so you don't hear footsteps. What you hear is the tired groan of sagging timbers. I hear it now. I know it's Mam. Everyone's climb has a different rhythm to it. I wonder if she's seen or heard me sneaking up here. I hope she doesn't come into my room because I don't want to know what the phone call was about. She doesn't.

From the floor below comes the click of a turning key. She's in Dad's workroom. She moves about. Drawers slide in and out. Dull thuds like books falling. Or being thrown. I lie back on my bed, afraid almost to breathe. What is she looking for?

9

Our History teacher, Mrs Moore, is talking about the Irish Civil War. Families torn apart by conflicting loyalties, the killing of Michael Collins, the mutual savagery of men who'd fought side by side for independence only a few short months before. She tells us how her own grandfathers took opposite sides and, though they lived in the same town, never spoke to one another for the rest of their lives, even after one's son married the other's daughter. I like history. 'Fantasy for grown-ups', Dad used to call it. But today I have to pretend an interest. I haven't really switched on since I came back to school. Going through the motions is all I'm doing.

Weird how when you act normal for long enough, you actually do begin to feel normal again. Normal enough to get by anyway. It's like you put on the green school uniform and you're one of the crowd again and you can half believe your life is more or less like everyone else's.

At first, Dad took it badly when we went back to school after the summer break. In his eyes this was yet another sign that we were deserting him. Neither myself nor Sean were sleeping in his room by then. Mam hadn't taken her turn, which bothers me, though, in fairness, Tom wouldn't have let her even if she'd wanted to. He's on better terms with Dad, but still clings to Mam, night, noon and morning.

Maybe I really was deserting Dad. Maybe he sensed a new coldness in me. I couldn't get the phone call out of my head. What had he lied about? I don't know why, but all I could think of was that there'd been another woman in his life. Maybe I've watched too many soaps. It's not like he ever went out very much, except to go for a drink with Martin once in a while.

Besides, this isn't exactly some big anonymous city we live in and news spreads fast, especially news of affairs and such carry-on. But the Angie in me insists that he often went around the country doing readings or meeting people he was working on cartoon shorts with, and staying overnight, and sometimes flew over to London to meet his publishers or some ad agency people he did work for.

If I was bothered and bewildered, Dad was even more so. Back in his weird no-man's-land again. The night before school started up, he was dead quiet for hours. Then he said to Mam,

'Sean and Eala go to school. You take care of Tom and fix up the house and make the dinners. What do I do?'

'I've plenty of jobs for you, Jimmy, don't you worry,' Mam said.

'I should have a real job. Fixing things or making things or something.'

None of us had an answer. Mam got us through the awkward moment, but I could tell it took a huge effort. I can't remember what she said. It was like one of those black holes everything disappears into. You're there, you're listening, but at the same time, the words are being sucked into some part of your brain that doesn't think, that only hides things.

All through that first week of school, Dad refused to speak to any of us. When Brian came over he got the same frosty reception. Dad wouldn't play football, run on the treadmill, watch TV. Not even *Father Ted*. Mam had trouble getting him out of bed in the mornings. I tried a few times. He'd tell me to 'Feck off', which was funny first time around, but soon got fair annoying. Sean said we should leave him alone, which really got my back up. We argued every morning for one reason or another and I'd head off as early as I could, glad to be out of there for a few hours.

Then things began to change. We still got the cold shoulder from him, but he talked to Mam more and more. On the Friday of the second week back at school we were playing at happy families again and Dad led the way.

It was one of those grey days that couldn't decide if it was morning or evening. I dragged myself downstairs thinking, *Thank God it's Friday*. I was wrecked. I don't get much sleep these nights. So wrecked that the surprise staring me in the face at the kitchen table didn't register in my brain at first.

When I was five years old, I asked Santa Claus to bring me a tricycle. Dad often talked about that long-ago Christmas morning. I don't remember any of it, but apparently I woke them at six o'clock. I was tearful. I'd checked under the Christmas tree in the sitting room and – no tricycle. So Dad brought me back down. 'But look, there it is, love,' he says. I'm looking straight at it, but I'm in such a state of shock and pure tiredness I can't see the bright crimson tricycle. Only when Dad puts me sitting on it do I realize that Santa has delivered after all.

That's how it was when I sat down for breakfast that morning. Pure spaced-out from lack of sleep until Mam brought the teapot to the table and sat beside me.

'Look at that little scamp,' she said. 'He won't eat a thing for me and Jimmy's got him to finish the bowl.'

I looked up from my muesli and there they were. Tom on Dad's lap and both of them grinning at me. Sean arrived at the table and his usual sleepy-sour daze went all wide-eyed. And then wider-eyed.

'Hey, it's Rip Van Winkle,' Dad said.

When Sean was a kid, the Rip Van Winkle tag really bugged him. He never said anything at the breakfast table except, 'What are you looking at?' Dad, being the tease he was, could never resist stirring him up in the mornings. Now the greeting delighted Sean and he jumped at the chance it seemed to offer.

'We're playing football this evening, right?' he said.

'Yeah,' Dad said. 'Maybe I'll try the treadmill too.' He counted me in. 'Fancy a work-out on the treadmill, Eala?'

'No sweat,' I said and he thought I was hilarious.

Accountancy I don't like so much. Unfortunately Mr Lynch, our accountancy teacher, is a young guy with a really dull voice that suits the subject. Last class on Friday evening, it's guaranteed to put you to sleep. As Jill says, 'Great face, shame about the voice.' I wonder if she'll ever say anything to me again after our big scene in the lunch hall earlier. Every time Mr Lynch turns to the whiteboard, she's gaping at me like I have two heads on me.

We were down in the lunch hall for the mid-morning break. The noise was doing my head in. Squeals of laughter, screeching chairs and everyone speaking more and more loudly to make themselves heard. Added to which, Jill was in tragic mode. Again. Things were going pear-shaped in the O'Brien household. I was nursing a small carton of orange juice and wishing it was cider or beer. Or better still, a grenade I could clear the hall with.

'My dad comes home from work every evening and he's going, "Is she still here?"' Jill said. 'And this is, like, right in front of Win. He says he won't speak to her until she tells him who the father is. He's convinced it's someone in town but, no, "some fellow from college" is all Win ever says.'

I felt this tightness in my stomach and at the back of my brain. I didn't want to know about any of this. I heard Angie telling me what to say. *I don't care, Jill, I've enough on my own plate.* But I didn't want a row either, so I said, 'Why doesn't she go back to Dublin? Why stay and listen to all that crap?'

'She's got no money and the Lone Parent Allowance won't come through for weeks yet. Plus she'll have to find the deposit for a new apartment, which Dad refuses to give her. Then there's all the baby stuff she has to buy and –'

'So, let the sugar daddy stump up,' I said, my patience stretched to the limit. And it was fair lousy, I know, but when I saw her tears welling up, all I wanted to do was make them pour down. 'Or was it, like, a one-night stand or something? Was so twisted, she can't remember who it was?'

Which drew a few tears, but not as many as I'd hoped for. Jill shielded her eyes so as not to attract attention to herself in the crowded hall. I was shaking inside, fit to burst.

'Why are you like this, Eala?'

'Because you're always moaning about Win and little Richard and –' I didn't realize how loud I'd got until the volume in the hall suddenly dropped. But I didn't stop. 'What's it about, Jill? Are you trying to prove your life is more tragic than mine or something?'

'Eala?' She was staring down at my hands.

'What?' I looked down. I'd squeezed the carton so tight that all the juice had poured out over my fingers and on to the table and down on to my uniform. Only when I saw the mess did I feel the wetness. I got up and walked away through the giggling gaggles of airheads.

As Mr Lynch drones on, I tell myself I had every right to say what I said. Why did she have to go dragging me down like that, making me feel so uneasy, spoiling the pleasant turn our life at home has taken? Making me fear it won't last?

Every evening when I get home, Dad's waiting at the window again. Not his workroom window, but the half-basement window. It doesn't matter. That first glimpse of him is like a shot in the arm – and these busy evenings I need it. First off, Dad and me go for a walk. We turn left at the front gate and head towards the river. The junction where the accident took place is in the other direction. We haven't ventured up to the town square because Mam says he's not ready yet for crowded streets and traffic and all that. He always walks on the inner edge of the footpath and when we go along the River Walk that winds its way out from the town, he insists that I take the side nearer the water.

The Walk extends only half a mile or so and he's always in a hurry to get back. He has no interest in the swans and ducks any more. Most mornings he comes down here with Mam and Tom and he's bored out of his tree with the place by now. I tell him about school. He tells me about Tom's latest adventures – my baby brother is slowly morphing back into a wrecking ball again.

Then there's the treadmill running and the football out in the Bernabéu. The games are hotting up. Not exactly rougher, but more competitive. And Dad is starting to get back some of his old tricks. Like kicking the ball against the side-wall so it bounces out behind you as he slips past. He does it slowly, but we give him time and once in a while he gets it spot-on.

We switch teams every day. Two against two. Yesterday, it was me and Brian against Dad and Sean. It's like the old saying, *If you can't beat them, join them*. So I'm one of the boys now. And I keep it that way. I never answered Brian's text. I waited to see if he'd try again. It was like a test. I don't know if he failed or I failed, but there was no second text. The way I see it, he won't be hanging around for long more anyway. Sean's told me that Brian is off to college next month to do Architecture. If the buildings he designs are half as big as his ego, they'll all be skyscrapers.

After the football, we scatter. Brian heads home. Sean goes up to his room to study. It's his final year at school and Mam can't believe he's so focused already. I can't believe it either. To be honest, I don't care if he spends every evening in the fantasy world of superhero comic books, as long as he helps keep Dad happy.

So after the football I go and take over The Surprise Addition and let Mam have some time alone with Dad. Normally, the very idea of smooching parents would be too gross to think about. But ever since I saw them last week down there I've felt, I don't know, so hopeful. More hopeful than before anyway.

I'd been keeping Tom out of mischief, trying to get him interested in the Lego collection Sean and me built up as kids. We used to fight all the time while we played with the blocks. Tom didn't need anyone to fight with – he fought with himself. When he couldn't make the blocks fit together, he flung them across the sitting-room floor.

'Want my gween twactor,' he said.

I searched everywhere and couldn't find it. He'd soon be screaming for Mam, I was thinking. Then he went over to the window and pointed down to the drive.

'Gween Twactor!'

I warned him not to move from the sitting room and went out and down to the bottom of the steps where the green plastic tractor lay on its side. I glanced over at the half-basement window. The curtains were open an inch or two. I saw Mam and Dad lying on the bed, his head resting in her lap. She gently stroked the scar above his temple. His lips moved. *Whatever lie Mam spoke of on the phone to Martin can't have been so serious then, can it*, I thought? I wanted to stay there watching them, but Tom had started to knock on the sitting-room window above me and I went back inside. It felt like I was walking back into a different house.

The bell goes and the school day is over. I pack up my things, keeping my head down until I know Jill has left the classroom. I curse her silently for making me blow up like that, for leaving this sour taste in my mouth. For the first time in a week I'm nervous about getting home and finding Murphy's Law in operation again. If anything can go wrong, it will go wrong. '*La loi de Murphy*', Dad used to call it, of course. That was Dad. Laughing everything off with a grin and a shrug of the shoulders.

I make my way out by the yard behind the school because I've someone else to avoid. Miss O'Neill, our music teacher. She wants me to audition for the next school show. *West Side Story*. The school show usually happens in November, but next Easter is the hundredth anniversary of our school and the show will be part of the celebrations.

Miss O'Neill's a small, heavy woman. Her arthritic hip has left her with an odd, rolling kind of walk. She wears long black shapeless dresses brightened up with a different multicoloured scarf for each day of the week.

'No red wig this time,' Miss O'Neill told me the other day. 'And no cute orphans, Eala. Believe me, Bernstein was a real composer and this is the real thing.'

'I won't have time this year,' I said.

'There'll be no clash between the show and basketball practice this year, if that's the problem.'

'I won't have time for basketball either. Not for a while.'

'Well, you should make time,' she said in her usual abrupt, no-nonsense way. 'We all need time for ourselves or we forget who we are.'

I told her I'd think about doing the show. I actually like

Miss O'Neill's directness. Forget political correctness or sweet pretence. One day in class, someone called her Ms O'Neill.

'Mizz?' she said. 'You make me sound like some kind of insect. I'd prefer you didn't saddle me with that idiotic modern invention. "Miss" it is and "Miss" it will remain.'

As I head home, I notice that the trees along our street are putting up a longer fight than usual to hold on to their leaves this year.

10

'Not the fecking river again,' Dad complains.

We're standing at the swinging gate into the River Walk and he won't budge. It's a beautiful evening. A rose-red sky beyond the treetops, the rustle of birds playful among the dry leaves, the river bubbling across the stones of a makeshift ford. The old Dad would've been going, 'See that? Listen to this!' Then again, the younger me would probably have been going, 'So?'

'It's nice and quiet,' I tell him.

'Exactly,' he says. 'Too quiet.'

I link his arm. It feels as unyielding as a metal stanchion. Sometimes I forget how strong he is.

'Come on, Jimmy.'

'Why don't we go up to the town.' He points back towards Blackcastle Bridge and before I know it he's pulling me along beside him, his arm locked on mine. Up around the corner from the arched stone bridge lies the town square and it'll be busy as hell this time of evening.

'Judy's not going to be too happy about this,' I say.

As we draw closer to the town centre, he slows down a little. There's a long stream of cars and the footpaths on the bridge are busy too. He's looking more apprehensive. That drag of his foot every few steps is more exaggerated than usual. Now I'm thinking, *What if we bump into Clem Healy or his brother Sham or his drug-pushing father?* I've seen them around town a few times since the accident, but only ever in the distance. They make themselves scarce once they've spotted me. After each glimpse of them, I feel sick for hours.

'Let's go back, Jimmy,' I say. 'Sean and Brian will be waiting for us.'

A couple of girls dressed in our green school uniform are heading towards us. First or Second Years, probably. I don't recognize them. I realize I've pulled my arm away from Dad's. I feel pure rotten for doing that. He's a few steps ahead of me as the young ones pass. They're gaping at him like he's The Incredible Hulk or something. I'm furious, but for Dad's sake I don't say anything. I'll remember those faces.

At the bridge, he takes a sharp left by the old castle and walks straight into a young woman who's turning the corner. She's power-dressed in a pin-striped suit and carrying a designer briefcase. She's not hurt, but her pretty face is twisted into a weird mask that's half offended, half disdainful, like Dad has deliberately invaded her space.

'For God's sake, look where you're going,' she seethes.

'It was an accident,' I tell her.

'Yeah,' Dad says, fingering the scar on his temple. 'Wrecked my head, it did.'

I have to get him away from here, but he's too busy gazing into her pale blue eyes, which freaks the woman out and she breaks into a little trot. Dad turns to watch her go. Fascinated.

'She's got a fine ass on her, hasn't she?' he says and I'm dumbstruck.

He heads into the town square. I follow him, though my legs have gone to jelly. The footpath is wide, but he walks close to the shopfronts. So close that people keep bumping into him at the doorways as they emerge. He doesn't apologize. He doesn't speak at all until we come to the Castle Inn. He stops up. Thinking. Remembering?

The Castle Inn is the pub he and Martin sometimes went to. It's the only old-style pub left in town that isn't fake. Tobacco-stained wallpaper, little nooks and crannies, timber that's darker than its own shadow. Dad often talked about the elderly landlord, a Cork man, who spends his days dreaming of going back down to Clonakilty 'where I belong'.

'Wherever you hang your hat, that's your home,' Dad told him once. The words of an old song, apparently. But the landlord's a cranky type and answered sourly.

'I don't wear a hat.'

Which we all thought was hilarious when Dad told us. Things aren't so funny now as he stands here oblivious to the odd looks we're getting from passers-by. The effort of racking his brain shows too clearly on his face. God knows what the effort of trying to shut Angie up about that woman is doing to my face. *How does that feel, Eala,* she's saying, *having a dirty old man for a father?*

'Jimmy? We should head home.'

'Will we go in for a pint?' he asks.

'I don't have any money, Jimmy. Another day maybe.'

'No sweat,' he says. That old phrase again. He reaches into the pocket of his denims and takes out a ten-euro note.

'Where did you get that?'

His eyes go shifty. I know he's about to lie to me.

'I found it.'

'Jimmy?'

'I found it, right? In the Bernabéu. Yesterday. Or Sunday, was it?'

He gives a sudden start. There's this old wino heading towards us with his arms outstretched like he's Dad's best mate. He's wearing a quilted bomber jacket that's been slashed open in a few places. He has, maybe, four teeth, all of them splintered and nicotine-stained. Dad was always a soft touch for these guys. 'There but for fortune,' he'd say, if Mam or me got on to him for giving them money they'd waste on booze anyway. I can smell the beer from five yards off. And the stale vomit.

'Howzit goin', Jimmy?' the wino says. There's a peeling scab from an old cut on the bridge of his nose. It's leaking yellow gunge. 'I heard you got an awful rattle on the head.'

I try to get Dad moving, but he's planted to the spot.

'Do you remember me at all, Jimmy? Dick Russell, remember? Up on the left wing when we played soccer together? Remember the one I scored against Saint Michael's in the Tipperary Cup Final?'

'No,' Dad says and his voice is quaking.

Drunk as he is, the wino realizes he's put his foot in it. He searches his addled mind and finds another line.

'But you're looking grand, all the same. With all that hair, like,' he says. 'Are you at the books again? Have you any new ones?'

People have to steer round us in the middle of the footpath and aren't happy about it.

'Books?' Dad says and I have to call a halt to this.

'We really have to go,' I tell Dick. 'Sorry.'

'No bother,' he says. 'But you wouldn't have a loan of a few bob for a burger and chips, would you, Jimmy?'

Dad's hand goes into his pocket, but I pull him away. He's forgotten about pints and pretty asses. He looks baffled. When he looks baffled, he looks dumb. I don't want to think stuff like that.

'Who was that?' he asks.

We're back on our own street. There's a cold breeze blowing into our faces. The leaves are falling like crazy. It's like they're sniggering at us, like they're whispering, *Remember what happened the last time we fell, ha ha!*

'I don't know, Jimmy.'

'Why did he ask me for money?'

'I don't know, Jimmy.'

'What was all that about new books?'

'He just wanted to know if you got any new books lately.'

'Why?'

I'm at a dead end. At least we're near the house. He's trailing after me now, I'm in such a hurry.

'Is he the Man?'

'God's sake, Jimmy, will you stop asking bloody questions? I'm sick of it. And don't ever say anything like that about a woman again, do you hear me? It's revolting. Filthy.'

He's hurt. More than hurt. Wounded. Skewered.

'Forget I said that, Jimmy. Please.'

He's got on a dopey half-smile, half-grimace. It's like he's telling me he deserves what he got because he's some kind of simpleton. We're at the front steps of the house. He digs around in his pockets and holds out the ten-euro note to me.

'Will you put that back in Judy's purse?' A half-whisper that makes the scream inside me sound even louder.

'No sweat, Jimmy.'

He doesn't follow me up the steps. Instead, he goes around by the side of the house. I don't follow him either. Tom's green plastic tractor is on the top step. I kick it down on to the drive and the front wheels come off. I open the front door and Mam is by the kitchen door at the end of the hallway. She does this pure obvious, looking-at-her-watch, where-the-hell-were-you thing.

'Where's . . . where is he?'

'He went round by the back, what d'you think? He's run away or something?'

'You were gone so bloody long,' she says. Seething, she is. 'I was worried sick.'

Neither of us moves. Me from the front door. Mam from the kitchen door. There must be – what? – thirty feet or so between us, but I can see every line on her face. The smell of the curry dinner she's been making turns my stomach.

'You didn't answer your mobile,' Mam says. 'That's so bloody irritating.'

'I didn't bring it.'

'Well, you should have.'

It's like she's deliberately needling me. And two can play that game.

'We went up town, right?'

'You what?' she goes. 'You know we have to do this slowly, step by step and he's not ready to deal with crowds and traffic noise and all that yet.'

I cut her off. I have to know what he lied to her about. Maybe there was another woman after all?

'He wanted to go for a pint and he had a ten-euro note. I asked him where he got it and he lied to me. He lied to me. Does he lie to you too?'

Her eyes slide away from mine. She's looking at the family portrait hanging there on the wall. We had it done a few weeks after Tom was born. Sean and me aren't impressed at the idea and it shows. Sour faces on us both. The Addams Family. That was Dad's joke.

We hear the door of Jimmy's room below us open, an upward rush on the narrow stairs. Three steps at a time. Sean. He stops where the stairwell opens on to the hallway, halfway between Mam and me. There's a bitter twist to his expression and he aims it at me.

'What did you say to Dad? You've really gutted him.'

'I told him to stop asking me questions. I got thick, right? Like you never do?'

'Not with Dad, I don't.'

'What about the night before the accident? You and your mobile and your jilted-lover crap.'

'Shut up,' he says. I know I've got to him because his eyes aren't so much burning now as ready to leak. 'We sorted that out, Dad and me.'

'Sorted it out? Yeah, right. He bawled you out and you did a runner next morning so you wouldn't have to face him.'

'It wasn't like that. I had to go into school early. We had a game in Cork that day and the bus was leaving at eight.'

'So what was your big guilt-trip about, then?' Angie's telling me to shut up now too, but I ignore her. I want to lay into Sean and not stop until I break him. 'How come you couldn't even go see him in the rehab centre all those months?'

'Lads, calm down, please,' Mam says. 'If we can't stick together we might as well pack it in.'

A piercing howl from out back startles us. Argos. The second howl isn't from Argos. It's from Dad. Sean turns and races down the stairs and we're after him in a flash. The howling grows louder. From both of them.

11

I can't believe what I'm seeing out here in the Bernabéu. Brian lies slumped near the high wall between ours and Mrs Casey's garden. Blood pours from his nose. He's passed out. At the foot of the wall, one of Dad's sneakers rests on top of a shrub. I can't see Dad, but I can hear him. He's in our neighbour's garden exchanging yelps and howls with Argos above the rush and scuffle of a fight.

Sean crouches for a moment beside Brian. He's shouting, 'Brian! Wake up, Brian!'

Then he's up and away. Shouting again.

'Jimmy! Get out of there! He'll tear you to bits!'

He jumps, grabs the top of the wall and pulls himself up. I reach Brian. Not a stir out of him. I turn him on his side. The bridge of his nose is off-centre. Broken, it looks like. Mam is beside me with a bundle of tissues in her hand. She goes about stopping the flow of blood. Over at Mrs Casey's the mayhem continues.

'Jimmy, make a break for it! No, don't hit him!'

Sean's screams are joined by Mrs Casey's. She's leaning out of a window on the top floor of her house. Her dyed red hair is wild, electrified. She looks like some kind of mad, toothless glove puppet.

'Get out! Get out of my garden! Leave my dog alone, you savage!'

Sean jumps down into her garden and I run to the wall. I scramble up, tearing my knees on the rough plaster, but I don't care. At the centre of the overgrown lawn, Dad and Argos do battle. Dad's wielding one of those long bamboo sticks for holding up tall plants. He's whipping at Argos and the German shepherd is lunging at his arms. There's blood on the sleeves of his white Real Madrid jersey and all along the dog's back. Sean reaches Dad and starts pulling him away. The dog makes a lunge at him, but he dodges to one side. Dad whips Argos again.

'I'm calling the Guards!' Mrs Casey shrieks and shoots back inside.

Sean gets a proper hold on Dad, dragging him back towards the wall. Argos keeps up the barking and the threatening growls, but he's had enough of the fighting. I slip back down the wall. I feel sick. What if she does call the Guards? What'll happen to Dad then?

Mam is holding Brian up in a sitting position. He's come to. She holds the red-stained tissues to his nose. He's pale and dazed and seems like he might pass out again. Mam's looking in my direction, but beyond me. As he hangs over the brow of the wall, Dad's tracksuit bottoms are slipping down so that half of his backside is exposed. I want to scream at the ridiculousness of it all. He's holding his right arm and grimacing in pain. Mam stares over at him like he's a total stranger.

'Eala, help Brian here, will you?' she says, without a hint of urgency. 'We'll have to get them both to A and E.'

I take over from Mam and she goes over to Dad, who's made it down off the wall with Sean's help. Argos whines and it's like he's having an argument with himself about whether he won or lost the fight. Brian is so wobbly and shivering so hard, I can barely keep him upright. His glazed-over eyes seem to see nothing.

'Are you OK, Brian?' Stupid question, but what else can I say?

'Jimmy clocked me,' Brian says and, of course, I've known this all along, but haven't let myself think it.

Dad's sitting against the wall and won't move or let Mam see the damage to his arm. I can't hear what he's muttering to her. Sean comes over to us. He kneels down, his head bowed.

'Sorry, man,' he says. 'I shouldn't have left you alone with him.'

Brian is following some dizzy thought in his head. He wavers, but I catch his fall.

'We were kicking around,' he says. 'And the barking was really getting to Jimmy. Next thing, he tells me he's going to rescue the dog. He's being kept prisoner in there, Jimmy says, and I try to stop him, but . . .'

Mine is the spinning head now. I'm holding Brian tighter than I need to because I'm the one ready to fall. This whole farce is my doing. A few careless, tired words and this is what happens. I need to tell Mam, let her know there's some reason for all this madness. That it isn't Dad's fault. Not entirely.

Brian stirs himself. We help him to stand up. He takes the

soggy mess of tissue paper from me and the blood spills from his nose again and down the front of his red Che Guevara T-shirt. He throws away the tissue and uses the T-shirt to stop the flow.

'Is Jimmy all right?' he asks.

Take a good look at that pale and battered but still good-looking face, Angie tells me, *because this is the last you'll be seeing of Brian Dunphy*.

'His arm's reefed,' Sean says and he mutters under his breath. 'Psycho.' He turns and shouts at Dad. 'You're a psycho!'

'Sean, shut up and get the car keys,' Mam says.

He storms off towards the house. Dad is on his feet in a flash.

'Sean, I was trying to set Argos free and he attacked me.'

He's forgotten the pain and his arms hang down by his side. His white jersey and blue French tracksuit bottoms are covered in blood and sweat and clay. His face is streaked too. He looks like the wino we met earlier, complete with begging expression.

'Judy,' he says. 'Why did Argos have a go at me? I was going to bring him out to the country where he belongs.'

'He didn't understand,' Mam tells him. There's not a lot of sympathy going on in her voice. 'We have to go to the hospital and get you and Brian fixed up.'

'I'm not going back to the hospital,' he protests. 'You don't want me any more, is that it?'

'It's a different hospital and we'll be coming straight home once we're done, right?'

She puts her arm round his waist and he surrenders to her. Sean is at the back door of Jimmy's room.

'There's a squad car out on the drive,' he says. 'What are we going to do, Mam?'

'I'll talk to them,' she says.

'Are they going to nick me?'

Mam doesn't answer. She releases herself from Dad and leaves him standing there. He's terrified. She's fixing her hair and her dress as she goes and I'm fit to say, *How can you worry about what you look like at a time like this?* Maybe she sees the resentment in me because her glare is icy, like she's telling me to keep a lid on it. She takes her mobile from the pocket of her cardigan as she goes.

'Eala, bring Brian inside and find him a sweater,' she says, and going by Sean, adds, 'Sean, bring *him* in and clean up his arm.'

Him? She might as well have said *it*, she sounded so bitter. The Bernabéu's gone dead quiet. I can hear Argos's every wheezy breath and the evening cold wraps itself around me. Our summer is over.

We troop inside to Jimmy's room. Nobody speaks. I keep expecting Dad to apologize to Brian, but he doesn't. He sits on an armchair by the back window while Sean cleans his wounds. Sean doesn't go about it very gently and I don't insist that he does. Brian sits on the bed and I wipe the blood from his face and neck, taking care not to hurt him. He's stuffed two little twists of tissue paper into his nostrils. His eyes are blacking up. He looks ridiculous. But not ugly. I get one of Dad's zip-ups on him and it's like dressing an exhausted child.

Out on the drive, Mam is talking to the Guards beside the squad car. Her cardigan is pulled tight beneath her folded arms. Wisps of hair, unloosed from the green hair-clasp that matches her dress, play about her face in the breeze. She's smiling. She looks scarily beautiful. Both of the Guards are young guys and not exactly hiding their fascination with her. All three of them head out next door to Mrs Casey's.

'Are they looking for *the Man*?' Dad whispers at Sean.

'Put a sock in it, Jimmy,' he warns.

I stay by the window, waiting for them to return. Maybe I'm just trying to avoid looking at Brian, knowing I won't be seeing much of him ever again. After too long a while, I see the two Guards get back into the squad car and reverse slowly on to our street. But they don't drive away yet. Mam waits on the footpath, looking up and down the street and I wonder why. Here's why. Fiona Sheedy's little red Toyota Starlet pulls in beyond the squad car.

Of course, I'm thinking. *Tom*. Someone has to mind him while we drive to the hospital. I'd rather take him with us, but it wouldn't be fair. He's seen enough accidents and emergencies already. At least he's slept through this whole episode and I'm glad of that. *You're not The Surprise Addition any more, Tom*, I'm thinking. Dad's The Surprise Addition now. And God knows what the next surprise will be.

Mam comes to the open window by the bed.

'Lets go then,' she says. 'We're getting a police escort through town. Won't that be fun.'

I've never heard such a cynical tone from her before. The sound of the police siren is ringing in my head, though in reality, it hasn't actually started up yet.

12

Friday evening in the Accident and Emergency waiting area is busy, but not hectic.

'Hectic comes later,' the nurse taking Brian and Dad's details joked. 'Then it's *ER* minus the pretty faces.'

They took Brian away to the X-ray department an hour ago and we haven't laid eyes on him since. Sean went out for a smoke half an hour ago and hasn't come back yet. Dad's in one of the treatment rooms. He might have been seen earlier if it wasn't for the boy racer and his bimbo co-driver. Seems he flipped his car over trying out handbrake turns in a supermarket car park. She's inside having a broken arm seen to. He's barely got a scratch on him and has spent the last hour on his mobile describing the accident to his mates like a kid down from a carnival ride. He hasn't mentioned the girl once.

There's a scattering of others in the ranks of chairs and all of us are watching the reception nurse's every move like it's a play in a theatre that's too brightly lit, and we can't catch a word she's saying. At the far end of our row, an elderly couple sits. It's impossible to tell which one is more in need of attention. They seem equally sickly and shrunken, their clothes hanging loosely on them. But they hold hands. They have each other. *Which is more than Mam and Dad will have in old age*, I can't help thinking.

When the A and E entrance door opens behind us we all look back, our heads pulled on the same puppeteer's string. It's Starsky. He's wearing the leather jacket with the collar turned up. His white sneakers screech on the polished floor as he approaches, making a farce of his fury.

'This is assault, Judy,' he says. 'I could do him for this. I damn well should.'

Maybe it's not fair, but I'm thinking, *You didn't have to tell your father it was Dad who hit you, Brian.*

'Look, we're really sorry Brian got hurt.' Mam's voice rings as harshly as the scrape of her chair going back when she stands to face Starsky. She's almost as tall as him. He rolls his shoulders and gains himself another inch. He's not convinced it's enough. 'He's been very good to Jimmy and we appreciate that. I wish this hadn't happened, but it has. What more can I say?'

'What more can you say?' Starsky shakes his head and his bouffant hair flutters in slow motion. 'I'm out there busting my ass trying to put young Healy away and pinning down Trigger on a drugs charge. And this is the thanks I get?'

'No one's asking you to put Clem away,' she says. *Not no one, Mam*, I'm thinking.

Starsky steps away, walks a tight circle and comes back.

'Isn't there somewhere Jimmy can go?' he asks. 'Some kind of sheltered community. Until he's learned to cope, I mean. Short-term, like.'

Mam raises her chin, the tendons tighten along her neck. Judy's *hauteur* multiplied by ten.

'As a matter of fact, there is,' she says. That cynical tone again. 'I can put him in a nursing home, maybe; have him sit with a bunch of people twice his age. Or, better still, I can have him locked away in a psychiatric institution. What do you reckon?'

'There must be something else,' Starsky says, but whatever that something is escapes him. Escapes me too.

Starsky takes another short walk. It's like he has to move his body to kick-start his brain.

'The plan was we'd go up to Dublin tomorrow to sort out Brian's accommodation for college,' he says. 'What if there's complications? What if he's not able to start his course? And Mary? Mary's climbing the walls.'

I don't know Brian's mother, but Jill says she's nice, though most of the neighbours on their street think her stand-offish.

'Jeez, Judy,' he pleads. 'What am I supposed to do? Pretend this never happened? And if it happens again, something more serious maybe, do I keep turning a blind eye to it? Someone's going to get hurt, badly hurt. That's the bottom line.'

'It won't happen again,' Mam says and he throws his hands up in exasperation.

'You can't watch over him twenty-four-seven, Judy.'

Starsky drifts away to the reception desk. I listen hard, though I pretend not to. I catch a few words. Overnight. Ward 310. As the nurse directs him towards a corridor to our left, a gang of drunken young fellas make a loud entry to the waiting room. The cold chill I feel isn't from the breeze sweeping through A and E. I glance across, but Clem Healy isn't among them, nor is his brother. One of the gang is bleeding from a cut above the eye. Another is half carried, half shunted along between two of his mates. They tone down the aggression in their voices when they spot Starsky eyeing them with contempt.

Like the rest of us, they're told at reception that they'll have to wait. Unlike the rest of us, they're not so accepting. Still, knowing that Starsky's in the building, they keep a lid on their frustration. When they sit down a few rows back from us, I get the gist of their complaint. The pubs will be closed before they get sorted. The memory of Starsky fading from their soused minds, they keep up a loud, brain-dead banter.

'Some freaking health service!'

'They should all be taken out and shot, them politicians.'

'Too right; shoot them and then sack the lot of them.'

'But, sure, they'd already be dead?'

'Wha'?'

'If you shot them, you wouldn't have to sack them.'

'So sack them first and then shoot them.'

'My ankle's right sore.'

'Shut up, Skinner. Why bother sacking them if you're going to shoot them anyway?'

Oddly enough, in spite of the racket, it's actually easier to talk. I mean really talk. Honestly. I tell Mam where Dad's idea for rescuing Argos came from. She won't let me take any blame.

'He doesn't always know where the boundaries are any more,' she says.

'I know.'

Mam looks at me, through me, reading my mind in that weird way mothers have.

'What?' I say and I'm off covering my tracks and it's so obvious, but I can't stop myself. 'I mean I know about the boundaries thing. Miss U told us, remember?'

'Something happened downtown,' she says.

'No way. We met one of those winos Dad knows . . . used to know . . . and it upset him.'

She doesn't believe me. Or she believes me, but knows there's more. Her put-upon look of accusation rankles. *I'm not the liar here*, I'm thinking, *Dad is*.

'Mam, a few weeks ago I heard you on the phone to Martin. You were upset. What did Dad lie to you about?'

She examines the palms of her hands, following the lines there with her fingers. I notice how her fingernails are bitten to the quick and how some are bloodied at the edges. I wonder if it's her blood or Dad's.

'I wanted to wait until we'd sorted it out before I told you,' she says. 'Or, at least, get to the bottom of it. I didn't want to make this any more difficult for you and Sean. You don't deserve this, Eala.'

'None of us do, Mam.'

She puts her hands away into her folded arms. And it's not the tight grip from earlier as she spoke to the Guards. She's gone pure limp. Every part of her. She sinks down in her seat.

'We had . . . we have these insurance policies,' she begins. 'You know, life insurance, medical, income protection, that kind of thing. Martin does all that stuff for us. So after the accident we needed to draw on some of these policies. Hospital bills to pay, mortgage and all the day-to-day bills. Things have been getting tight since I took this unpaid leave. Very tight.'

'And the insurance companies haven't paid up?'

The tips of her fingers burrow at her brow, leaving deathly pale patches that fill in slowly with a purplish pink.

'Well, when you're signing up for these policies, you have to send copies of birth certs, passports and whatever. To prove you are who you say you are, basically. And . . .'

'And?'

'And Jimmy's birth cert is faked.'

'Faked?'

Mam nods, sits up straight, stretches her back as if to get out from under some great weight. And how dumb am I? All I can think of is that birthday party we had for him when he was forty; and the cake Mam bought was a bit small, but we stuck forty candles on it anyway and he lit all of them and the cake got so hot the icing started to melt; and everyone's screaming laughing because we can't blow out the candles because they're special ones Mam bought that keep lighting up again after you think you've blown them out; and he has to pick up the plate the cake's on with oven gloves and bring it outside the back door so the house won't go up in flames . . . *And it wasn't even your birthday, Dad ?*

'Martin thinks that somewhere along the way, Jimmy got into some kind of trouble and had to change his identity. Or had it changed for him . . .'

So whose birthday was it, Dad, who were we singing 'Happy Birthday' to?

'. . . he was twenty-two when I met him. Or that's what he told me. We shouldn't be talking about it in this awful place.'

But what better place to have your world turned upside down once again than this roomful of drunk and damaged, half-daft and fear-filled people? Turned upside down and emptied.

'I don't think we should tell Sean yet,' Mam says. 'He's so volatile, God knows how he'd react. Especially after today.'

She takes my hand. Her fingers are bony and sharp and she has no idea how tight her grasp is or how painful.

'I know it's been hard for you too, Eala, but I know I can trust you to be more sensible, more level-headed.'

Maybe. Maybe not. Whatever sense or level-headedness I ever had seems to be fading fast. Mam lets my hand go. Maybe it's the fluorescent light in here, but our skin – the skin on the backs of my hands, on her face – is mottled and it's like we haven't washed for days.

'All this hassle with the insurance means I'll have to go back to work, Eala. I've no choice. You understand, don't you?'

'So who takes care of Dad?'

'We'll find someone to come for a few hours during the day,' she says. 'I'll be on a three-day week for a while so that'll make it easier.'

And Dad emerges from the corridor of treatment rooms, led by a red-haired nurse who looks about fifteen, but a tired fifteen who's seen so much that nothing will ever faze her any more. Dad's right arm, his whipping arm, is bandaged up. He points at the young nurse.

'She's gone and given me a jab in the arse,' he calls across the waiting area at us. 'It's well sore.'

One of the loud-mouths guffaws and Dad dips his head. It's like he's onstage and has lost his nerve. We go and rescue him. He's had stitches put in two wounds. Seven stitches in all. And a tetanus jab, which is all he wants to talk about as we make our way out by the lobby of the hospital. I imagine going back inside and making my way to Ward 310, to Brian. But that's all I do. Imagine it.

Outside, among the smokers gathered by the main doors, we find Sean. He's talking on his mobile phone. He ends the call abruptly when he spots us. I get the feeling he has something to tell me. I hang back and let Mam and Dad go on ahead. Sean catches up with me.

'What?' I say.

His eyes slither about and I can't get a fix on them. He's definitely got something to tell me, but now he's having second thoughts. Why do I feel so sure it's another bad news story featuring Dad?

'What?'

'Nothing,' he says. 'Nothing . . .' I can tell before he speaks again that it's going to be a lie. 'I was . . .' He's stumped again. He looks down at the phone in his hand and finds a way to rescue himself. 'I been talking to Brian.'

Now my head swerves in another direction. Angie's whispering in my ear. *I bet Brian wants to go out with you, Eala.* Shut it, Angie. My heart's on speed.

'He's had a major row with the old man, above in the ward,' Sean says. 'He's not going to college. Told Starsky he never wanted to.'

'So what's he going to do?' I ask, stupidly disappointed.

'He wants to be a carpenter. Fair cool, isn't it?'

'Who does he think he is?' I say. 'Jesus?'

I watch Dad tag along after Mam in the stark sodium yellow light of the hospital car park. A big, loping, hunched man dragging his left foot every few strides, fiddling with his outsized watch, sneaking looks from side to side like he's checking no one's following him. The back of his white Real Madrid jersey is manky with dirt and grass stains. The number 6 is still quite clear, but the name above it – Zidane – is obscured.

Who are you, Dad? Who are you, Jimmy?

13

I won't sleep tonight. The court case starts tomorrow afternoon. Mam said I didn't have to go to school in the morning, but I'd rather be anywhere than at home these days. I've rewound the image of Clem Healy falling from his bike so many times that I'm beginning to see it all as if it's recorded on a CCTV camera. A black and white version of the real thing growing more grainy with each rewind, and eerily silent. As silent as our house had become in the weeks between Dad's battle with Argos and the arrival of the Ice Queen.

Dad was due back to see the psychiatrist a few days after his showdown in Mrs Casey's garden anyway. I can't blame Mam for giving Dr Reid the low-down on Dad's battle with Argos. So Dad got to pop some stronger pills. And become a pure zombie. But there was a bright side to it as the owl said to the pussycat in the middle of the night. That's one of Dad's old ones. In fact, there was a brighter side to his being doped up to the eyeballs. He seemed barely to have noticed the changes happening around him. And there'd been more than a few.

Sean stopped talking to him. Brian slipped off the radar altogether. I never expected his unlikely kindness to last anyway but, in fairness, a broken nose is a better excuse than most. If he couldn't have Sean and Brian, it seemed he didn't want anybody. He refused even to watch TV with us in the sitting room. Always had some excuse and when we started lighting the fire there in the evenings, he latched on to that too.

'I don't like fires,' he complained. 'Why do we need a fire? The house is warm enough.'

When we stopped lighting fires, of course, he didn't want to be with us either. Instead, he spent most of his time in his room, staring at the walls. No football, no treadmill running, no Xbox, no helping Tom to load Lego into the green tractor.

'Jimmy silly,' Tom would complain and get a half-hearted lecture from Mam that led to another of those pathetic, pointless rows we all slipped into too easily. It never mattered how these rows began. The subject always ended up the same. Mam's being back at work.

'Couldn't you have at least waited until after the court case?' That's Sean for you. The Lord of Logic. He tears strips off Mam for abandoning Dad and he's the one won't talk to him?

'You'd prefer to live on the side of the road in a caravan, would you, Sean?' I say.

'Shut up.'

'You shut up.'

'I'm warning you, Eala.'

'Go jump in the river.'

'Lads, please.'

And so it went, day after day, until the Ice Queen came and cast her spell. Marta Pelova is Dad's care assistant. I gave her the Ice Queen title. Her hair's been dyed blonde so often, it's strawy and has no sheen to it. Her features are perfect, but strangely not at all beautiful. She has the personality of a snowball. With a stone at the centre. Dad loves her.

Mam wanted all of us to be there when she interviewed the Czech woman. All stiff-backed politeness, the Ice Queen sat at the kitchen table. Her mouth was the only part of her that smiled as Mam introduced each of us. It's hard to guess what age she is. Somewhere between twenty-five and forty is the best I can do.

'My home is Moravia,' she told us. Dad was fascinated with her accent. 'In Czech Republic I am nurse. I live in Ireland five years. First I work in nursing home, then in private. I am care-giver for special needs and people who die.'

We looked at Mam, who was as dumbfounded as we were. We as in Sean and me, that is. Dad didn't seem to grasp the strangeness of what she'd said.

'You mean palliative care?'

'Yes. Palliative care,' Marta said, unembarrassed by her mistake. 'It is difficult so sometimes I want change. Special needs is good change.'

I was ready to flip, thinking, *Doesn't she have any cop-on, talking like that in front of Dad?* Mam was on the same wavelength.

'We don't use the term special needs, Marta, OK?' she said.

Once again, Marta showed no sign of discomfort. Dad continued to smile shyly at her and I wished he'd stop making an ass of himself.

'This is not problem,' she said.

94

I could see Mam was having second thoughts. I felt relieved. Sean did too. We were sure this was the last we'd see of the Ice Queen. We were wrong.

'So,' Mam said. 'When can you start? Next Monday at eight in the morning?'

'This is not problem,' the Ice Queen said.

'I've a pile of homework to do,' Sean muttered and stalked away.

'Me too,' I said and made to follow him.

'That's our house for you, Marta,' Mam said and laughed to cover up her annoyance with us. 'Busy, busy, busy.'

'This is not problem,' the Ice Queen repeated annoyingly.

I don't understand why Mam didn't see and still doesn't see what I saw in those pale blue eyes. Indifference. Like Dad was another client, another job. Tough luck, those eyes seemed to suggest, but I've dealt with worse. Indifferent or not she has this magical power over Dad and Tom. It's like they'll do whatever they're told so she'll favour them with one of her icy smiles. I wonder if it might even be that she rules by fear. Whatever force it is, it isn't love. As far as I can see, love doesn't work. I've tried.

In the week after his raid on Mrs Casey's, I did everything I could to lift Dad's spirits. Our usual early evening walk was off the agenda. The psychiatrist suggested we keep him out of stressful situations for a while. Exercise in the Bernabéu and on the treadmill were out too until he'd adjusted to the new dosage. His body had slowed to a crawl. I didn't want the same thing to happen to his mind. He needed to be pushed, have his memory jolted and I knew Mam wasn't going to do it any time soon. She's way too cautious.

First I had to sneak the Undertones CD and the *All Dogs Go to Heaven* DVD from Dad's old workroom. It was two o'clock in the morning before I got a chance to slip in there unseen. The key made too much noise in the lock, but I waited and no one seemed to have woken. I slipped inside and closed the door behind me. The blind was down, blocking out the street light. Then I almost jumped out of my skin. Someone was standing in the corner of the room.

'Dad?' I whispered and quickly corrected myself. 'Jimmy?'

My eyes adjusted to the darkness and my memory kicked back in at about the same time. It had been so long since I'd been in Dad's workroom that I'd forgotten the wooden mannequin. Added to which, someone had moved it to a different corner. Mam, I guessed, that day she went searching in there. The mannequin's not a full figure, just a head and torso. It wears a peaked cap with the Timberland name and logo. Another of Dad's jokes.

I stepped carefully across the floor because, under my bare feet, I felt the books and papers Mam had scattered in her search. I turned on the lamp attached to Dad's drawing board. A set of drawings for the last book in the Terry the Tank series was still clipped to the board.

The stories are basically the same in each book. Terry's got no one to play with. His friend Rosie the Mechanic in her psychedelic boiler suit and red bandana tries to comfort him. Then he sees a family of ostriches or teapots or whatever playing in the meadow. In this last book of the series, he persuades Rosie to turn him into an elephant. There's a page of cloudy smoke and exclamations – *Bang! Bang! Ouch! Ouch!* – as she works and Terry emerges as a metal elephant.

He races down to play with the real elephants, who think he's dodgy at first, but then play with him.

So he's having a whale of a time, but gets so excited he starts firing live rounds from his trunk and they all run for cover. He's crying his eyes out when the baby elephant comes back and then Rosie arrives and makes him see that he should be himself and that way he'll be accepted for what he is. In the last unfinished drawing, Rosie is walloping Terry back into shape as a tank in another exclamation-filled cloud.

Looking at the drawing, I realized that any half-decent illustrator could finish the book and who'd ever know? It was the saddest thought. It was like Dad didn't matter any more outside of our own four walls. I searched for the Undertones CD and the *All Dogs Go to Heaven* DVD. I wasn't even sure I still wanted to try them on him. But next day I did. A Saturday, so I had plenty of time alone with him.

At the breakfast table, Dad was pure out of it. The slow movements of his hand lifting the teacup, the listless shovelling of muesli into his mouth, the vacant stare. I wanted to hold him tight, squeeze the life back into him, tell him that everything would be all right. When we went down to his room, I did. I hadn't done that for a long time. Held him, reassured him. All I managed to do was embarrass and confuse him.

'But everything's A-one now,' he said. 'Innit? I'm not a nutter any more.'

'You never were,' I said.

I felt broken-hearted. I split away and put on the Undertones CD. Not too loud so they wouldn't hear it upstairs. 'Jimmy, Jimmy'.

'I don't like that,' he said before they'd got to the first words. He lay back on the bed, his eyes closed, his feet still touching the floor.

'Give it a chance,' I said. 'It's called "Jimmy, Jimmy". I bet you'll love it.'

'Why do they have to shout so much?'

'It's punk. *Joie de vivre* punk.'

He yawned. 'You've Got My Number' was faster still, but didn't keep him from nodding off. Later that morning and five minutes into *All Dogs Go to Heaven* he got right thick.

'This is kids' stuff. What you take me for, a fool?'

After the music and the film failed to lift the veil on his memories, I spent the time with him reading aloud. He liked that. He'd lie on the bed and gaze out by the window. I wonder whether he even followed the story. I know he didn't recognize the book, though he'd read it to me and Sean when we were young and often dipped into it himself.

The book was called *Coral Island*, written way back in the nineteenth century by J. M. Ballantyne. It was the first book he'd ever owned. There are fourteen different editions of it on the shelves in Dad's workroom. He often told us how a description of a coral reef in that book was his first experience of actually seeing in his mind a picture painted entirely by words. When I reached that passage, I dared to hope again that a memory might be sparked in him. I might as well have been reading from the telephone directory. But I ploughed on. A few chapters each evening and we were close to the end before the Ice Queen came.

After her first day with him, I picked up the book again.

'We'll finish it this evening,' I said.

'Marta already did,' he said. I was pure gutted.

'We can read another one then.'

'Marta's starting a new one tomorrow. She said it's good for improving her English.'

My brain shut down; my heart too. They've stayed shut down.

So the other day when Jill broke her silence with me and texted to say she wouldn't be in school for a few days, that there was a major crisis at home, I didn't bother to answer.

And yesterday, when Miss O'Neill asked me if I was going to audition for *West Side Story*, I nodded in a vague way that might have meant yes, no or maybe.

And this afternoon, when I sang 'Tonight' on the stage of the school assembly hall, there was no music in me and the acoustics in there are so weird it was like more than one of me was singing.

'A bit on the sharp side, Eala,' Miss O'Neill said and I couldn't have cared less.

14

The bell for the mid-morning break is less than five minutes away. Mrs Doran is too young to have grey hair and too bouncy to be teaching something as boring as economics. At least you stay awake during her classes. She's always liable to fire a question at you out of the blue. But this morning I'm on the edge of my seat for a different reason. And, for the moment, it's not the court case. Jill is back in school.

She wasn't here earlier on and arrived only after Mrs Doran's class had already started. The light sheen of foundation she's wearing doesn't mask the shadows under her eyes. I should feel sorry for her. I don't. I look across at her and all I can think of is her neighbour. Brian. It's not only our house he's disappeared from. I never see him around town these days and Sean hasn't mentioned his name since that night at the A and E. Maybe he's gone to college after all. Not that it matters. It's curiosity, like, nothing more.

When I watched Jill come into our classroom I thought, *No way am I going to listen to her sob story.* I've changed my mind. She's bound to know where Brian is. The bell rings. I get to Jill quickly and catch her off-guard. She's still putting away her economics textbooks.

'Well, Jill. You all right?'

She looks up from her bag. A picture of holy suffering.

'Hi, Eala.'

Suddenly she's on her feet and wrapping her arms round me. Nothing unusual in that. Not for Jill. She's into hugging. Sometimes she might have seen you only a few hours before, but she greeted you like she'd been away for a year. But this hug is different. Tighter and it lasts longer. Our classmates are still filing out, taking their time to witness her antics. Some think the scene is touching. Others can't help smirking. A few squirm at the absurdity of it. I'm with this last bunch. I'm still debating about pulling free when Jill lets go. She takes a deep breath like she's about to reveal all. I hear Angie's voice in my head. *Don't let her start, Eala; tell her you need to find Brian because . . . because . . .*

'Have you seen Brian around lately?' I ask. Angie asks. 'Because he took a loan of one of Dad's DVDs – *All Dogs Go to Heaven* – you know, the film Dad worked on. And I really need to get the DVD back.'

Brilliant, Angie says. *Like Brian would borrow a kiddies' film?*

Jill's stumped. Her lips move, but she doesn't know what to say. Or maybe she knows what to say, but she's too polite to put it into words. Angie's too quick for her anyway. *Squeeze out a few tears, Eala.*

'I've so little left of Dad, I . . .'

I tell Angie to get lost. Because of the foundation cream, Jill's blush has a weird green tinge to it.

'I haven't seen him, but I'm sick of listening to the racket from his workshed. Win had to go in there a few times before she went back to Dublin and ask him to turn off that saw thing or whatever it is so Richard could sleep,' Jill says.

'He's not gone to college, then?'

She shakes her head. She's waiting for me to ask about her sister. I don't. As I turn away, she holds my arm.

'Win's planning to give Richard up for adoption,' Jill says.

'She's better off,' I tell her. 'Maybe the kid's better off too.'

Only now do I notice how stuffy and downright putrid the air in the classroom is after a few hours of stale breath and body smells trapped without an open window to escape through. For some reason I think, *This is what prison smells like*.

'You're fair messed up, Eala,' Jill says and I'm surprised at how dead calm she is. 'I mean you were always kind of sarcastic, but funny, like. Now you're pure cynical and . . . and cruel. I know it must be hard for you, but . . . Eala, you really need to talk to someone.'

Which really sets me off.

'Someone like you, maybe?' I say. 'Like I could get a word in edgeways with you moaning on about Win and her little sprog.'

'Do you want to know why I came to school today?' Jill asks, and I'm thrown.

'Same reason we all do.'

'Because of the court case,' she says. 'I wanted to be here for you. Which is more than you're prepared to do for me.'

I'm flabbergasted. I look at Jill, but she's studying her fingernails. No nail polish. It must be the first day since she was about ten years old that she hasn't painted them.

'I don't need all this crap today.'

'You can't walk away from people,' she says, all goo-eyed. 'People who care about you, who . . . I'm going down to the lunch hall.'

Laughter comes bursting out of me as she heads towards the classroom door through the maze of benches. This is totally mad, but I can't stop myself. I'm laughing and shouting at the same time.

'Look at her! "You can't walk away," she says, and then she walks away!'

In the far corner of the room, Angie's doubled over with laughter too.

15

The courtroom is a kip. The high windows are so grimy that the afternoon light has turned to a dirty dusk before it reaches inside. Blistered and peeling wall paint is spotted with greeny-black mould. The place smells like a toilet that hasn't been flushed since it was last used about a hundred years ago. It's full of dark timbers, sticky to the touch. A judge's high bench lords it over the witness box, the double row of pews for the legal people and the Guards, and the steep bank of seating where the rest of us sit.

Mam, Sean and myself are sitting in the second row of seats. Behind us sit Martin and Fiona Sheedy. In the front row and over to our right are Clem Healy, his brother Sham and his father. It's the first time I've seen Clem Healy up close. He's small, weedy and seriously aened. He looks about twelve, though I know he's going on fifteen. His father, Trigger, is short, thickset and shaven-headed. In his black suit, he'd pass as a night-club bouncer, the kind who won't let you in and lets you go figure out the reason. His buttoned and tieless shirt collar is embedded in the flesh of his thick neck. Sham is a twenty-year-old copy of his old man except that he wears a rapper's oversized threads.

Clem was the first person I saw when we came in here. I felt physically sick with hatred. It didn't help that he had his hoodie up and was grinning stupidly. When he glanced in our direction he didn't seem to realize who we were. Either that or he didn't care. Then the grin evaporated and he was a rabbit in the headlights. Sean had caught his eye. Clem nudged his brother, who took up the staring match with Sean. Trigger joined in too.

'Stop it now, Sean, please,' Mam whispered. 'We'll have none of that macho nonsense, do you hear me?'

Martin leaned forward to Sean and they exchanged a few quiet words. The staring match ended. Trigger turned to his son and pulled the hoodie roughly down. The kid flinched, expecting a blow from his father, but it was Sham who delivered an elbow into his ribs.

We had to sit through three cases before they came to ours. A mugging, a house break-in, a joyriding incident. Two boys and a girl. Thirteen, maybe fourteen years of age, all of them. Ordinary kids you'd walk past on the street and not look twice at. All three got suspended sentences. There wasn't a lot of remorse on show.

Our case began about half an hour ago. A Guard gave evidence of the chase down by the River Walk and the arrest. Another gave details of tyre marks on the footpath. Starsky, wearing a bouncer's suit not unlike Trigger's, said that Clem Healy had, at first, claimed that Dad tried to knock him off his bike, but later admitted he'd been lying. In spite of Clem's denials, Starsky felt sure that someone had been chasing the kid that evening. He also offered his opinion that Clem had been carrying *illegal substances*.

The judge told Starsky he wanted proofs not opinions.

Then a middle-aged woman whose car had stopped at the junction pointed at Clem Healy when asked to identify the cyclist who caused the accident. Soon as I saw her, I knew she was the woman who held Dad until the ambulance arrived. I hated her for it. It should've been me holding him. But the worst part was yet to come.

Dr Reid, the psychiatrist from the rehab centre, outlined the damage done to Dad. He had this distinguished air of grey-haired wisdom about him. Dad had another French phrase to describe old guys like that, but I couldn't remember it while Dr Reid spoke and I still can't remember it now. At first, his evidence was full of incomprehensible medical terms. The prosecuting solicitor, a young, dark-haired and efficient woman, soon got to the heart of the matter.

'What, Dr Reid, in your opinion, is the long-term outlook for the victim?' she asked, sweeping off her glasses for effect.

'At this point, I'm forced to conclude,' Dr Reid said, 'that, notwithstanding some recent progress, a return to previous intellectual capacity is not a realistic prognosis. Behavioural problems, anxiety and depression are also likely to be ongoing.'

'In a word, then,' the counsel said, 'Mr Summerton has been condemned to a life sentence?'

'Mr Summerton and his family both. Yes, I'm afraid so.'

I already knew this, of course. It didn't matter. I was sitting there, not moving, but I felt myself sinking into a bottomless pit. Dad wouldn't have understood the psychiatrist's words but, all the same, I was glad he didn't have to hear them. Even if he did have to be at home with the Ice Queen. Beside me, Sean sobbed while Martin comforted him with a hand on his shoulder.

When I was seven or eight, we spent a summer holiday in Salthill. I wanted to go up in the Big Wheel opposite the long promenade and look out across the silvery waters of Galway Bay. Though she was pure terrified of heights, Mam sat in the bucket seat beside me. All the way up and then down again, she leaned back as far as she could and held on to my hand as if I could have stopped her falling should anything disastrous happen. I thought of that day as Dr Reid spoke and she clung to me.

After the psychiatrist finished his evidence, I was to be next. It didn't happen.

For the last ten minutes, the microphone at the high bench has been switched off and there's a discussion going on that we can't hear between the judge, the solicitors, Starsky and a tall red-haired young woman.

Clem Healy is rocking back and forward nervously and it's fair annoying. His father is bristling with impatience and we hear a muttered, 'Get on with it,' from Sham. The judge, an older man with half-moon glasses perched low on his nose, switches on his microphone.

'No interruptions, please,' he says. 'Is that clear?'

Trigger looks back at the people behind him, passing the blame. The judge switches off his microphone again. I don't like how this is going. Mam doesn't either. She shakes her head as if she's refusing to answer some terrible question she's asked of herself. The discussion at the high bench is over. Clem Healy's solicitor leads the young woman over to the witness box.

From this distance she looks like a size-zero model and her elegant walk seems weirdly out of place in this dingy courtroom. I can't figure out who she can be. Another witness to the accident – with a different story to the one we've been hearing? Starsky's back in his seat near the solicitors' benches. His head is lowered.

'Miss Delahunty,' the solicitor begins. 'Can you give us a synopsis of your psychological report on the accused?'

Christ, I'm thinking, *another bloody psychologist* and I know too well what her intention is. To get creepy little Clem off the hook. I turn and shoot Fiona Sheedy a filthy look. I can't tell if it's a smile or a wince I get in return.

'Yes, well, having examined Clement,' the catwalk psycho says, 'I've reached the following conclusions. Firstly, it's clear that he suffers from attention deficit disorder and a variety of more serious learning disorders related to this and other problems, all of which point to a significant developmental deficit. There's an especially low reading age, low scores on intellectual indices and inadequate social skills, which are exacerbated by familial difficulties.'

'In short,' the defending solicitor says, 'Clement Healy is simply incapable of being fully responsible for his actions?'

'Yes.'

Mam has withdrawn her hand from mine. She stares vacantly at the diseased walls. Sean's muttering to himself, beating a fist into his palm. Below us, Clem Healy is watching the psychologist's click-clacking, high-heeled retreat to her seat like he's still trying to figure out what she's said. His solicitor beckons to him and his father digs him in the ribs to catch his attention. He jumps up and, in a weird half-run, makes his way to the witness box.

The judge takes off his glasses. He surveys the gallery where we sit and somehow I know he's short-sighted and can't actually see our faces. Maybe this is what they mean when they say that justice is blind. He starts to speak, but has forgotten to turn on his microphone.

'We can't hear you,' Trigger calls out and the judge eyes him threateningly. Starsky's staring back at him too and he makes a slicing gesture across his neck. Trigger smiles. The microphone comes alive with a piercing whistle. The judge taps it like a drum. Clem Healy can't keep still, hopping around in the witness box like he needs to go to the toilet.

'As a guilty plea has now been entered on behalf of –' the judge shuffles through the file before him, – 'of Clement Healy and, taking into consideration Miss Delahunty's report, the case can be decided without further evidence or submissions.'

Sean leans forward, gripping the back of the seat before him.

'I am not persuaded of any malicious intent in this case, only the extreme recklessness of an intellectually challenged young boy. My sympathies go out to Mr Summerton's family. However, I do not consider that a custodial sentence is appropriate in this case. I, therefore, have decided on a sentence of forty hours' community service . . .'

Clem Healy spins round. He's smiling broadly at his father.

Sean stands up.

'You can't do this!' he shouts at the judge. 'You can't let him walk!'

'Sit down, please,' the judge says. 'I know this is difficult for you all, but –'

'You know nothing,' Sean answers. He's flushed and wild and I know this isn't going to end here today in court. 'Come back to our house for an hour and you'll see what it's really like.'

There's a Guard at one end of our row now and Starsky climbs the steps reluctantly to take the other end. Mam's head is lowered, her hands over her ears. Martin is trying to pull Sean back down on to the seat. Clem Healy is skulking away behind his solicitor.

'You're dead!' Sean calls after him. 'Dead!'

'Clear the courtroom,' the judge says and switches off his microphone.

'OK,' Starsky says. 'Can we leave quietly, please? Sean, leave it, OK?'

We file out slowly between the rows of seats, the Guard behind us, Starsky in front and beckoning us forward. It's like we're a gang of prisoners being led down to our cells. Single file and each of us alone. As we go by, Starsky says,

'Sorry you had to go through all of this for nothing, Judy.'

Mam shrugs. Sean stops and I try to pull him on after me. He's almost as tall as Starsky and in his face.

'Some cop you are,' he says. 'You couldn't catch a cold at the North Pole with your trousers off.'

In the corridor outside the courtroom, it feels like everyone is watching us. Waiting for more. Sean slips by me, hurrying to be out of this hellhole. Martin's at his heels. I can't see the Healys and I've lost Mam and Fiona. The noise of chatter and footfall is doing my head in. The heated, sweaty smell of the crowd is sickening. I'm drowning in it. I can't breathe. Seeing stars, hearing them burn out with a loud hissing.

'Bastard!'

Sean again. The crowd has parted and I see Clem Healy talking on his mobile and Sean's fist coming out of nowhere and slamming into the side of the raised hoodie. The mobile falls on the floor. It stays in one piece and slides towards me. Sean's holding the kid's shoulder, preparing another punch. Trigger grabs a hold of Sean's arm from behind. Martin catches Trigger by the shoulder and Sham is trying to pull Martin off his father. It's like a crazy conga dance. Everyone's watching them so they don't see me stamp on Clem Healy's phone and make bits of it. Starsky rushes across and steps in between Sean and the Healy sons. Martin and Trigger are squaring up to each other. Each has a fistful of the other's shirt collar.

'Anything happens to my son and you lot will be sorry you ever crossed my path,' Trigger grunts. 'You don't know who you're messing with here.'

'You're a scumbag, Healy,' Martin says before Miss Understanding emerges from the crowd and eases him away from Trigger, whispering in his ear, patting him on the back like he's a child.

'Da,' Clem Healy complains. 'I lost me phone.'

His father slaps him across the back of the hoodie.

'Well, go and find it.'

But Starsky's had enough of them.

'Get out,' he says and pushes the Healys towards the courthouse exit.

'But the young lad's lost his phone,' Trigger objects.

'Make yourself scarce, Healy, before I cuff you for causing disorder.'

Tears flow down between the spots on Clem's face. His nose is running too.

'What if Mammy rings?' he pleads.

'She won't ring, you dummy,' Healy says and punches him so hard on the shoulder, the kid hits the wall.

A shiver runs through me. Someone catches my arm and I pull free. It's Mam. And she looks at me downcast, defeated.

16

When I realized that Mam had invited Fiona Sheedy back to the house, I said I'd go with Martin in the Mercedes. Sean was already in the back seat of Mam's car. The courthouse car park leads on to a one-way street and we've hit the evening traffic. I don't mind the delay. I'm in no hurry to get home anyway.

Martin's always driven these big Mercedes cars and when I was a kid I loved travelling in them and pretending I was some kind of princess or celebrity. I loved how smoothly they moved, how silent they were inside compared to our old banger of a station wagon. I'd sit in the back seat talking non-stop to my invisible friend. Once, Kathleen, sitting in the passenger seat, asked me what my friend's name was. And in all innocence, I told her it was Angie. Whatever it was that she and Martin felt, neither of them reacted badly because I remember nothing else of that journey and it didn't stop them spoiling me rotten every chance they got.

We have a lot in common these days, Martin and me. He thought he was Dad's best friend, but Dad's still afraid of him. Twice in the last few weeks Martin has tried to break the ice, but to no avail. My childish notion that I'd been

Dad's favourite was well and truly buried too. It was true that I'd always spent more time with him than Sean had. Talked more with him. Now, all those hours seemed like missed opportunities.

When I try to remember what he'd told me about his young days, all I ever come up with is some funny incident or other because that's all I ever got from him. The day he and his pals were caught stealing apples from an orchard because the ground level was lower inside the garden wall than out on the road and they couldn't climb back out. Or the time they persuaded one of his pals to jump from a six-foot-high wall with an open umbrella to see if he'd float down. He didn't. He twisted his ankle and grazed his elbow. That kind of thing.

We're inching our way towards the junction with the main road. The sky is darkening above the street lights. We stop again opposite the shopping centre at the edge of town. I'm staring at the multistorey car park there and a memory flashes into my head from seven, maybe eight years ago of Dad. Lying to me.

Another of his funny incidents. He'd been down in Cork talking to some people he was doing a cartoon short with the day he told me the story. He'd left at six in the morning and got back around midnight. I worried all day. I had this obsession at the time about multistorey car parks. If we went somewhere and parked in one, I'd be paranoid about getting back before it closed so our car wouldn't be locked in for the night. He still hadn't got himself a mobile phone back then and I imagined him sitting in a dark car park a long way from home. When he came to my bedroom, the tears started. So he tried to cheer me up with one of his boyhood adventures.

It was the story of this cranky old man who lived on the street where he and his pals played football every evening. Most of the people living there made no big deal of it when the ball ended up in their small front gardens. This old fellow, Bert, was different. Any ball that came over his wall, he confiscated.

But Bert was more than cranky. He gloated in the boys' misery when they'd lost yet another plastic football to him. He put all of the balls on the window sill of his kitchen facing the street. Eventually, ten footballs were piled high there.

I listened to the story and my stomach tightened into a knot. I knew what happened next. One day, Dad and his pals saw Bert go to the shop – and leave his key in the front door. Dad was the youngest so they volunteered him to go inside and steal back their footballs. He went in. Bert came home unexpectedly. Dad was trapped under the kitchen table for hours before he could sneak back out.

Except I knew it wasn't Dad in the story. He'd read it to me from a book the previous year. And not one of his own books. Now he was telling it like it had all happened to him. Before he got to the end, I blurted out,

'Dad, that story is out of a book you read to me. *The Football Thief.*'

He rubbed the tiredness from his eyes.

'Well, actually,' he began. 'The man who wrote that book has the same agent as me and I met him a few times in London. We're about the same age and read the same comics when we were kids, went to the same films and all that stuff, and one evening we were swapping stories about the old days over a few beers. Well, he really liked that one and asked me if he could use it in a book.'

'But you should've written it,' I said. 'Did he pay you for the story?'

He laughed and tucked me in and kissed my forehead.

'Maybe I should've asked,' he said. 'The thing is, though, I never told anyone about this before. Maybe we should keep it as a secret. Our secret.'

Which was like asking me if I'd like a whole box of chocolates to myself. It was stuff like that had me believing I was his favourite. Why have I only remembered this now? Have I hidden it from myself? And if I have, is there more stuff like this buried deep in my brain? But there are bigger questions still. Were all of his 'funny incidents' really fictions? Was every last thing he'd ever told us about himself one great big lie?

'Have you found out anything about Dad yet?' I ask Martin.

I don't know if it's the question or the suddenness of it that unsettles him more. The slow driving becomes a more difficult task. Or he pretends it to be. He keeps turning towards his side window as he drums the steering wheel. Hiding his face from me.

'You did.'

'Eala, I haven't spoken to Judy about this yet.'

'Please. Tell me, Martin.'

I'm playing the part from last year's show again. The orphan girl winding her rich benefactor round her little finger. I might not be Dad's favourite, but I know I'm Martin's. I'm his Angie. A weird thought, but true. I don't hear the Angie in my head, but I see her and she doesn't look all that happy.

'There's this tracing agency I used a few years ago to trace a guy over in England,' he says. 'I was trying to buy a house and this guy had been left it in someone's will, but he'd never shown up and these people found him for me. Anyway, I asked them to check out your Dad's papers – see where it might lead.'

'You mean like private detectives?'

'Nothing as dramatic as that, really. Most of the searching is in documents. Registers. You know, births, marriages and deaths. Tedious work and it takes time.'

'But they found something?'

'Not exactly.'

We're stuck behind the first car at the junction. The driver's too cagey about edging out on to the main road, though he's got plenty of time. Martin blasts the horn. Martin doesn't do stuff like that. He sits back, twists the cramp out of his neck.

'These people, this agency, they know the territory very well,' Martin explains. 'They're not too hopeful about the search.'

'You mean we might never know who Dad was? Is?'

'I'm afraid so.'

'So we're never going to get this insurance money, are we?'

'The chances are that even if we discover Jimmy's real identity, they won't have to pay up,' he says.

The car in front makes a break for it at last and we're free of the crawl. Cars speed towards us in the opposite lane. I look at the faces of the drivers and passengers. Are they all who they pretend to be? I find myself trying to pick out the ones who might have changed identities, but they whizz by too quickly for me to decide.

'How can these agency people be so sure they won't find something?' I ask because, insurance money or not, I have to know my dad's story. Everyone deserves to know that, don't they?

'They've done so many of these searches, they get to know the ones that are going to end in a blind alley. And they get to know why.' Martin's still avoiding my eyes and that makes me uneasy and the long pause doesn't help either. 'They think Jimmy's new identity was either issued to him by the Ministry of Justice in the UK or he bought his papers on the black market.'

'Which means?'

'There's half a dozen possibilities, Eala, and more.'

'He's done something seriously bad, hasn't he?'

'Or had something seriously bad done to him,' Martin says. And Dad's greatest fear comes to mind.

'This is what *the Man* is all about, isn't it?'

Martin turns to me. I know Mam's told him about this obsession of Dad's. He's glad to have this stop-go traffic to negotiate.

'Maybe not. Fiona Sheedy has a theory about that and I think she may be right.' There's no escaping Miss Understanding. 'She says the Man might very well be Jimmy himself. The old Jimmy.'

'That doesn't make sense.'

'I think it does. Deep down, Jimmy vaguely understands that he used to have another life. That he used to be a different kind of person, if you like. He may think of that person as completely separate from him now. Some kind of shadowy figure he imagines is always close by. That has to be very troubling for him.'

'But that doesn't explain the fake birth cert,' I tell him.

'No, it doesn't,' he says. 'But listen, Judy doesn't need to know about the insurance money. Not yet, OK? She's been through enough already today.'

We cross over Blackcastle Bridge. The River Walk is in darkness over there. No swans this evening or none that I can see. I should ask Martin to turn left here so we'll reach home from the river end of our street. I don't. For almost a year now, I've avoided the other end, the junction where Dad's old life ended. Which hasn't been easy and, often, especially when I'm with Jill or whoever, I feel half daft as I insist on taking the long way round from town. It's like being a kid and walking all the way from school avoiding the lines on the footpath. Now I'm thinking, *What was the point? I'm there every night in my head anyway.*

'Why did he do this to us, Martin?' I ask. 'I mean it's bad enough he didn't tell Sean and me. But why would he not tell Mam? I always thought they were so close, so together.'

'Think of the start in life he had, Eala,' he says. 'Losing his parents so young had to make him very insecure. It was always going to be there at the back of his mind, this fear of being abandoned by the ones he's closest to. So he meets

Judy and maybe he's afraid to risk losing her by telling her this secret of his.'

'But all these years and he still doesn't say a word? Whatever he was hiding had to be something really major. There's no other explanation.'

'Of course there are other explanations.'

'Such as?'

Martin's getting all edgy again. He leans forward to the steering wheel, his neck doing that weird snapping-stretch thing. I don't know if he's thick with me or with himself as he tries to dream up some excuse for Dad.

'Such as . . . such as this, right? Jimmy didn't have a regular family life, did he? He grew up in foster institutions where you have to build these walls around you to survive. You don't talk about yourself, your past, your emotions. Then he hooks up with Judy and, as time goes on, it's looking like, you know, the real thing, which makes it even harder for him to open up. He's got so much to lose. And more to lose still when they married and you and Sean came along.'

'If he really loved Mam, he'd have trusted her with his story no matter how bad it was,' I tell Martin sharpish. We're beginning to grate on one another.

'He loved Judy. Believe me, I can vouch for that.'

How the hell would you know, I'm thinking, but I hold my fire. I don't want to add Martin to my blacklist. It's full enough already. We pass along through Friary Street and as we go by the high gates of his house, Martin finds a way to steer us into more neutral territory.

'I'm moving out of the house,' he says. 'Moving into one

of the apartments I built out by the golf course. Can't sell the damn things anyway with this recession.'

'But why would you move?' I ask, genuinely surprised. 'It's a lovely house.'

'Too many memories. I should've listened to Jimmy.'

'He said you should move out? When?'

'After Kathleen left,' he says and smiles. '"Wuthering Heights", he called it. "And you're no Heathcliff," he says. He was a ticket, wasn't he?'

'Yeah.'

'He was dead right too. You know, as soon as I made up my mind to leave that house, it felt different. *I* felt different. And I couldn't figure out why at first. Then I got it. Angie was gone. I'd let her go. We should never have stayed in that house after Angie.'

A strange thought enters my mind. Martin lets Angie go – and she comes to me. The town square passes by in a blur of street light. The Long Mall too except that I notice Mrs Casey's sweet shop is closed earlier than usual. We reach the junction where Dad was hit and I'm sitting up straight, my body rigid, my hand gripping the armrest on the passenger door like something's going to happen. Nothing does. Nothing might ever have happened here for all these people walking or driving by know or care.

'Do you think Mam and Dad will split up?' I ask.

'Judy's completely devoted to your dad,' he says. There should be more. There isn't.

Angie's in my ear. *Little Orphan Eala and her sugar daddy*. How dodgy was that school show last year anyway? Young girl goes to live with older man? My stomach sickens.

I think of Dad, a vulnerable, orphaned kid. Is this why he never talked about the foster homes he lived in or the people who took care of him? The people who were supposed to be taking care of him.

We pull into the drive and park beside Miss Understanding's car. I hate it when she's alone with Mam. I don't trust her. I should go inside and break up their little chat, but I'm too spun out. Dad appears briefly at the half-basement window. The Ice Queen is there too. She stares straight at me. Martin raises his hand, a little hesitant wave. And they're gone.

'Eala, keep an eye on Sean,' Martin says. 'I'm afraid he might do something foolish. Those Healys are dangerous people and the last thing Judy needs is hassle from that lot.'

He's looking up at the bay window of the sitting room. His eyes wide and bleak. Mam's up there, leaning back on the sofa and staring up at the ceiling while Tom bounces up and down beside her. She looks pure washed out, emptied. I can't see Miss U, but I know she's doing the talking because Mam nods her head as though agreeing with whatever the psycho's saying.

'Are you coming in?' I ask and unbuckle my seat belt. The sensation of release doesn't last very long. For all its size, the inside of the Merc feels claustrophobic. I can't breathe deeply enough. My fingers can't remember where the door handle is.

'No.' He shakes his head. 'I've got some stuff to do at the office.' He doesn't sound like he's looking forward to it.

I'm pushing against the door as it opens and I almost tip out. Martin doesn't notice. He's still watching Mam. The air I craved is so cold it finds every inch of my flesh instantly.

'Did you and Mam go out together before Dad came along?' I ask.

'We were kids. And it lasted all of two months,' he says with a rueful smile. 'If you think I'm small now, you should've seen me back then. I was a year older than Judy and I looked like her kid brother.'

'I know the feeling,' I say.

'Take care, Eala,' he says and the best I can do in response is to raise my hand goodbye.

I wait as the Mercedes reverses on to the road and pulls away. A minute or two passes. The crawling cold tempts me to go in; the street light tempts me to wander out, escape for a little while longer. I go with the street light.

17

Sometimes you only know where you're going when you get there. This is one of those times. I'm standing at the junction where Dad's mind was sucked into a black hole. I'm not sure what I expect to find here. Dad's MP3 player still lying in the gutter? His blood still staining the footpath? I go down on one knee, peer closely at the filthy concrete coated with cigarette butts and blobs of flattened chewing gum. There are plenty of stains, but they could be any disgusting thing. A man goes by speed-walking a greyhound. He keeps looking back and wondering what the hell I'm doing until I get up from the footpath. I walk slowly along by the gable wall Dad cracked his head against. I don't find any trace of his blood there, no cracks in the plaster, nothing.

Why didn't you ever talk to me, Dad? Why didn't you trust me with your secret? I'm crying and Angie's at my shoulder. *Yeah right, Eala, and if he had told you, you'd still be whining like you are now, feeling sorry for yourself because that's what you're doing, isn't it? Feeling sorry for yourself and waiting for someone to come along and hold you, that someone being Brian, right?* I tell her to leave me alone. I run towards home, but I can't shake her off. *You're such a loser, Eala.*

At our driveway, the noise of the pebbles underfoot as I run drowns Angie out. I go in by the narrow side passage by the half-basement. The light's still on in there, but the curtains have been pulled. Halfway through the passage, I'm plunged into darkness. I'm stupidly afraid. I feel my way along by the wall, the palm of my hand chafed by the rough cement finish.

Turning the corner into the Bernabéu, I'm met by a cloud of cigarette smoke blown by someone in the shadows by the back wall. My heart skips a beat. But it's only Sean. Angie's here again. *You thought it was Brian, didn't you? Ha ha, as if!*

'Jesus, Sean,' I blurt out. 'You frightened the bloody life out of me. What are you doing?'

'What does it look like I'm doing?' he says and blows some more smoke in my direction. I don't know if it's deliberate, but it pisses me off anyway. I have to hurt him, hit him with something, make him feel as rotten as I do.

'Some show you put on over at the courthouse,' I say. 'Just what Mam needed to see, wasn't it? Her macho super-hero son lashing out and drawing more trouble on us.'

'Get lost, Eala.'

'I won't get lost,' I say, which sounds pure infantile, but I can't shut myself up. I remember Dad's words from the night Sean clocked our baby brother.

'Do you feel better now you've hit a child? Do you feel more like a man?' I ask.

The words are etched on Sean's brain too and it shows. His cigarette hits the ground so hard that sparks fly up and pepper the skin along the side of my leg. I aim a kick at him, but he blocks it off and he's in my face, his fist raised towards me and I make myself laugh because that's what we do, Dad, isn't it? Laugh away every last question, every last problem. What did the clown say when he went to the bar? Remember that one, Dad? The jokes are on me, ha, ha!

'Well? Do you? Feel more like a man?'

'Stop saying that,' he warns, his fist pressing up into my chin. 'That dumb kid is out there walking the streets, probably peddling his old man's shit when he should be in prison.' His voice is breaking up. He pulls away from me. 'He should know what it's like to be locked up . . .'

He's walking around in a crazy circle, his eyes somehow finding enough light to glisten with in this dark.

'And what it's like to spend two years inside and never have one, not even one visitor.' I'm already freezing out here, but the chill that hits me now goes way deeper. Where's all this detail coming from? 'And coming out those prison gates and no one there to meet him and nothing but a plastic bag with a few clothes and a certificate for some prison art competition and a bundle of comics. And the first job you get, they fire you when they find out you've done time and . . .'

A bundle of comics? The only part of me I can move is my lips and that takes some effort.

'Are you talking about . . . is this Dad you're talking about? In prison?'

'I should've told Mam before now,' Sean says. 'Told the both of you. I didn't know what to do.'

'Told us what?'

His back is to the wall. He slides slowly down until he's on his haunches and bent double. He wipes his eyes with a careless hand, looks up at me. I want to sit too, but I'm pure riveted to the spot.

'The night before the accident Dad told me he'd been in jail,' he says. 'He was sixteen. Two years he got for breaking a beer bottle over a guy's skull.'

I can almost hear the white noise of the frost going about its work among the leaves of grass. I imagine standing here so long that the frost will cover my shoes.

'He used to sneak out from the Home where he lived and go to this, like, punk club. One night he meets this girl and they get on right well. When she asks him where he lives, he decides, you know, upfront is best. So he tells her he lives in a foster home, which she seems to be OK with, and they arrange to meet the following week. She never shows up, but her ex does, along with five of his mates.'

'Where did all this happen?' I have a thousand questions, but this is the first one I can get my tongue around.

'North London was all he said. I was in such a state of shock I didn't think to ask what club it was, who was playing, where the foster home was. How dumb am I?'

'So they came after him? And?'

'Dad's out behind the club waiting for her. He told me there was this long redbrick wall with *Palais de Dance* written across it, that he'd never forget. How ironic is that?' Sean says, shaking his head. 'And these guys, they come along chanting this punk song at him, 'Borstal Breakout' – borstal is like a prison for young –'

'I know what a borstal is.'

He looks at me like he doesn't understand how I could be angry with him. *Because Dad chose to tell* you, *dumbo.*

And I don't know which is worse: the pain of hearing this story or the pain of Dad's having told Sean and not me.

'Then they jump Dad and start doing him over. Dad breaks away. The bottle's on the ground and he grabs it when one of the guys pulls a knife and he splits him open, cracks his skull.'

From out front, the noise of shuffled pebbles reaches us. The Ice Queen leaving, I suppose. A light comes on in the kitchen. Mam passes by the window up there and I step closer to the back wall so she won't see me. Sean's looking up at her too.

'I only kept it to myself because Dad asked me to,' he says. 'He wanted her to hear it from him. I kept thinking, *When he's himself again he'll tell her.*'

'He should've been honest with her from the start,' I say. 'She'd have understood.'

I sit on the window sill outside the basement room. There's no light from in there. Above us, the sky's busy shunting clouds along. The world never stops. No matter how exhausted you feel, it keeps dragging you on and on and there's no rest. Not for the wicked, not for anyone. Right, Dad?

'He was afraid is all,' Sean says. 'First time he opens up to anyone, it ends in a scrap that puts him in jail. And remember what Mam's first job was? When they met up? Working with battered wives. She'd have been well impressed, wouldn't she?'

He's right, I suppose, but there's still a lot of missing pieces here.

'So he changed his name because he had trouble getting work?'

'He changed his name?' Sean says and I realize Mam hasn't told him yet. I'm glad. Now he knows what it feels like to be left out. He gets to his feet. No threats now, no hovering over me with his fist.

'Martin was trying to sort out some insurance stuff and they copped that Dad's birth cert was faked.'

'But if we tell Mam, maybe –'

'No,' I say. My mind clears. I know what we have to do. Not do, more like. 'We don't tell Mam. Martin says the insurance money won't be paid over even if we find his real identity. And, think about it, Dad's already attacked Argos and clocked Brian. And if the psychiatrist at the rehab centre finds out about this, what's he going to think except that Dad's got form? And where will that lead? To Dad landing in some kind of institution or whatever? We can't let that happen.'

'I suppose,' Sean says. 'Still doesn't feel right, though.'

Next door, Argos lets rip a few barks. I hear the scrape of his metal feeding bowl along stone paving, the murmur of Mrs Casey's voice.

'Nothing feels right any more,' I tell Sean.

18

'They say that men find it difficult if not impossible to carry out more than one task at the same time. That may be true. But the sad fact is that in musical theatre, it's true of both sexes. The better singers can't act. The better actors can't sing.'

Miss O'Neill leans against the piano at the foot of the assembly hall stage as she delivers more or less the same speech she gave last year and the year before. There's a lightness about her movements today and her tone is brighter. It's like she's acting out the life she really wants to have, rather than the one she's stuck with.

'We've got more time than usual to prepare this year so, for the first few sessions, we'll concentrate on the acting. What we're aiming for is to become the part. And we'll start with some role-reversal exercises.' We did these last year too. They didn't work out very well. She claps her hands. Wake the dead that clap would and I quake inside. Today is not a good day. 'Michael, Marie and Jill, let's be having you.'

There's the usual embarrassed shuffle to the front, the standing around gaping at the floor and trying to work up the nerve to follow Miss O'Neill's directions. As I watch them play the part of parents who've discovered their daughter's going out with some waster, the bad feeling that was there when I woke this morning invades me again. A tightness in my stomach, an aching in my lower back. It's like I'm waiting between a roll of thunder and the lightning to come.

I keep asking myself what I'm doing here, what right I have to be singing and dancing? And why did I take the main role Miss O'Neill offered in the first place? But I know why. I've been mooching around in a kind of silent rage because Dad is happy and, once more, his happiness is not of my making and I'm not even included in it.

'We've got Jimmy a place at the Head-Up Day Services Centre,' Mam announced a few weeks ago.

'The what?' I said.

'The Head-Up Centre,' she explained. 'You know? That prefab building behind the old dance hall on Rock Street. A few hours on Tuesdays and Thursdays is all.'

I didn't know of it and I didn't like the sound of it. I was the little girl of that long-ago Christmas again, not seeing what was under my nose. I mean I've been up and down that street thousands of times. How can I not have spotted a sign or something? Or maybe there isn't one. Maybe they prefer to hide all these brain-injured people away.

'Doing what?' I asked.

The coffee mugs she scrubbed had been ringed with stains for years. Now it seemed like the most important thing in the world for her to clean them.

'Oh, there's . . . there's relaxation exercises and, you know, help with social interaction and . . . The thing is they've got no official funding so they're pretty limited in what they can do until they raise more money. They run that charity shop on the Long Mall.'

I've actually been in that shop a couple of times and never knew what charity it supported. All I remember of it is the smell of stale clothes and a small Asian woman reading a book behind the counter and Jill going, 'These could be dead people's clothes!' Fast fashion is more her style.

'Fiona thinks he's ready for it.'

I was drying the plates she'd washed. I wanted to fling the one I'd taken from her across the kitchen. Instead, I fired off another empty round at Miss Understanding.

'She won't be happy until Dad's locked up somewhere,' I said.

'Don't be like that, Eala,' she said. She wiped her forehead with the back of her wrist. A few drops of water fell on to her cheek. *The tears she should be crying, but never does*, Angie was telling me. 'Look, our miserable health service has little or nothing to offer Jimmy. This Head-Up organization tries to fill some of the gaps and he needs what they have to offer. So do we.'

She went on, but I wasn't listening. To me, all her talk sounded like excuses for seeing even less of him than she already did now that she was back at work. I might have gone ballistic, but I didn't feel I had the right. What was I doing for Dad anyway? Nothing. I couldn't bring myself to. Whenever he was near me, all I felt was resentment.

Sean was late in that night as usual. Half eleven or so. I don't know where he goes or what he gets up to now that he doesn't hang around with Brian any more. Why they've fallen out I have no idea. Maybe it's just as well. At least

Sean's not drinking these times and I don't see any sign that he's doing hash either.

So. In he comes to the sitting room, misery written all over his face as usual. Mam, still in her happy-clappy mood, soon went fast-forward to the subject of Head-Up. How some woman called Foran started up the local centre two years ago after her son suffered a brain injury. How they're slowly building up the services there. How this whole recession business is making it even more difficult to get government funds. I gave Sean one of those sneaky, I-told-you-so looks and he turned on Mam.

'He'll be sitting round a table with a bunch of spastics making baskets,' he said. 'What good will that do? You don't want him here is all. Tuesday and Thursday, your days off work. That's very handy for you, isn't it?'

'Don't you dare call those people spastics,' Mam fumed.

'I just did.'

The first role-reversal exercise is falling apart from lack of inspiration. The parents and daughter are standing there saying nothing, avoiding eye contact with one another. And I'm thinking, *This is the closest they've got to reality in the last ten minutes.*

'OK, then,' Miss O'Neill says. 'That was very good. Now, we'll have Eala and . . .' There's giggling and hoarse laughs coming from behind me. Miss O'Neill does another of her thunderclaps and it drills into my brain. '. . . And Derek.'

She's been caught between two minds over her choice of male lead. Benno Brophy or Derek Rice. Benno's a quiet fellow. Minds his own business. Nice-looking and shy. My guess is he didn't really want the part because he's not keen on the limelight. Derek, on the other hand, is mad for it. He's been doing dance, singing and acting classes since he could walk and talk. Last year when Brian got the main part ahead of him, Derek mysteriously came down with some virus and dropped out of the show. That's Derek for you. Either he's top dog or he doesn't run.

I stand up and take my place alongside Miss O'Neill. One look at Derek's face as he makes his way through the jumble of chairs and feet and I know he's going to start messing.

'Right,' Miss O'Neill says. 'Boy, girl. He hasn't shown up for their date last night. She knows he was with someone else. That sort of thing. Eala, you're the boy. And Derek, keep it clean, right?'

But he's already doing this camp, gay thing behind her back. Hand on hip, limp wrist and fluttering eyebrows. I shouldn't be surprised. His own brother Frankie, who's gone to college in Dublin, is gay and while he still lived here in town, Derek was one of his main tormentors.

'That's so original, Derek,' I mutter at him. Which only makes him ham it up some more.

'Tone. It. Down. Derek,' Miss O'Neill warns, frost at the edges of every word.

He does. But only a little. I'm fed up of his prancing around and lisping. *Shut him up*, Angie is telling me. *Stick the knife in him and twist it*. And I do.

'Frankie's not the only queen in your family, Derek. Singing lessons, dancing classes. All a bit gay, don't you think? For a fellow, like?'

If he's stunned, I'm dumbstruck. I've never said stuff like

that before, never even thought that way. Jill is hiding her eyes, blushing for me. I don't know what to do, what to say.

'You're some wagon, Eala,' Derek says. Then he leers at me. 'I owe you one, right?'

'Thank you both for that little display of homophobia,' Miss O'Neill says.

She's disgusted with me. Not half as disgusted as I am with myself. I wish I could tell her about the glimpse I've had into Dad's past, tell her how I've been shaking inside ever since that cold evening in the Bernabéu. But how could I even begin to?

'OK, let's leave it at that,' she tells us. 'Tomorrow evening we'll try another role reversal. You lot can pretend to be adults for a change.'

'What'll you pretend to be, Miss O'Neill?' Derek says.

'I'll have my brain removed overnight,' she says as she rises stiffly from the piano stool below the stage like she's nursing a dead leg. 'And pretend to be you, Derek.'

He isn't happy about that one, but he has more sense than to get thick. The main part is more important to him than his pride. We scatter. Jill catches up with me near the assembly hall door. We haven't spoken for weeks. She's not sure she wants to talk to me and I don't make it any easier for her to decide. I say nothing. I keep walking. She's got the part of Graziella, the leader of the Jet girls. It's the kind of part Angie would prefer. A more streetwise edge to her. And I'm stupidly jealous. Out in the corridor, Derek and his pals are up ahead and he's mouthing again.

'O'Neill's such a lezzy, I bet she's into role reversals big time,' he says.

The strangled laughter of his hormonally challenged pals echoes around the corridor. One of them hits another a friendly slap in the head and the whole mad gang of them go racing out the front door like dogs chasing a bone.

'What a bunch of losers,' Jill says.

At least she hasn't started with the latest chapter of the Win-and-sprog story. In fact, now that I sneak a glance at her, I realize she's not doing tragedy today. Contentment, more like. So much for missing little orphan Richard. I feel like bursting her bubble.

'Maybe we're all losers,' I say.

'It's just a bit of craic,' she says with a smile. 'Win said this morning that the thing she misses most about school is being in the show every year.'

'She's back?' I ask and I know I shouldn't have.

We reach the double doors at the front of the school and I'm pushing at the handle, but it's stuck. I get thick with myself. Jill steps in and opens the door. Inwards. Why am I getting all fussed up like this? Why does the night air make me so dizzy?

'You won't believe this, Eala,' she says. 'It's like we live in a different house and it's all down to Richard. Mam and Dad went up to Dublin and convinced Win to come home. Not only that, but we're going to take care of the baby while she's in college this year.'

I don't work too hard at being enthusiastic.

'Great,' I say.

'Yeah,' she says. 'And Dad is totally, like, beaming when he comes home from work and even if Richard is asleep in the sitting room, he has to go in and take a look.'

She sniffles. I pretend not to notice. Outside it's bitterly cold as we walk out by the avenue towards the street. The trees are bare along both sides. In the darkness of evening, the branches are lit from below with floodlights and seem so fragile that you wonder if they'll survive the frost. I'm shivering. Jill stops up, suddenly flustered.

'I've to . . . I've to meet Benno down at the sports hall,' she says and looks beyond me towards the school gates.

'You're with Benno? You never told –'

'I texted you loads of times, but you didn't bother to read them, obviously.'

I turn to see what's bothering her over behind me. Under the light globes on the high piers of the school gates, Brian stands. Hands in pockets, his shoulders hunched, chin buried in the scarf round his neck. Great pose, Brian.

'Are you going out with him?' Jill asks.

'No.'

'Keep it that way, Eala; for your own sake, keep it that way.'

Jill hurries off down the path that leads to the sports hall.

'Can we talk?' Brian asks.

'No,' I say, but I don't move and I don't know why I don't move.

'We have to talk about Sean,' he says.

19

This is starting to get ridiculous. We're walking, what, ten minutes now and neither of us has said a word. We're down by the river, which is a great idea if you want to acclimatize yourself for an Antarctic expedition, but not if you ever want to feel your fingers and toes again. The breeze blows into our faces. The water flows in the opposite direction and is so high it's within inches of the riverbank.

'You could've rung me,' I say. 'You've got my number.'

I almost laugh, but it's more mad than funny that I've come out with the title of one of Dad's Undertones songs.

'I knew you wouldn't answer,' Brian says. I sense him watching me, but I stare ahead.

We're moving more slowly. It's like walking and talking is suddenly as difficult as singing and acting at the same time. I'm looking for swans, but I don't see any. Maybe they have more sense than we two have and are sheltering somewhere. We're close to Blackcastle Bridge. From back here where the only street light is out of action it feels like I'm peering from the dark at a place I'll never reach because my legs ache with dread of hearing what he has to tell me about Sean.

I'm not sure I even care about what my brother gets up

to. I hate him so much for being the one Dad confided in. I know Dad was worried that Sean might go totally off the rails, that he had to deal him a major dose of reality. Keep going the way you are and you'll end up in jail for clocking some kid with a beer bottle. Fine. But fair to me? No. The way I see it, I'd have been better off going wild, hanging out on the streets instead of being the sensible type. Then I'd have heard his secret first. Then I'd have got closer to him than I ever actually got.

'Say whatever you have to say, will you?' I tell him. 'I'm pure freezing here.'

Brian stops up and I face him. He looks older. Beaten up. The bridge of his nose is slightly flattened after the break. Under his left eye, there's a recently healed scar and I can't honestly remember if that was Dad's doing too. I think I prefer this version than the pretty one.

'Sean is stalking Clem Healy,' he says.

'How do you know?' My breath flutters and sets my heart thumping. 'You two don't even talk any more.'

He's not so sure he should have started this. He looks around him like he's the one being stalked.

'I know because he asked me to help him. I told him no way. He knows what those Healys are like, but he's planning something. I'm sure he is.'

'What am I supposed to do about this? Like I don't have enough to deal with already?'

'Look, Eala, all I know is the kid is terrified. And my guess is he hasn't told his old man yet because that guy will go ballistic if he hears what's going on. He's done time for assault before. Assault and worse.'

'Yeah,' I say. 'Like drug-dealing. You should know.'

And the swans come. Not a bother on them. Two, three with their young. Seven in all. Floating upwards against the current. The whole crazy world of people nothing to them. Brian tracks them too. He's leaning on the stone wall. I watch him watching the swans.

'Before we came to town, we used to live in this small village outside Cork,' he says. 'And there was this field near my grandfather's house, really low-lying it is and it gets flooded every year. I mean, there isn't even a river there. And every year the swans come to that field. Incredible, isn't it? It's like they know, man, like they know exactly when that water's ready for them. I really missed that when we came to live here.'

'Why did you move?' I ask.

'Dad got a promotion,' he says. 'So we all had to follow him to this dump.'

I don't know why I feel so touchy about him insulting our town. It's not like I'm pure in love with the place or anything.

'You're old enough to move away if you want to,' I say.

Act your age, not your shoe-size, Angie tells me. I'm tired. Tired of being angry, tired of being hyped up all the time, tired of pretending I don't like Brian.

Angie's having a good chuckle at me. *If this was Jill crying on your shoulder, Eala, you'd be gone in a flash*. I blink Angie away. I don't avoid Brian's eyes when he turns to me. I wait for something to happen, but he doesn't know what to do. No, of course he knows what to do. He's having second thoughts about whether he wants to do it with me. And now that he's taken a good long look, he's decided maybe not. He looks at the river again. *It feels like he's stolen something from me. Something I've never had. I'm all hollowed out, so empty it hurts.*

'I should head home,' I say.

We walk down towards the turn into my street. The river whispers like a spreading rumour. *She thought he fancied her; how dumb is that? Big deal*, Angie says. *Plenty more fish in the river.* The sea, Angie, and I can't swim.

'How's Jimmy doing?' he asks.

'If you really wanted to know, you'd call around and ask him yourself.'

'I know I should,' he says. 'But I can't.'

'Yeah, you've fallen out with Sean so Jimmy can go take a run and jump. I'll walk the rest of the way on my own, thanks.'

'That's not why.' He's come to a halt again, but I keep moving.

'Right, so it's what, then? Starsky won't let you? Or your mother?'

'Not exactly. It's . . . complicated.'

As I turn the corner into my street, I look back at him. He hangs in the shadows, trying to look dark and mysterious.

'Stuff your *complicated*, Brian.'

I'm already on our street when I hear him again.

'I'm sorry, Eala.'

I stop up like it's me who's been hit with the hard-helmet missile. Except I don't fall over. There's a gang of kids coming towards me with their hoodies up and though I can't see their faces, I feel sure Clem Healy is among them. They drift closer. No Clem. Angie's at it again. *You can't go wobbly like this every time you see a hoodie, Eala, you wear the flipping things most of the time yourself, ha, ha!*

'Stuff your *sorry*,' I call out and the kids are looking around to see who I'm talking to and looking at me like I've lost the plot because Brian's back around the corner. They go by me.

'Eala,' Brian calls and I hear the kids repeating my name, hamming up the plea in Brian's voice and laughing their pimply little faces off.

Then I remember his story of the swans and I feel like a pure airhead for falling into his sweet-talking trap. I bet he knows that Eala's the Irish for swan. So, he invents this cute little fable for me like I'm a five-year-old being tucked in for the night.

'And stuff your feckin' swans,' I tell him and the young lads are in hysterics over at the river wall.

'Eala?' Brian says. 'Eala.'

I keep walking, keep hoping he'll follow me.

He doesn't.

20

The madness never ends. And the horrible thing about madness is that it's as funny as it is sad. So I stare in by the half-basement window at the brightly lit room and a part of me weeps and the rest of me wants to guffaw like the boys back at rehearsal or the kids on our street a few minutes ago.

Dad's bed is a trampoline for Tom. He bounces up and down, clapping and laughing as Dad, decked out in one of his blue Zidane jerseys, dances with the Ice Queen. Dad can't dance. He never could and never wanted to. But he's having the time of his life in there. Grinning from ear to ear as he looks down at the Ice Queen's feet, trying to get the moves right.

For the Ice Queen it's a more serious business. She's got this stern, determined expression and though she's smaller and thinner than Dad, she pulls him about so easily he might be weightless. It's like one of those dumb celebrity dance programmes on TV. Because I can't hear the music out here on the drive, the whole scene seems even more farcical.

Mam's car isn't here. I check the time on my mobile. I ignore the 3 MESSAGES RECEIVED. Almost half past six.

It's the first time Mam's been late home since she went back to work. Then again, this is the latest I've been home too in a long time.

As they begin to twirl around, Dad's left hand is on the Ice Queen's waist, his right arm outstretched alongside hers. His head is thrown back, his eyes closed. They speed up and I know they're spinning too fast. The Ice Queen takes off and flies across the floor towards the bed. Tom dodges away in time and she lands beside him. Dad stands there with his right arm still raised and starts to laugh. I hear the Ice Queen because she's shouting.

'Stupid man. Stupid, stupid man. You hurt me!'

I rush forward and bang on the window. Tom waves at me. He's laughing so hard that two great yellow trails of snot hang down from his nose. Dad's not laughing. His head is bowed and he plays with his watch. The Ice Queen turns to the window. I can tell she's pure relieved it's me and not Mam standing here. She looks right through me like I don't matter and I'm away round the corner of the house like a raging Argos making for the back door.

The path alongside the gable end is slippy with evening dew and I slide right down on my bottom and it's wet and it hurts and why can't life stop playing these ridiculous games with me. I get to the back door and charge in. Dad still stands at the centre of the room, but now the Ice Queen is holding him. His head is resting on her shoulder and she's rubbing her hand along the scar above his temple.

'Jimmy, Jimmy,' she says. 'Marta make mistake. Not Jimmy.'

I can't get any words out. I can't move my legs. I feel

Tom's arms clutching me. He's hiding his head in the folds of my skirt. Whimpering, which kicks me into gear.

'Don't touch him,' I warn her. 'You have no right to touch him.'

She steps away from Dad. She's afraid, but not of me. Afraid she'll lose her job more like. Bet your life you'll lose your job. Dad doesn't know what to do or where to look, which makes him seem so gormless I totally lose it.

'I heard what you said to him. How dare you. Soon as Mam hears about this you'll be out on the street where you belong.'

'I said I was sorry,' Dad tells me. 'And Marta said she was sorry. So it's OK. It's not problem.'

'It's not *a* problem,' I say.

Tom is sobbing and holding on tighter to my legs. I want to push him off me. What's happening to me? Don't I love anyone any more?

'He can't even speak English now because of you.'

'Eala.' She stresses the *a* at the end of my name, stretching it out until I'm at breaking point.

'I was just kidding,' Dad says. 'Course I can speak English.'

'Jimmy, you don't let her touch you. D'you get it? And you don't touch her. She's a stranger. It isn't . . . it isn't right. Right?'

His forehead seems to bulge and throb with the effort at understanding. He starts pressing the buttons on his watch and the beeps are horrible to hear and his confusion is horrible to see. Horrible.

'She's not your friend, Jimmy,' I say.

'Yes, she is. She's one of my best mates. Her and Alan.

And she's the ballroom dancing champion of Moravia. Right, Marta?'

'Alan?' I say.

'I go home,' the Ice Queen says.

'Yeah, why don't you?' I say. 'Go back to Moravia and whatever you got up to over there besides ballroom dancing. Pole dancing, was it? Or, no, lap dancing, maybe?'

I don't know where all this is coming from, but it feels good to throw some dirt at this woman. I'm getting to her. The ice in her pale blue eyes is melting. Tom lets go of me. He sits on the floor and sobs into his fists.

'Maaa . . . meee,' he sniffles.

'Aw, To*mas*,' the Ice Queen says and the name comes out like 'dumb ass'. She takes a step forward. I move between her and Tom.

'His name is Tom not To*mas*. And don't you come near him.'

Dad moves at last. He walks over with that dragging step of his and picks up Tom.

'Aw, To*mas*,' he parrots.

'His name is Tom,' I insist. 'Call him Tom.'

'Names don't matter,' Dad says.

'They do matter. You have no bloody idea how much they matter, Jimmy.'

The TV screen catches my eye. A DVD on freeze-frame and I freeze too. The girl with the mad red curly wig. Her mouth wide in mid-song, her eyes raised heavenwards. I know this DVD so well, I can tell what the next line of the song is and it sings itself in my head, though I don't want it to.

'You had no right to play this DVD,' I tell the Ice Queen.

'But Jimmy love this "Tomorrow".'

The glare of headlights coming directly at the front window blinds me. Mam's car pulling into the drive. The lights go off and the Ice Queen now stands within arm's reach of me. It feels pure weird like she's not walked towards me, but floated.

'I'm going up right now to talk to my mother about you,' I say. ' So pack up your –'

'You are not good for Jimmy this way,' she says. I could easily hit her and she knows it, but she doesn't back away. 'You love too much.'

I'm in her face.

'English, dumbo, we speak English here,' I say and I remember Jill telling me about a young Polish kid who was bullied in First Year with these exact words. I'm sickened. From above us, I hear the front door close out and Mam calls.

'Hi all!'

Pure upbeat, like 'I have a life again'. *Lucky her*, Angie says. Before me, a weird transformation takes place. The Ice Queen morphs into Miss Understanding Mark Two. Her eyes are wide with sympathy. A tear emerges. One tear.

'My father is dead last year,' she says. 'I am not happy also.'

I sweep by her and head for the stairs. First chance I get, Mam, I'll burst your happy little bubble.

21

I've been here all evening in my room except for the five minutes it took to eat my dinner. I'm waiting for Mam to snap so I can have a go at her. She's had to cook the dinner, get Tom ready for bed, sort out Dad for the night. I told her I had to study, that I was falling way behind at school. Which is true. The falling behind bit. As for study, I haven't opened one book. I tried to listen to some music, but I don't have the heart for it tonight. Four hours have passed and I'm fit to explode.

It's not easy to get this door open without a creak, but I manage. Not a stir from the house below. Quiet there is, but no peace. Not in my head anyway. I head down the stairs. No light under Sean's door, which means he's out on the street, trailing Clem and heading for a showdown with the Healys. The door of Mam's room is slightly ajar. Tom's asleep, cuddling into his green tractor. Weird, the things kids can find comfort in. Pity it doesn't stay like that.

I find Mam in the sitting room. It's stiflingly hot in here, though we don't light the fire any more. There's something bleak and empty about a fireplace when there are no dancing flames. The TV's turned off and she's listening to a CD. She's stretched out on the sofa in the sitting room like she's posing for some boho photo shoot. Her eyes half closed, her fringe a veil, her thighs showing as her dress slides up. I want to grab the glass of red wine from her hand and throw it in her face. I want to ask her why she's listening to music again after all this time.

It's one of her choral things. Arvo Pärt, her favourite composer. *The Woman with the Alabaster Box*. I know the piece because I've heard it so often in the past, though not since the accident. A few years ago, she and Dad went to a concert of this guy's music in Dublin and she came home in an ecstasy because Pärt himself had unexpectedly shown up. 'She's fallen in love with a beardy old Russian monk!' Dad joked. 'Estonian, actually,' she said, 'and unfortunately he's married with kids.' I was ten or eleven and I remember being right thick with Mam. What was I like? What am I like?

'Eala,' she says, her eyes still drowsy. 'Makes me want to go back to the choir, that music does. Soon maybe.'

I don't answer. She wants to go out singing her hymns while our lives are going down the tube?

'Did you get loads done?'

'No,' I say. 'Do you want to know why?'

Her head does a kind of lazy roll and she looks at me.

'Because I caught that woman dancing with Dad. Dancing.'

'I knew about the dancing,' Mam says. 'Marta asked me if it was OK and I thought why not? It's good for his coordination and why shouldn't he have a bit of fun?'

'But it's crazy,' I said. 'She's supposed to be a carer, not a flippin' dance instructor.'

'Eala, she was making conversation with Jimmy the other day and mentioned the ballroom dancing and he kept pleading with her to teach him. She did the right thing. She came to me first.'

'Yeah, well you didn't see what I saw. Dad gets the steps wrong and she goes flying and she called him stupid! "Stupid man", she said.'

'But we all lose the rag now and again with him. We can't wrap him in cotton wool, you know. And she was very apologetic.'

'I don't believe this. She tells you she's making a monkey of your husband and you're going, "Fire away,"' I said.

'Sit down, Eala.' She taps the sofa, raises a hand towards me and I pass up the invitation.

'Well, here's something you don't know, then. Sean's stalking Clem Healy.'

She sinks further back on to the sofa. *It's the wine*, I'm thinking, *and the hushed tones of the* a cappella *singing from the CD player. She's half-cut and the world is all harmony and nothing's a problem.*

'I'll talk to him,' she says and I wait for more, but nothing comes.

'Don't you care about anything any more? Apart from your job. You stay so late, you must really love it.'

'I wasn't late at work. I went for a drink.'

'Some stranger is fondling your husband. Your son is playing with fire. And you go on the razz? With who?' And it dawns on me. 'Miss Understanding.'

'With Fiona, yes.'

She puts the glass on the coffee table and sits back again,

but not so elegantly. All coiled up and dishevelled, she lets her skirt ride up embarrassingly high. *For God's sake, cover yourself up.*

'At work today,' she says, 'I fell apart.'

The first thing I feel is disappointment. She should have fallen apart here at home because then I could let myself fall apart too and we'd pick one another up. *Isn't that how families are supposed to work*, Angie asks? The ones that aren't terminally dysfunctional, that is.

'I had to visit this young girl,' she goes on. 'Same age as you. She's had a child and there's not much support at home. Her mother's gone. Her father's a complete waster. Her brother's in jail. And this girl, she hasn't got a clue how to take care of the baby. You know, proper diets and all that. As for budgeting her money, forget it. And yet she's on cloud nine thinking this baby is going to put right everything that's gone wrong in her life. And I know in my heart and soul it's a disaster waiting to happen. I've seen it time and again. Her mother was exactly the same and it ended in a terrible mess and what can I do about it? Not a damn thing, it seems.'

'At least she has someone to love,' I tell her. 'And it might work out. It's working out fine for Win and her child. More than fine. The baby brought the whole family together. And her dad's a totally changed man.'

'It's a very different situation, Eala,' she says.

'Because this girl you met is poor or something?'

'Not poor. Or not only poor. But troubled, very troubled,' she says, and I don't like the worried expression that passes across her face as she stares at me. 'I haven't been paying attention to you, Eala. I've taken you for granted, haven't I? Solid, sensible Eala.'

'There's nothing wrong with me.'

'We're all under pressure, Eala.' Mam plays with her wedding ring, slides it off and on. 'Today of all days.'

'Today?'

'This day last year?' She gives me a quizzical look. 'The accident?'

My legs can't bear the weight in me. I sit down on the sofa beside her. How can I have forgotten this worst of anniversaries. The music of unaccompanied voices is starting to freak me. They sing a line that's all harmony. Then there's too long a pause before the voices come again and seem to clash. Another long pause and it's harmony again and on it goes, pause after pause like they can't catch their breaths, like they're dying. I lean back on the sofa and close my eyes. I'm totally wrecked. I see the Ice Queen, hear her. You love too much . . . And maybe she's right because for all my efforts I seem to be slipping further down Dad's list of favourites below the Ice Queen and some guy I've never heard of called Alan.

'Who's this Alan guy he talks about?' I ask. 'His new best mate.'

'He's one of the clients at the Head-Up Centre,' Mam explains. 'His parents got the place up and running. You'll meet them at the Christmas concert.'

'The Christmas concert?' I'm up on the edge of the sofa. I imagine Dad and the others acting out some childish nonsense on stage while we sit cringing in the audience. 'Like some kiddies' school show? No way am I –'

'It's nothing like that. It's a fundraising concert,' Mam

says. 'Some local acts and a raffle and that kind of thing. We have to support it.'

'Will this Alan guy be there?'

'Yeah. He's a lovely fellow is Alan. Such a pity he may be moving on soon,' she says, and I don't like the sound of this.

'Where's he going?'

'Well, he's on the waiting list for a residential home in Limerick and there's a good chance he'll get a place there.'

'They're putting him away?'

'It's not some institution or anything, Eala,' she says. 'It's a house for four or five people and there's twenty-four-seven supervision and –'

'Is that your plan for Dad too? Dump him in a home? I bet this is another of Miss Understanding's bright ideas.'

Mam withdraws the hand she'd offered me. Her lips are purple and ugly from the red wine. She does a couple of those dopey exaggerated blinks that drunks do. Then she tries to glare at me all offended, except her eyes won't stop crossing.

'Jimmy's not on any waiting list and even if he was, he'd be waiting for years there are so few places. Anyway, this is his home,' she says. She lets her eyes close and stay closed long enough to get focused again. 'And another thing – I wish you'd stop using that nickname for Fiona. She's been a good friend to me and we need our friends. You do too. What's happened between you and Jill?'

'Nothing.'

'We don't agree all of the time, Fiona and me. In fact we disagree quite a lot, but that's what friends are for, right?'

'Like I don't know anyone else besides Jill?' I say. I can

feel myself veering off into fantasy and I don't stop. 'Well, I do actually have someone.'

She blushes a little. I blush a lot. Angie thinks it's hilarious. *Another invisible friend, Eala, ha ha!*

'I'm glad,' Mam says. 'Am I allowed to ask who this someone might be?'

Then, for once in his life, Sean comes to my rescue. We hear the front door open and swing shut with a bang, his school bag hit the hallway floor with a thud. He's home earlier than usual. Mam sits up, straightens her skirt and brushes a hand through her hair. She knocks back what's left in the wine glass.

'You have to talk to him,' I say.

'I know, I know.'

Sean opens the sitting-room door, but hangs at the doorframe. He floats somewhere between cheerful and smug. His iPod earphones pop and whizz. He looks from Mam to me and back again.

'What?' he asks too loudly and switches off the music. 'What?'

'Where were you?' I say, jumping in because Mam's way too slow about it.

'Mind your own business.'

'Sean,' Mam says.

'But I'm not even late. What is this? Guantanamo Bay Interrogation Centre?'

'Are you following Clem Healy?' Mam asks straight up and she's gone well beyond sober and on to Judy's *hauteur*.

Sean turns to me. He does a few quick calculations in his head and the result is a filthy look.

'You've been talking to Brian,' he says. 'Is that all you've been doing with him?'

'Sean.' Mam stands up too quickly and knocks over the wineglass. It rings and tinkles across the coffee table and when it hits the floor, the stem breaks neatly from the bowl. 'There was nothing in it anyway,' she says, all flustered with embarrassment and maybe dizzy too. She seems to have forgotten what the argument was about. 'For God's sake . . . for God's sake . . .'

'I've never touched that kid, Mam, and I never will. I swear,' Sean says, and all she does is accept his promise with a nod.

He goes and gets his school bag from the hallway. As he passes the top of the stairs leading to Dad's room, he pauses and looks down.

'Well, Jimmy, how's it going?' he says.

'Good, I'm good, it's all good,' I hear Dad say from below. 'You coming down for a while? Play some *Premiership*?'

Sean taps his loaded bag.

'Have to do some homework, Jimmy. Catch you later, right?'

'Later. No sweat, Sean, no sweat,' Dad says and it comes out like a descending scale of notes that might easily have fitted into Mam's mournful choral music.

And it's the saddest thing to see her face now, the saddest thing.

I should offer to take Sean's place, but I don't. As soon as I hear Dad's door close down below, I escape to my room, to my bed. I turn off my bedside lamp. I long for sleep, but every time I close my eyes, I see Mam's face. I pull the covers over my head like they'll block out the image.

I try to think of other things and it's the girl Mam spoke of earlier that comes to mind and Win and their babies. I think of the baby Mam might have had and how differently things might have worked out if Dad could have held it tenderly like he held Richard that day in the Bernabéu. I see his face lighting up, his eyes brightening, his brain kick-starting as he realizes he's a father. I see him sharing all the tasks having a baby involves, taking on the old responsibilities again and, nappy by nappy, bedtime story by bedtime story, becoming the man he once was, the father he once –

'Judy?'

It's Dad. I ease the duvet down from over my head. The door is wide open and Dad is silhouetted there. He's got a bread knife in his hand. I'm frightened of him. Sick in my heart that I'm frightened of my father.

'What's the bread knife for, Jimmy?' I ask, breathless with dread.

'The Man might be about,' he whispers. 'I thought this was Judy's room. I can't sleep with Argos barking. I think that crazy lady next door puts him up to it.'

'Course, she doesn't.'

'She does an' all,' he says. 'She's got it in for me. I've seen how she looks at me.'

'Jimmy, why don't I go down to your room and let you sleep here. That way you won't hear Argos.'

'No.' He checks out the landing behind him. 'I'll pop into Judy's. Which door is hers?'

He's wearing football shorts and a black and white striped Juventus jersey. The house is cold and I shiver for him.

'Better not, Jimmy,' I say. 'Tom's in there and he'll wake up if you go in. You know how hard it is to get him to sleep. Give me the knife, Jimmy.'

He wanders in, dragging his foot every few steps. There's something rattling in his pocket. It can't be matches, can it? He sits on my bed and places the bread knife on my duvet.

'Have you got a box of matches in your pocket, Jimmy?'

'Yeah,' he says. 'I'm hiding them. He might start a fire.'

'The Man?'

He nods. I put my hand out. He reaches into his pocket and gives me the matches. He's got that old '*profonditées de l'existence*' expression of his. It reminds me of my innocence back then. There I was, imagining that look had something to do with his work. Figuring out some plot point. Chasing some new idea. I should've known it was just plain sadness, his past catching up on him, overwhelming him.

'I'm fed up, Eala,' he says. 'I don't know what to do with myself.'

His shoulders are hunched and he fiddles with his watch. If he gets really agitated, I'll have to pop him another downer, another sleeper too maybe. I'm trying to remember where I put the tablets. I'm in charge of them when Mam's not around or when she's tied up with Tom.

'I don't want to live here any more,' he says. 'I've stayed here too long. You can't stay in the same place too long.'

'Why?'

'The Man,' he says. 'He'll suss you out.'

'Where would you like to live, Jimmy?'

He thinks about it for a bit. Whatever resentment I felt towards him evaporates as I watch his childlike indecision.

'On a boat on a river, maybe,' he says, which I find odd because he doesn't seem to like the water when we go down to the River Walk. When we used to go down to the River Walk. Maybe this isn't only some random thought of his.

'Did you ever live on a boat?' I ask.

'I think so,' he says. His eyes narrow in concentration. 'Or was it a dream?' The seconds counter on his digital watch can't be right, it moves the time along so hesitantly. He presses one of the little controls and flinches when the watch beeps. 'Maybe living on a boat's not such a good idea. Water can catch fire, you know.'

I wonder where this latest obsession comes from, this fire thing. From his prison days or the years in residential homes? I know we've been told that the brain injury can make him imagine weird stuff. But I look at his worried frown and it seems to me that all these fears – the Man, fire, water catching fire – are the kinds of fears a very young child might have. I can't help thinking that they might go right back to the time when he still had a mother. There are more secrets. I feel certain of that.

'How much would it cost to go to Moravia?' Dad asks.

'A fair whack, Jimmy,' I say, trying to keep things light because I'm this close to cracking up. 'There's four of us and –'

'No, I'll go on my own,' he says. 'There's nothing but hassle with you lot. Always fighting and arguing and ordering me about.'

I'm gutted, pure gutted. Why do you keep letting me down, Dad? Can't you see what you're doing to me?

'Or if Moravia is too expensive, I could go out to Alan's house in Borris. It'd be nice to live out in the countryside. And Alan never fights with me.'

I slip back under the duvet and wait for him to go. A horrible, tense emptiness invades me. My legs feel like I've hit the wall in some endless marathon. The bed rocks lightly like a boat might when he lifts his weight from it. I hear him shuffle away, shuffle and drag. I hear the carpeted stairs sag step by step beneath him. The creak of his door when it comes might be in another house, it's so far away.

The press above the fridge in the kitchen. That's where I left Dad's tablets. The trembling inside me is frightening. My heart races. I have to calm down. I need something to calm me down. One tablet. Just this once.

22

The Head-Up Centre prefab is a pure wreck of a place hidden away behind the old dance hall on Rock Street. The outside walls are stained with black damp, the windows wet with condensation that drips down and rots the timber sills. I've never been here before and already I hate it. Sean does too. Tom is cranky and clingy, which is his way of saying he's not comfortable either among the Christmas Fundraising Concert crowd. Mam is all smiles as she floats around the reception area from one group to the next offering sausage rolls and chicken wings like a perfect hostess. Dad's talking to his new friends. He seems perfectly content.

To one side of Dad is the strangely beautiful young man who, earlier on, poured the Coke we're sipping at. He has this weird combination of deeply sallow skin and red-gold hair and eyebrows so dark they're almost black above the hazelnut eyes. It turns out he's Alan, Dad's latest best mate. I don't know why, but I expected Alan to be closer to Dad's age. He doesn't look much more than twenty-four or twenty-five and walks with a stick. Sitting in a wheelchair on his other side, is a woman who's maybe in her mid-thirties. Her head moves constantly from side to side like she doesn't have any control over it, but her gaze is fixed on Dad. She seems to find everything he says pure hilarious.

'It's a freaking freak show,' Sean mutters.

'Sean bold,' Tom says. He's hanging on my neck like I'm a banana tree and my ears are the bananas.

'We're here for Dad,' I remind Sean. 'Relax, will you?' Which is easy for me to say because I slipped one of Dad's anxiety tabs before we came.

Our conspiracy of silence over the prison story hasn't brought us any closer. The opposite if anything.

'Shut it, Eala.'

'Sean bold,' Tom says again. He might be a toddler, but he really knows how to get under his brother's skin. He'll keep this up until Sean spills over. Bold this, bold that.

'Listen, Saddo, if you don't zip it up, I'll knock seven colours of shit out of you.' Which is typically dumb of Sean because what else is Tom going to say but . . .

'Bold, bold.'

Tom's pointing a finger at Sean for all to see as he raises his voice, but there isn't time for an argument to develop. I don't know who this man approaching us is, but he smiles like we're his oldest pals. He's somewhere in his mid-sixties, greying at the temples. His coffee-brown linen suit is casual but expensive. He extends his hand to me.

'My name is Peter Foran,' he says. 'I'm Alan's father. And you're Jimmy's family, am I right?'

He shakes hands with Sean. I don't know what to say. I leave it to Sean to come up with something. Not a great idea.

'What happened to Alan?' he asks straight up.

'I'm Eala,' I say, trying to rescue the situation. 'This is Sean. And the little monkey here is Tom. Say hello, Tom.'

"lo Tom,' my little brother pipes up.

We all laugh. Peter tickles Tom's nose and I wonder if he's remembering his son at Tom's age.

'Five years ago,' he says, 'Alan was beaten up outside a nightclub in Dublin and left for dead. He's come a long way since then. We all have.'

'Did they ever catch who did it?' Sean asks and I'm cringing at his persistence, but Peter doesn't seem to mind.

'Two of them left the country. Didn't have the moral courage to face up to what they'd done. The third one served six months in jail and died of a heroin overdose last year. These people punish themselves in the long run.'

'And if they don't care what they've done?' Sean says.

Peter shrugs. He's so relaxed in himself, he reminds me a lot of the old Dad. Reminds me too of what Dad might have become, still managing to look cool in his sixties.

'I spent the best part of three years fantasizing about how I'd make those people pay for what happened, Sean,' he tells us. 'Three wasted years. I wanted revenge, but I should've been asking what my wife and Alan wanted.'

At the far side of the crowded room, a woman speaks into a microphone.

'Ladies and gentlemen, can we all take our seats now in the Rainbow Hall. Our show begins in five minutes.'

'No way am I going in there,' Sean says as people file past us and along the corridor. 'What are they going to do – the frigging Nativity or something?'

'Keep your voice down,' I tell him. 'You heard what Mam

said. It's a few local acts doing their bit for a good cause, right?'

But Sean isn't listening. He's spotted something or somebody up ahead and he's not happy about it. We're pressed forward towards the Rainbow Hall by the people following us. The corridor is too narrow for escape.

'I knew it,' Sean says, fire in his eyes.

I see what's grabbed his attention. Up by the door to the Rainbow Hall, Mam is chatting with Peter Foran. No smiles exactly, but a kind of worrying lightness and ease about them.

'That big heart-to-heart was a pure set-up,' Sean says. 'Mam put him up to it. Does she think I'm a psychopath or what?'

'What's she supposed to think?' I snap back at him. 'And you chasing this Healy kid around.'

'I'm not chasing anyone,' he says and we're sucked into the Rainbow Hall.

Earlier in the afternoon, we were given a tour of the Centre. The art room where I avoided looking too closely at the drawings and paintings and the misshapen bits of pottery on display because I didn't want to see any of Dad's efforts. The exercise room with yoga mats on the floor and some of those big balls you do stretching exercises with. The computer room wasn't much bigger than a closet and had all of two ancient-looking computers.

What they call the Rainbow Hall isn't part of the prefab. It's actually the old dance hall Mam used to go to when she was my age. She told me about it when we did the tour. The blinds on the long windows were drawn. A kaleidoscope of molten colours swirled around the bare white walls. In the background, some New-Age-type music shimmered. A soft, electronic pulse below the twitter of birds and the patter of rain. It's supposed to be relaxation music, but I'm pretty sure it would drive me spare if I had to listen to an hour of it.

'We used to have hops and discos here,' Mam said, the colours playing across her face like sweet memories. 'We had great craic.'

'We?' I asked. Dad's tablet hadn't kicked in yet and I was pure uptight.

'My friends, the girls I went to school with.'

'And Martin?'

'Yeah, Martin too,' she said distractedly. 'It seems so much smaller than I remember it.'

The colours are still swirling in the Rainbow Hall as I carry Tom inside and Sean follows, grumbling to himself. At least the tinkly music isn't playing. We find seats, but not beside Mam. She's near the back, flanked by Peter and the small, middle-aged Asian woman from the charity shop. His wife, I'm guessing, because Alan has her brown eyes and her dark unblemished skin.

On the stage there's a few amps and microphone stands and, over to the left, one of those digital pianos. Emblazoned on the wall behind is a multicoloured sign in a rainbow shape. WELCOME TO THE RAINBOW CABARET!!! I get this horribly cruel image in my mind of Dad and Alan and a few others colouring the sign in, the tips of their tongues sticking out as they work.

'If you're really quiet,' I tell Tom, 'I'll buy you a huge bag of sweets on the way home, OK?'

He nods. I know he won't make a sound. He's got that

serious expression on his face, an expression that's become too familiar. Troubled and yet curious. We had such an easy time, Sean and me, such a good time all through our childhood. Nothing can ever change that, can it? The hall darkens. Then the stage lights come on.

I scan the crowd, but don't see Dad and wonder if he's helping backstage. Along the centre aisle between the double rank of chairs, Peter Foran makes his way towards the stage and takes the little flight of steps to its left in three long-legged strides. As he crosses to the microphone centre stage, he looks much younger than he does close up. He doesn't seem in the least nervous as he begins.

'You're all very welcome to our second annual fundraising Rainbow Cabaret. For your entertainment we have some well-known local celebrities and a few surprises from among our own group here at the Head-Up Centre. And a raffle, of course.'

'Oh, for Christ's sake,' Sean mumbles and I know he's thinking what I'm thinking. Not Dad. Please, don't come out on that stage, Dad. I swear I'll totally lose it with Mam if this turns out to be a sick farce.

'As many of you will know, we've been making steady progress in developing our services here at the Centre,' Peter Foran continues. 'And I'm happy to say that we're close to agreement on funding from the health services for some of our rehabilitation activities. Of course, there's much more we can do and need to do and our long-term ambition has always been to provide not only day-care facilities, but also to offer the opportunity of transitional and independent living in a fully equipped and supervised residence.'

I can't focus on what he's saying. All I can think of is Dad limping out on to that stage. Doing what? Then it hits me. Dancing? Dancing with the Ice Queen? I'm shaking so much that Tom cuddles closer as if to warm me.

'Raising funds in this time of recession is more difficult than ever, of course, but we may soon be in a position to make a major announcement in this respect. The details have yet to be ironed out but, suffice it to say, that the New Year may see the most exciting development yet in our efforts to provide the services and facilities that all ABI sufferers deserve. So on that positive if slightly mysterious note, let me introduce our first act. Please put your hands together for Vanadium!'

'Van wha'?' Sean says.

'Vanadium,' I tell him. 'It's one of the heavy metals.'

'Where'd you learn that?' he says sourly. 'From Brian?'

Vanadium is a gang of skinny kids with great hair. Early learners as far as musical abilities go. But they try hard and they're having fun. Nothing much wrong with that. They do a White Stripes cover. 'The Hardest Button to Button'. Great choice, lads. Sean moans all the way through and doesn't clap when they finish. Next up is an Oasis cover. 'Wonderwall'. Tom loves it. He jigs away to his heart's content on my lap. Their last effort is a Black Sabbath special and they go at it like they're possessed. It's called 'Paranoid'. These guys are not into subtlety. The crowd urges them on and Tom joins enthusiastically in the clapping and makes me clap too. Sean's not impressed with either the band or with me.

'Lighten up,' I say, though I feel like a maniac trying to clap away the dread. Not Dad. Please, not Dad.

The applause for Vanadium dies down and Peter Foran

returns to the microphone. He's pure beaming from ear to ear and all this cheerfulness is getting to me. I know it's fair lousy of me, but I wonder if he's happy because his son will soon be dumped in that home over in Limerick.

'And now for something quite different,' he says. 'Please welcome to the stage the one and only Alan Foran.'

I don't join in the applause. Tom's my excuse. I move him to a more comfortable position on my lap. Sean doesn't clap either, but Tom does. Alan Foran limps along with his stick to the mike.

'My name is Alan Foran. The first piece I'm going to play for you was recorded in nineteen fifty-eight by the American jazz pianist Bill Evans who died on the fifteenth of September nineteen eighty. It's called *Peace Piece*.'

The kaleidoscopic colours are switched on again. Alan limps over to the piano and sits down. My head goes down and I'm thinking, *Please don't let this be too awful*. He plays two slow single notes down low, two chords further up, the second one kind of off-key, but somehow right. It's a simple pattern repeated and repeated until I'm wondering if this is all there is to it. Then the right hand comes in, high chiming notes, but not a melody. It's beautiful.

I look up and see that Dad has taken a seat in the front row and I realize that he's not going to appear on stage. There's nothing he could do up there and anyway his was a different kind of talent, but a talent that, unlike Alan's, is gone forever. And I'm like some little girl discovering that her father isn't the biggest, strongest, most gifted man on the planet. And it grieves me and I need to tell someone how much it grieves me.

As he watches Alan, Dad's expression is one of quiet pleasure and admiration. Alan follows the liquid colours flowing along the wall before him so intently that it's almost as if he's reading the music in them. The left-hand pattern never changes, but his right hand gets busier and busier and yet not loudly. The tune ends, but not until the last far vibrations have dissolved does the crowd break into applause.

Alan waits patiently for silence to descend again. He doesn't go back to the microphone, but his voice carries anyway.

'I'd like to dedicate this next piece to my very good friend, Jimmy Summerton,' he says.

23

Christmas on the town square. Lights strung across the street and around the edges of the shop windows. Music pouring out of every second shop and from tinny speakers scattered around the square. Music that all seems to come from the same album. *Aren't You Sick of Christmas Songs? Volume 3.* Shane MacGowan and Kirsty MacColl sound like they never want to sing 'Fairytale of New York' ever again once they've finished this tired effort. But there's no escape for them any more than there is for me. If you stand here long enough, you realize the songs are repeated in a never-ending loop. I've been standing here long enough.

People rush about and you can almost see the credit cards burning rectangular holes in their pockets and handbags. And everywhere the message is the same. Happiness for sale. But you'd better hurry before the recession bites big time. I wish I'd asked Brian to meet me somewhere else, somewhere quiet. I hate standing here by the entrance to Supersnax. Hate being gawked at, being invited inside by brainless skangers for 'a burger and whatever you're having yourself'. I don't even know why I said Supersnax because I never go in there. Serve me right if he doesn't show up. He wasn't exactly bursting with enthusiasm.

First chance I got when we left the Head-Up Centre, I texted Brian. CAN U MEET ME AT SUPERSNAX 6.30? Half an hour later he got back to me. SURE. Which seemed to me like a shrug. I felt like texting back. FORGET IT. After all the texts he'd sent me in the days following our frozen pilgrimage along the River Walk I felt sure he'd want to meet up. HOPE IT WORKED OUT OK WITH SEAN and TXT ME IF U GET CHANCE AND U OK? and PLEASE TXT ME. I hadn't answered, but I kept the texts on my phone. Now, one by one, I delete them and it's too weird, but the phone seems a little lighter after each one goes.

'How's it going, Eala?'

He catches me off-guard and the phone almost spills from my hand. It's not quite the Brian I know. He's had his head shaved. I'm not sure I like it much.

'Awright?' Sometimes Dad's cockney greeting slips out like this when I'm distracted.

'Got the skull trimmed for Christmas,' he says and I realize I've been making my misgivings a bit obvious.

'Different,' I say.

'You don't like it.'

'It'll grow on me.' I say, which is pretty original of me. He laughs and looks around the brightly lit town square. I can tell he's into the whole Christmas thing.

'I was going to take a look at the crib down in the cathedral,' he says. 'What d'you think?'

'You're messing, right? You're not one of those religious freaks, are you?'

'Course not. No, my grandfather did all the timberwork on the crib there when we moved up from Cork. He was some carpenter, he really was.'

'Why not?' I say and I feel his hand touch my back briefly as we make our way against the flow of the Christmas crowd and head down towards the cathedral. One part of me is thinking, *Who does he think he is, touching me like that?* The Angie part of me is going, *Hold me, why don't you?* There are so many people around that the silence between us doesn't feel too awkward. Angie warns me. *Don't scare him off with your hard-luck story now, Eala.*

We climb the steps of the cathedral. I can't remember the last time I was in here. Up at the far end, there's a queue filtering along by the passage behind the altar where the crib is. Mostly young couples with their kids, happy families that leave me aching with loneliness. We join the end of the queue. There's a little fair-haired girl about Tom's age in front of us and she keeps peeking back at me with the sweetest smile from behind her father's legs. I can't even force a smile for her, which makes her curious and then pure serious and I feel bad about casting a shadow over her day.

We get to the life-size crib and Brian peers in over the shoulders of those in front of us. I catch glimpses of the garishly painted statues. Joseph and Mary, some sheep, a donkey. Brian guides me in, his hand light on my shoulder. I expect to see the baby Jesus lying there with his hands raised like he wants to be lifted, comforted. But the little basketry cot is empty.

'There's no baby Jesus,' I say before I can stop myself.

'He hasn't been born yet, see?' Brian says and I get this

weird feeling of *déjà vu*. 'They don't put him in there until Christmas morning.'

I've asked this same question before and got the same answer and I remember when. The year of the tricycle. And there's nothing sweet about the memory.

Christmas Eve and Dad's been out for a few drinks with Martin and the five-a-side gang. Mam's arranged to meet him here at the crib. I'm doubly disappointed when he doesn't show up. No baby Jesus and now no Dad. Mam's furious. That much I'm sure really happened. Am I imagining the rest, knowing what I know now? Or knowing how much I don't know, more like.

We're back home from the cathedral and Mam's giving us our bath early so that Santa doesn't catch us on the hop. She's getting Sean and me all excited with reports of Santa's whereabouts. And in comes Dad to the bathroom, all silly grins and wobbly on his feet. Trying to squeeze a laugh out of Mam, who's stopped smiling. Telling us he's sure he saw a sleigh in the sky coming in from the Holycross direction. Trying once more to cuddle Mam and . . . Did she really say what I hear in my head? *Why do you have to drink your way through every bloody Christmas, Jimmy?* The memory ends there, try as I might to dredge up more of it.

What was that all about? Had he been drinking away the pain and loneliness of Christmases spent in prison? In foster residences? Or did Christmas recall for him some far more fearful memory? The thought bothers me. I try to brush it away, thinking, *There's no mystery about Christmas being the saddest time of all for an orphan*.

I slip away from Brian and edge through the crowd. He

doesn't seem to notice. I have to get out of this place. I feel panicky and I'm thinking, *Why didn't I go back home and take another of Dad's tabs before I came here?* My breath catches like I'm underwater. I push my way out of the scrum and wait for Brian. He takes longer than I want him to. On the wall above me, there's a small mural. One of the Stations of the Cross. XXIII. *The Virgin Mary cradles the dead Christ.* I feel like heading home, but Brian comes along at last.

'You all right?' he asks. Concerned, watching me too closely. I turn away. *Drama queen*, Angie says. Not Angie, I tell myself, there is no Angie.

'Can we go somewhere quiet?'

'It's Christmas, Eala. There are no quiet places.'

'We could try The Bridge Cafe.'

'Sure.' He sounds disappointed.

We walk back up towards Blackcastle Bridge where a woman comes towards us laden down with shopping bags. We split to let her through. The gap remains as we go on. We could be strangers who happen to be walking at the same pace. He's probably thinking the same thing I am – *What the hell am I doing here?*

The cafe is actually called *Le Pont*, but it had been The Bridge Cafe for years before and the new name never stuck. It's small and not too packed. We get a seat by the front window. It's a mock French kind of set-up with red-chequered tablecloths and candles lighting the centre of the tables. There's music playing, but at least it's not Christmas stuff. Edith Piaf singing '*Hymne à l'Amour*'. I know because Mam has the CD at home and used to sing along with it all the time, and Dad would whine, 'Who let the cat in?' And she'd chase him out of the kitchen, flapping the tea towel at him and – *Shut up, Eala, that life is over, gone, dead and buried.*

I wrap my arms tightly about me because I'm afraid to let my hands loose, they're so shaky. Brian orders two coffees. There's maybe a dozen people here, mainly couples, and everyone's minding their own business. Brian sips at his coffee. I see my reflection in the window. Short black hair and hoodie, big needy eyes and a face like a wet week in Bognor Regis. That's Dad again. *Shut up, Dad.*

'What's wrong, Eala?' Brian asks.

'I shouldn't have texted you,' I say. 'You don't need this and, anyway, I probably don't mean anything to you.'

'You know that's not true.'

'I don't, actually.'

He places his hand, palm up, on the table like an invitation. I take it and I'm off like he's fired a starting gun.

'We were at the Head-Up Centre where Dad goes a few times a week and they had this fundraising concert. There was this fellow about, I don't know, twenty-five, that got beaten up outside a nightclub and walks with a stick, but he's so brilliant on the piano and all I could think was, *Don't let Dad come on stage.* And, of course, he doesn't because he can't bloody well do anything now.'

I'm crying. *Some show you're putting on,* Angie says, and I can't tell if this is real or if I really am hamming it up.

'And next thing Alan – that's the guy's name – he starts playing this incredible, laid-back, jazzy version of 'Tomorrow' and my heart . . . I was like a pure fool, thinking I should be the one up there performing for Dad in my curly red wig and singing 'Tomorrow', but that's never going to happen now. Ever. And it's my own fault because I wouldn't let him and Mam come to the show until the last night and there was no last night. Oh God, I'm such a drama queen. I'm freaking you out, aren't I?'

'You're not freaking me out,' Brian says and both of his hands cover mine now. 'I'm so sorry about your dad . . .'

I want to tell him everything else that's bugging me, but I've pushed my luck far enough already. The touch of his hands feels too good to risk losing. Another couple has come in and taken a table opposite ours. They're too close to us. They're too close to one another. All pecks on the cheek and hand games and wide-eyed with a mutual fascination they think will last forever. Martin and Kathleen were probably like that once. Mam and Dad too.

Brian shifts about in his seat and takes out a small, flat, gift-wrapped package from the inside pocket of his jacket. He places it on the table beside my cup.

'Something for Christmas,' he says. 'I hope you like it.'

'But . . . I don't have anything for you.'

'I don't deserve anything,' he says.

'Why would you say that?'

'I can be a drama queen too, can't I?' he says with a smile. 'Are you going to open it?'

I do. Very awkwardly. My fingers like scissors ripping the paper apart. A silver bracelet and much more expensive than the beaded one he broke so long ago I'd forgotten all about it. *This one will break too*, Angie says. *Everything breaks. And whatever there is between you and Brian, that'll break as well when he gets tired of your sob stories and of feeling sorry for you and your dad.* But I shout her down in my head. *I'll take this*, I tell her, *and I don't care whether it's love or pity because I can't get by on my own.*

'I don't know what to say, Brian.'

He shrugs. I don't know what to do. I get inspiration from Romeo and Juliet at the next table. I lean over and kiss him on the lips.

24

I'm dancing with Dad. The foxtrot. We're in his room and the music is from way back in the past. From before my time, from before his time. Some old swing orchestra. I'll never be dancing champion of Moravia, but at least I've distracted him for a while from his latest obsession.

After that memory came back to me at the cathedral, I couldn't shake off the feeling that Christmas would really freak Dad out this year. I was wrong. He loved every minute of it. Even came upstairs to play Santa Claus to a sleeping Tom, arranging his presents by the end of the bed, drinking the milk Tom had left out for Santa and breaking off a chunk of the carrot left for Rudolph. I knew it wouldn't last. I felt so edgy I took another of Dad's anxiety tablets to stop my insides twisting into agonized knots.

Christmas Day he was beside himself with joy at all the stuff he got. A football signed by Roy Keane that Martin had bought at an auction and God knows how much it cost. Mam gave him a new parka jacket, a wool-lined hunting cap with ear flaps and a pair of strong walking boots. That's Mam. Practical. I got him a retro Brazil jersey with 'Pele' and the number '10' on the back. But it was Sean's gift that caused the most excitement in Dad on Christmas Day and the most consternation for the rest of us in the days following Christmas.

Dad never liked tennis. 'There was a time,' he'd often said, 'when at least the players had some kind of personality.' John McEnroe with his tantrums, Billy Jean King with her in-your-face feminism. Nowadays the players were machines, the matches as predictable as sunshine in the Sahara Desert. Since he got the Wii console from Sean, football has taken second place to the sport he once despised.

How Sean came up with the money for the game was a mystery to us. More than a mystery, a worry. So Mam asked him straight up. She tried to be pleasant about it, but too obviously so.

'That must have set you back a few bob,' she said. We were in the kitchen washing up after the turkey dinner. From below we could hear Dad's loud grunts as he served. 'I didn't realize you had so much left in your account.'

'I sold some of my stuff on eBay, right?' Sean said.

'Two hundred and fifty euro worth of stuff? Yeah, right,' I said.

'You bought him a lousy T-shirt, so I'm supposed to give him some cheap crap as well, is that it?'

'It's not a T-shirt, it's a jersey. And it wasn't cheap, actually.'

'Lads, please.' Mam wore her martyred expression. *As well as everything else*, it implied, *I have to put up with you two bickering.* 'And mind those bowls, Sean, please.'

He'd been putting way the delph and looked like he was ready to fling the last soup bowl at me. In the basement, Tom cheered. Another wicked shot from Dad, no doubt.

'As a matter of fact,' Sean said, 'I sold a bunch of Dad's Judge Dredd books and comics. I got forty-five euro for one of them alone.'

'You'd no right to sell Dad's stuff,' I said.

'My stuff, that he gave to me.' Sean banged a finger on his chest. 'Not you, me.' Meaning, *He told me his secret, Eala, and not you.*

'Look,' Mam put in. 'All I'm saying is that maybe we should have discussed what we'd get him for Christmas. I know that game keeps him active, but he gets so aggressive when he's playing and we need to keep him calm.'

'OK then, I'll take it back from him,' he said, heading for the kitchen door. 'I'll tell him it's not for zombies. I'll bring him over to the Head-Up Centre for a game of Tiddlywinks.'

'It's Christmas, Sean – they're closed,' I said and Mam didn't appreciate my sarcasm.

The kitchen door opened and in ran Tom, pink with excitement.

'Jimmy win,' he cried with delight.

Then Dad was peering in at the door and he puts on this posh English accent.

'Anyone for tennis?'

All day, every day he plays. He's the unbeaten champion of the house. We never let him lose. We know better. He loses the rag, shouts at the screen if a ball is called out at a crucial stage of a match. He plays like he's on a real court, lurching awkwardly all over the place and because he's such a big man, stuff tends to break when he thrashes about. He's knocked a picture off the wall, the bedside lamp twice and a small vase of Christmas hyacinths from the dresser.

We've tried everything to distract him, but he's always got some excuse. When we got out the *Father Ted* DVDs again, he said he couldn't understand the actors' accents. When I tried to bring him for a walk by the river, he goes, 'What if I fall in? I might drown, you know.' When Sean tried to coax him out to the Bernabéu to play football, he said the ground was too mucky.

So today I've tried something different. I've put on the *Ballroom Dancing for Beginners* DVD he got from the Ice Queen for Christmas. *With afection, Marta.* Two f's, Blondie. We've spent the best part of an hour working on the foxtrot. At first, I felt completely strung out. Aching with tiredness but telling myself I had to go on. Then I started to enjoy the dancing. Dad was totally focused, if not exactly graceful. Now his attention is wandering and he's beginning to get thick with himself. Soon, he's blaming me.

'You stood on my flippin' toe, Eala.'

'Your toe shouldn't have been where it was,' I joke.

'It's on my foot, where else can it be!'

We move off again.

'Left, not right,' he says. 'We turn left.'

'Sorry, Jimmy.'

'Marta's way better than you are,' he says. 'I'm fed up of this.'

There's an odd delay in my brain. His words should be hurting me. They don't. Not straight off. Maybe it's the tablets. The more I take, the more I need to take, it seems like.

'OK, let's leave it,' I say. 'We'll try again later.'

'Best of three,' he says, picking up his Wii console. When

he says three, he doesn't mean three games or three sets, he means three full-length matches.

'I've to meet someone,' I say.

'Two, then?'

'I've to meet someone.'

All of a sudden, it's like I want to tell him something real about my life, tell him I'm going out with someone. Which is kind of ironic because the last time I had a boyfriend was before the accident and I tried so hard to hide the fact that it was blindingly obvious to him and Mam what was going on. The teasing he gave me. I wanted that teasing now, that normality again, so badly. 'I've to meet someone, Jimmy.'

'All right then, one match,' he says.

'I've to –' I stop myself. 'OK, but no jumping around, Jimmy, right? You're wrecking the place.'

'No sweat. I bags first serve.'

Here we go again. I waste every shot. I don't want any rallies because that's what gets him hyped. He's not happy with my efforts.

'You're not trying,' he complains.

He starts to get clever. Lobbing easy shots back at me instead of smashes that steer the ball clear of my lousy backhand. Filthy looks fly at me when I whack the ball into the stands or completely miss it. The agitation begins. He's fiddling with his watch between serves. He starts slamming the ball hard again. Once, twice he launches himself at the virtual ball.

He takes off for a third time and trips on the edge of the Moroccan rug. He hits the bed. The bed collapses loudly on the floor like a bomb's gone off. He's not hurt. He looks around at the damage and then looks up at me. A smile. A big, stupid, mad smile and big, stupid, pleading, don't-tell-on-me eyes. Outside on the stairway, there's a race to the bottom. Mam wins. First at the open door, she can't contain herself.

'Jesus Christ, what's going on down here?'

She sees Dad sitting on the broken bed. Her hands knead their way through her hair.

'It was my fault,' I say.

'Yeah, it was Eala's fault,' Dad says.

Mam doesn't believe him and he knows it. He struggles to his feet and when he gets there, his expression has changed to defiance.

'I don't like that bed anyway,' he says. 'It's too small.'

He's staring hard at her. She tries to match the stare, but after a few seconds her head snaps to the side like a bird's. I get this terrible sinking sensation because I know what's coming. Behind Mam, Sean's afraid to come inside. At least Tom is having his nap and not here to witness this.

'I'm taking that game out of here this minute,' Mam says. 'We're all sick to death of this messing.'

She takes a step towards the Wii console by the bed. Dad blocks her path.

'No way,' he says. 'It's mine.'

He stoops down and gathers up the console and the controls.

'Jimmy,' she says and not kindly, 'Give me those. Give me those right now. You've caused enough damage already. I won't let you ruin our Christmas.'

His arm shoots up. I gasp. But he's only pointing at her.

'You don't want me, Judy,' he says. 'You won't let me into your bed.'

'Jimmy, please don't,' she says.

Sean sinks on to the last step of the stairway. Mam reaches to take the console from Dad and he backs away.

'You promised,' Dad insists. 'But you never did.'

'Give me the game,' Mam says. 'Give me the game. Give me the game.' The pitch of her voice is rising. I know how she feels. When there's nothing left to say, all you can do is say the same thing over and over again. 'Give me the game.'

'Mam, leave it,' I say.

'Jimmy, if you don't give me that game,' Mam insists. 'I'll . . .'

Sean charges out from behind her and makes for Dad.

'Give her the frigging game, Jimmy,' he shouts and he grabs at the console in Dad's hand. There's a tug of war, a rough dance. They're pushing at one another. 'I'll clock you, Jimmy. I swear I'll clock you.'

'Clear off,' Dad warns him. 'Or you'll regret it.'

The flush of anger is gone from Mam's face. She's pure pale. Her mouth's twisted up on one side like she's had a stroke. A strangled whimpering rises in her.

'Lads, stop it,' I say. 'Please, stop it.'

As they struggle, the point of Sean's left shoulder catches Dad on the nose and he reels back. He drops everything and throws a punch at Sean's chest. Sean catches him with a right to the stomach that tips Dad over the edge. It's a wrestling match now. They tumble on to the floor. They're poking, gouging, twisting one another's arms. The bedside table goes down and the ceramic lamp smashes. DVDs rain on them as they roll over and hit up against the shelving. Mam loses it. She's hysterical. They don't stop. They're really hurting each other now. There's blood and I don't know whose it is.

My first instinct is to ring Brian, but I can't. I'll lose him if he sees this madness. Then I hear Angie. Actually hear her. A real voice from behind me. *Ring Martin*, she says. I turn for the door. Tom's standing there holding his green tractor. His face is a blank. His blue eyes are dead. I sweep him up the stairs with me.

'It's a game, Tom,' I keep telling him. 'Only a game.'

I reach the house phone in the hallway. I scroll blindly for Martin's number and eventually I find it.

'Judy?' Martin says.

'Help us, Martin,' I say. My eyes close. I feel Tom's hand stroking my hair.

'Jimmy bold,' he says and I don't tell him he's wrong.

25

New Year's Eve and for the first time in my life, I'm not at home to celebrate it. Mam had planned to have a party. Martin and a few others. Some people from her work, I supposed, and from the choir. And Miss Understanding, no doubt. After what happened to Argos, there was never going to be a party. Maybe the dog is lucky not to have another year to face into.

This is our first public outing together and it feels like everyone's gaping at Brian and me. As loud as the crowded bar is, you can almost hear their slow brains ticking over when they look our way. The girls are probably thinking, *He's going out with her?* As for the fellows – Derek among them – I can tell they're going, *Go, Brian, another notch on the gun!*

I'm nursing my second cocktail. A Mojito, too green, too minty. Another first though I'm pretending, sure, I've tasted every cocktail out there, but I'm taking it handy tonight. My head's already beginning to spin. It's not the worst feeling in the world because the thinking part of my brain cuts out for minutes on end. Unfortunately, all the stuff I'm trying to forget comes back with a bigger bang when the spinning sensation passes. Sean killed the dog. He must have done it because Dad couldn't have, could he? But I can't be angry with him. I can't kick him when he's down.

After the fight and the little miracle Martin performed, Sean retreated to his bedroom. Something about the way he looked at me as he went, told me our secret, Dad's secret, might not be safe with him for much longer. I got Tom ready for bed – Mam was still down in the sitting room with Martin. He wanted me to read for him. I told him a story instead. The first Terry the Tank adventure. The one where he wants to be a giraffe. I don't know if he really got the connection between the long gun barrel and the giraffe's long neck, but he liked the story anyway and I had to repeat the whole thing again. Well, two thirds of it. He fell asleep at the happy part where Terry is playing with all the giraffes and before they cop on that he's really a tank.

I knocked back one of Dad's panic tabs and went to Sean's room. He didn't answer when I knocked. Which, in his case, means it's all right to go in there. The light was off, but the curtains weren't drawn. The yellow sodium street lamp outside mellowed the blindness of the dark room. Sean lay on his bed.

'You all right, Sean?' I asked.

'Yeah.' A deep intake of breath that said, *Come in*.

I closed the door behind me. I went to sit at the end of the bed, stepping over the clothes and books scattered around the floor. He has a new poster on the back of his door. A large-scale black and white sketch. In it, a man approaches wearing a long coat and a wide-brimmed hat that shadows his face. In the distance behind him, a young black boy stands, unsure whether or not to follow. The caption reads *The Dead Man*. Sean's drawn a line through the word Dead. The poster made me uncomfortable, made me wonder what was going on in his head besides opening up to Mam.

'How do you sleep with that guy staring at you?' I said, trying to sound light-hearted.

He looked at the poster like he was seeing it for the first time, examining every detail or every detail you could see in that light.

'Did you ever read any of those Judge Dredd books Dad gave me?'

'Do I look hormonally challenged?'

'Judge Dredd is, like, one of these avenger types,' he said and showed no sign of getting thick. 'Judge, jury and executioner sort of thing.'

'Is that why you're stalking Clem Healy? So you can be judge, jury and –'

'I never intended clocking him. I got this crazy idea into my head that I'd, like, haunt him like Dad's haunted by the Man. But what's the point? What's the point in anything we do?'

The tablet was starting to work, but only on the outside. My hands were dead steady. I checked. Inside, I was shaking so much I had to fold my arms tight across my stomach.

'So you've stopped following him?'

'Yeah,' he said and stared over at the poster. 'The weird thing, the really weird thing, is that in this book, *The Dead Man*, Judge Dredd loses his memory. And get this, it was Dad's favourite.'

'Did he get it back?'

'What?'

'His memory; did Judge Dredd get his memory back?' I asked.

'Yeah. It's fantasyland, remember?'

He massaged the ball of his shoulder as he lay there.

'Did he hurt you?'

'Naw,' he said. 'It was handbags really.'

I was thinking we never had a real conversation in our lives. None that didn't descend into a squabble. But even if another argument was the result, I had to know if he planned to talk to Mam. I couldn't let that happen.

'D'you hear that?' he said as I prepared to take the plunge. 'It's doing my head in. Dad's too.'

I listened and heard nothing at first, which made me worry even more about my brother. Then I caught the faint sound of a half-hearted bark from Argos.

'She should put one of those barking collars on him,' he said. 'Give him a shock every time he tries to bark.'

'That would be so cruel,' I said.

'Not much different to what we do to Dad. Zonk him out with tablets when he loses it.'

'To stop him hurting himself.'

'To stop him hurting us,' Sean said. 'I mean, I can defend myself. Just about. But you and Tom and Mam?'

'He'd never . . . He wouldn't . . .'

Argos tried a few more complaints, a dreadful mix of misery and pain.

'Are you going to tell Mam? About Dad going to prison? What he did?'

'Maybe it's time to,' he said. Then he turned towards the wall, hid himself away from me. 'I don't know. What kind of crap life is this for him? I wish he'd never woken up out of the coma. I wish he'd died.'

'How could you say such a thing?'

'It's the truth,' he said and drew his knees up so that he lay like a baby in the womb. 'We keep dodging the truth, all of us. Dad's slipping out of control and we're going, "He'll be grand; he'll be OK when he settles."'

'So, you want to tell her?'

'You decide,' he says and shrugs. 'I've had it up to here. You're better at this than I am.'

I wanted to tell him that I was already in bits. That every day I felt this awful sickness in my stomach, in my bones. That every night I cried without spilling one tear. That I felt sure I was going slowly and quietly mad. That the only time I felt even half sane was when I stole Dad's tablets and popped them. Or when I was with Brian.

There's a gang of seven or eight of us around the table in Brady's Bar. An easy-going crowd. No hairstyle excesses, no labels, no animal noises, no public groping. All that stuff is available here, but not at our table. The conversation is about albums, bands and I'm totally lost. I haven't looked at MySpace or YouTube or whatever for months and I can't even remember where my MP3 player is.

'You're very quiet,' Brian says, like he knows I'm keeping something from him. 'What's on your mind?'

'*Les profonditées de l'existence*.' The phrase comes unbidden and there's a bitter aftertaste to it. 'Something Dad used to say when he went all quiet in himself. I used it in a French exercise before Christmas and Mrs Claffey said it should be "*profondeurs*" not "*profonditées*".'

Brian's baffled. It shouldn't matter that Dad got the word wrong but, stupidly, it does. I sit up straight, blink some sense into my brain.

'Don't mind me. Had an early start this morning is all.'

Like father like daughter, Angie's telling me, *with your secrets and lies. Secrets aren't lies*, I tell her. Not always.

'Are you sure you want to go to this party?' Brian asks. 'I mean, I don't mind if we don't.'

We're supposed to be heading later to his friend's house. I've been trying not to think about it. Mam's at home with only Dad and Tom for company, but when she said this afternoon that she was going to have an early night, it was like she was telling Sean and me to make our own plans. Make that telling *me*. She wasn't talking to Sean. She might have done if he'd told her the truth about Argos.

'We're going to the party,' I tell Brian. 'One more drink and we'll head.'

As Brian goes up to the bar, I check out the place again to see if Jill is here. No sign of her. I wonder if I'm the reason she hasn't come to Brady's tonight. Probably. We didn't exactly part on the best of terms a few hours ago at the Jasmine Garden.

Back when we were twelve, we started this tradition of meeting up at the Chinese restaurant on New Year's Eve. We'd hold over our Christmas presents for each other until then and it was good to have something to look forward to after the thrill of Christmas was over. That first time we decided we'd keep this thing going until we were pure ancient and rotten rich and married with seven children and fourteen grandchildren or whatever.

Today, I was first to arrive at the restaurant. I was pure wrecked, but who wouldn't be after having been woken at seven by the screaming and banging at our front door? When Jill came, I knew I was going to feel a hell of a lot more tired. I took one look at her and thought, *She's got more bad news about Win and the sprog.*

'Did you have a nice Christmas?' she asked.

'Yeah, mad.'

She didn't get the joke. How could she? She wasn't on for smiling anyway.

'Ours was nice too,' she said. 'But sort of sad.' And Angie was groaning, *Here we go again.* I tried to head Jill off.

'I've something for Richard,' I said.

A mistake. The mention of Richard made her tearful. She opened the gift-wrapping on his present. I'd gone out of my way to come up with something different for the baby. A little white T-shirt that I took to the shop where Dad got his 'Housewife of the Year' apron printed up. My slogan went, 'Rock On/Little Richard'. I got them to print on a cartoon guitar between the lines. I don't know why I went to so much trouble. Jill choked back the sobs.

'It's . . . so . . . lovely,' she said.

'Little Richard? D'you get it? The singer, like, from the sixties? The black guy?'

She nodded, covering her face from the other diners. Her tears left me cold. I focused on the menu. The descriptions of each item turned my stomach. Food was the last thing in the world I wanted. She dried her eyes with the linen napkin from the table. A few sniffles and she was ready to roll.

'Win's got everything fixed up,' she said. 'The Lone Parent Allowance, the apartment, the crèche in college, so . . . so she'll be taking Richard back to Dublin next month after all.'

'Well, it's worked out then, hasn't it?' I said, but for some stupid reason I felt sad about it too.

'Yeah,' Jill said. 'But we got so used to having him around, it's pure torture letting go.'

The stifling, spice-filled air was getting to me. I knew I wasn't going to be able to eat. I knew if I stayed there another minute I was going to throw up. Suddenly, I was standing and the restaurant floor swayed beneath my feet. Her look of concern made me feel even worse.

'You know something?' I said as evenly as I could. 'It'll be such a relief when that child is gone because I'm sick to death of hearing about him and Win.'

'Eala,' she said. 'You're on something, some kind of downers. I can tell by your eyes.'

'There's nothing wrong with my eyes,' I snapped but, in fairness, she had a point. I could see two of her.

'Don't do this to yourself,' she said, calm as you like. 'You're pure out of it.'

I couldn't think of a smart answer, so I left her sitting there. Only now do I remember that we never exchanged our presents. The earrings I bought for her are still in my bag.

'Eala?'

It's Brian. The noise of the crowd in Brady's sweeps back into my brain and I don't catch what he says next, but it's so urgent that he grabs my hand and yanks me upwards to his side. His friends can't figure out what's going on either.

'We have to get out of here fast,' he says, his head snapping from side to side as he surveys the packed bar.

'Why?'

'Trigger Healy's over at the counter.'

'So? Why should we run from that scumbag?'

'Because I know he's going to get on to us over Sean.' He's getting impatient with me. 'Let's go.'

'But Sean doesn't follow that dumb kid any more.'

'That's not the point, Eala. Trigger doesn't forget and he doesn't do forgiveness either.'

He takes my hand and I follow. Someone taps me on the shoulder and I spin round. Derek. He's holding his pint at a precarious angle and his heads's floating about like a balloon on a string. Tanked out of his tree, he is.

'I can't wait to get my head on your lap,' he smirks. The last scene in *West Side Story*. The hero's dead and Maria holds him and sings and cries and whatever.

'Make sure you wash the lice out of your hair first,' I tell him.

Brian feels the drag of my delay and looks back. He throws Derek a filthy look, but I move on and we make it through to the door.

26

Outside on Friary Street, I'm trotting to keep up with Brian and it feels ridiculous. The cold air meets the alcohol in my brain and I stumble.

'Take it handy, Brian.'

He eases up as we turn off Friary Street into the town square. I realize we're heading the wrong way for the party.

'Where are we going?' I ask.

'I'm not up for this party, Eala, do you mind?'

'I don't care,' I tell him, but I don't want to head home yet either, and that's the direction we're taking. Some New Year's Eve we're having. I'm half afraid of what I'll find when we reach our street. Another squad car or Martin's Mercedes or an ambulance outside Mrs Casey's. We're on the Long Mall and right by her sweet shop.

'Can we sit down for a minute?' I say and don't wait for an answer.

I let go of his hand and park myself on the window sill of the shop. Brian sits beside me. He puts his arm over my shoulder. With his shaven head and broken nose and the small scar under his left eye he could almost pass as a bouncer if he changed into a black suit and got himself an earpiece. Except for his eyes. The windows to the soul. But eyes can change too. Dad's have. More like shutters than windows.

I can't put away the memory of how indifferently Dad looked at Mrs Casey as she stood on our doorstep this morning. We could see the outline of her frail and tiny frame inside an almost see-through nightdress. A dash of lipstick, hastily applied, made an anguished mask of her face.

'Don't you know what it's like to be alone?' she said to Mam. 'To have nothing, nobody, not even a dog to protect you?'

Mam tried to bring her inside to calm her down, but Mrs Casey refused. I tried to bring Dad away from the door, but he wouldn't budge either. Sean managed to get him a few feet back along the hallway.

'We didn't touch your dog, Mrs Casey,' Sean insisted, but I already knew he was lying and Mam was beginning to cop on too. 'And, anyway, he's better off dead than being tied up all day every day in your back garden.'

'The Man did it,' Dad said, which only added fuel to the flames of Mrs Casey's distress.

'I know what you're up to, Mr Summerton,' the old woman said, pointing a bony, accusing finger. 'You were forever on to me about moving to a smaller house. Don't deny it. And now you're making my life a misery trying to drive me out. You beat my dog and then you poisoned him and you're always watching me, always . . .'

'Mrs Casey, please,' Mam pleaded. 'This has nothing to

do with Jimmy. He was always good to you, you know that. And if he ever suggested you should move, it was out of concern for you is all.'

'I'm taking this further and no Guards will persuade me against it this time,' Mrs Casey said. 'I won't be driven from my home by anyone.'

'No one's trying to drive you from your home, Mrs Casey,' Mam said.

'And you're in on it too,' the old woman insisted. 'I know you work up in the health centre and those nurses and that Indian doctor fellow want me to go into a home and you're helping them get me out. I've lived in that house all my life and I'll die in there just like my Raymond did. If only he was around to deal with you people.'

Mam laid into Sean after Mrs Casey left. She was terrified that the old woman might get a stroke or something after the upset she'd had. She still is. Sean refused to own up to killing Argos. I knew why she wanted to hear that confession so badly. I weighed in too.

'Don't you get it, Sean? If it wasn't you, it was Dad. And it can't be Dad, right? Dad couldn't do stuff like that, right?'

'That stupid dog was driving the whole street crazy,' he said. 'Any one of the neighbours could've done it.'

All day I've been trying to avoid the thought of Mrs Casey ringing the Guards and the ISPCA or whatever and the terrifying consequences. Terrifying if Sean is the guilty one. Terrifying times ten if it's Dad. We haven't heard anything yet, but I feel certain that we will. The few drinks I've had have lost whatever pleasant effect they had on me. I'm back to being cold sober. Very cold and very sober.

'It must be close to midnight,' Brian says and I check the time on my mobile. There's a message from Jill.

'Twenty to.'

I read the message. NEXT YEAR WILL BE BETTER. JILL.

'Is that Sean?' Brian asks.

'No. It's Jill.'

'Does she know about us?'

'Not yet,' I say.

'If she tries to diss me, Eala, don't believe a word she says. Or Win either.'

'Why should they diss –'

He draws me closer and kisses me. His hands begin to move along my back, my stomach. I'm light-headed again, but more pleasantly. Some people pass by. A middle-aged couple, power-walking and tut-tutting. I don't care. We come up for air.

'I'm pure paranoid tonight, Eala,' he says. 'Had a major blow-up with my old man this evening. I've been applying for apprenticeships all over the place, but with this recession, I'm having no luck. I mean, how crazy is that? I can go to university and study architecture, but I can't get a start as a carpenter. Course, my old man says all I'm doing is making excuses for loafing around. So I lay into him over Grandad, which is how these rows always go . . . I shouldn't be bothering you with this.'

'I don't mind.'

And Angie's in like a flash, warning me again. *That's his trick, Eala – cry on your shoulder to soften you up and then . . .*

'When we moved up here, Grandad missed us big time.

So he came and stayed with us for a few months. That was when he built the crib in the cathedral. But he didn't settle here and he went back down. Two months later he died. A heart attack and nobody to call an ambulance for him. If we'd been there, he mightn't have died. I never forgave my old man for that. He says black, I say white. That's the story of my life. That's what has me so messed up.'

'You don't seem all that messed up to me,' I say, chasing away the gnawing sensation in my stomach with a joke. 'Apart from the haircut, that is.'

'I can't wait for them to head off to Morocco next month. Give my head a break for a few weeks.'

Brian stands up and takes my hand. We head down towards my street. His arm over my shoulder, the heat of his body warming me, the stubble on his chin brushing against my forehead every now and then, feeling good. In the distance I can see that there's not one light shining in our house. Not even the one over the front door. Mam's forgotten to turn it on. Mrs Casey's house is in darkness too. There's no ambulance, no squad car and Martin's Mercedes is nowhere to be seen.

I have no idea how Martin managed to wangle his way into Dad's room earlier in the evening, but I do know how he managed to emerge half an hour later with the Wii console in his hands. I wish I didn't. We sat waiting in the kitchen, all four of us. We could hear the scuff of feet, the groans of exertion, the occasional ominous silence. We couldn't tell if they were fighting or playing a match. Then it ended and we listened and tried to figure out if it was both or only one of them who climbed the stairs from the basement. And it was only one of them.

So Martin's standing there at the kitchen door. The tail of his white shirt is hanging out, the sleeves rolled up. His forehead's covered in sweat, but he's dead pale. He's holding the Wii console a little away from him like it's a dead rat or something. He comes in and drops it on the kitchen worktop.

'I challenged him,' Martin explains. He's leaning against the wall like he's out on his feet. 'Winner gets to keep the Wii console. I couldn't think of any other way.'

He looked at me and I could tell he knew what I was thinking. I was glad he'd got the console from Dad, but I hated him for it.

'He was so devastated, I had to offer him something,' Martin said then. 'I promised I'd bring him to play five-a-side with the old gang.'

Mam was too grateful to object, though she clearly had her doubts.

'I'll take care of him, don't worry, Judy.' He changed the subject before she could change her mind. 'By the way, who's Alan? He wants Alan to come along too.'

Later, as I crossed the landing from Sean's room, I saw their shadows, Mam and Martin's, stretching out from the sitting room and along the carpet in the hallway. Actually, it was one shadow. Maybe he was only comforting her.

From the far side of the river comes the sound of a dull, heavy thud like a rock falling into a quarry and it startles me. I press closer to Brian. A long whistling whine follows and we look up at the sky that runs riot with shapes and colours. We don't notice the black SUV until it pulls up beside us. The blacked-out side window slides down and Trigger Healy grins so widely, his shaved scalp wrinkles.

'Happy New Year, lads,' he says and Brian steers me away towards our house. Trigger reverses by the edge of the footpath, keeping up with us. 'I was going to buy you a pint in Brady's, Brian, but you scuttled off fair fast.'

'Leave us alone,' I say. Brian stares straight ahead and I'm disappointed he doesn't stand up to Trigger. He's scared stiff. *Maybe he owes Trigger money from his dopehead days*, I'm thinking.

'Eala,' he whispers. 'Don't.'

The SUV reverses over the speed bump by our front gate. Inside, Trigger wobbles like a lump of jelly.

'These speed bumps are cruel, Brian, ain't they?' Trigger says. 'Wreck the old suspension, they do. Good thing I have the Hummer and not one of those old Honda Civics. Fierce low on the ground they are, aren't they?'

Brian comes to a halt. Our drive is a few feet away.

'I'll see you tomorrow, Eala,' he says and I can't believe he's abandoning me like this.

'What are you driving yourself these times, Brian?' Trigger asks.

'I don't drive,' Brian says. 'You know I don't drive.'

His voice is shaky. His pained expression worries me. Trigger's leaning across towards us, pointing a stubby finger at Brian.

'I told you to get that kid off my son's back.'

'I did,' Brian says and he's almost pushing me on to our drive.

'Yeah, well, thanks, but it's too bloody late,' Trigger says. 'The kid's pissing the bed every night and –'

'What do you care about dopey little Clem?' I say. 'You've got him carrying your gear around town. That's what he was doing the evening he hit Dad, wasn't it?'

Trigger passes a hand along his shaven head and when it comes down, the hand has become a fist. I keep up a staring match with him and he's the first to slide away. He fixes his gaze on Brian.

'Ask lover-boy there what it's like to hit a wall at forty miles an hour.'

He revs up the SUV and takes off, leaving us a cloud of poisonous carbon monoxide to breathe in. The poison hits my brain at the same moment as the realization does.

'You were driving the car that crashed into the riverbank wall?' I say. 'The speed bumps are here because of you?'

'I wasn't driving, Eala,' Brian says. 'I was in the car, but I wasn't driving, I swear.'

I'm not sure I can walk, but I try a step anyway and it seems to work so I try another and another. I'm on our pebbled drive. This can't be happening to me. I get a few days of love and then this kick in the stomach. I've been going out with the guy who's responsible for destroying my dad's life, destroying all our lives.

'If those speed bumps weren't there, Clem Healy wouldn't have been cycling on the footpath and he wouldn't have crashed into Dad,' I say like a kid slowly doing a simple sum. One plus one plus one plus one.

'I swear, Eala,' Brian says, but he doesn't follow me. 'I was stupid, a stupid kid acting the rebel to get back at my old man. I got in over my head.' His voice begins to trail away. 'I wasn't driving. I was in the back seat and . . .'

I stop up. I can't look in his direction.

'How does Healy know about this?' I ask.

'His son was the driver, the older fellow, Sham,' he says. 'I'm so sorry, Eala.'

'It's too late for sorry,' I tell him and I make my way up the steps to the front door.

The sky is still celebrating. Great dandelion shapes appear and disappear, appear and disappear. I have trouble getting the key in the lock my fingers tremble so much. I ease the door inwards and close it back without looking to see if Brian is still there. The house is quiet, dark. In the kitchen I want to scream at the paper bag Dad's tablet bottles are in because it makes so much noise as I open it. *Mam's going to cop on to the missing tabs soon*, I'm thinking, but it doesn't stop me swallowing a few. A downer, a sleeper. And because that doesn't seem like enough to stop the pain, I pop one of the antidepressants too. I make my way to my bedroom and slip under the covers of the bed without undressing.

I know she can't really be out there, standing at the end of my bed, but she is. Angie. Watching me, murmuring, and her voice becomes two voices and more and then more. Murmuring. I don't know what it is the voices are saying, but I'm terrified because I'm certain they're talking about my future, about Dad's future, about all our futures. And they know what's going to happen and they know it's going to be terrible. And there's nothing that I or anyone else can do to change it. Everything I've done has only made things worse. What more can I do?

I pull one of my pillows close, wrap my arms round it. A hundred Angies are laughing, sneering. Is that a baby you're holding, Eala; is that your baby?

I'm so afraid.

27

The space inside my head is bigger and wider than the school assembly hall here. All the stuff that bothers me floats in the distance, not gone, but far enough away that I'm not panicked or fearful all the time. Everything has slowed down so much that it feels like the world might stop at any moment. I don't exactly feel better, but I know that without Dad's tablets, I'd feel an awful lot worse. Sometimes I do weird things like suddenly talking out loud to myself or maybe standing in the same spot for five minutes, not moving a muscle, not even wanting to, until I snap out of it. Fortunately, I've always been alone when I've thrown one of these wobblers.

I'm not at the assembly hall for rehearsals. I'm here because this is where Dad and his five-a-side pals used to play. And tonight is his big comeback. He's not over the moon about it. Coming over here in Martin's car, he hardly spoke a word even to Alan. Sean stayed home. If I hadn't found a way to get a plentiful supply of Dad's tabs, I probably wouldn't be here either. I never imagined I'd make such a clever thief.

Mam had to go to a conference in Kilkenny last Thursday,

so I told her I'd bring Dad's prescription to the shopping centre pharmacy after school. I knew Dad had enough tablets for the rest of the day and for the next morning. So when I got home, I took one of the downers and stashed the new supply of tablets in my wardrobe.

I was already feeling a little spaced out when Mam got in. I told her I'd been in a few shops down at the shopping centre after the pharmacy and must have left the bag in one of them. I said I'd gone back to each one, but couldn't find the tablets. At first she was thick at me, but I soon won her over. I worked up a few tears. I called myself names. I said I wished he didn't have to take all that stuff anyway. I didn't even feel guilty for lying. I still don't. At least Mam has someone to hold her, someone to hold on to.

'Don't blame yourself, Eala,' she said. 'We'll sort it out. Don't worry.'

Dad and Martin and the others have been playing for five minutes or so. Dad hasn't been doing very well. His yellow, retro Brazil jersey is already soaked with sweat. When the ball comes near him, he freezes or gets his feet in a tangle and scuffs his shot. It's like his sneakers are three sizes too big for him.

The other men are as bashful and afraid as Dad is. You can tell they're trying to keep the temperature of the game in check They don't want to hurt Dad or make him feel useless. They give him all the time he needs on the ball. Twice, Martin has managed to get him in front of goal with no one to beat and twice he's missed. Beside me, on the bank of seats at the back of the hall, sits Alan. He's a straight talker. Too straight.

'Jimmy's not very good, is he?' he says. He's already told me that Dad's carrying too much weight and asked if he's ever actually played football before.

'He's doing the best he can,' I say. 'He used to be very good.'

'He should think about retiring.'

'You don't have to be pure brilliant at something to enjoy it.'

He thinks about that for a while. Out on the court, the play has slowed down to a crawl. Dad is over at the far side and he's talking to Martin. I can tell by his body language that he's had enough. Martin walks away from him and, as he passes by one of the others, he says something I don't catch. Pat Dillon is chubby and red-faced and about ten years younger than Dad. He looks at Martin, uncertainty written all over his face.

'But you have to recognize your limitations,' Alan says, picking up where I thought we'd left off for good. 'I never try to play Chopin's *Fantasie-Impromptu* or, say, Liszt's *Après une Lecture du Dante*. I don't have that kind of dexterity or focus now. If I try, I get frustrated and then I don't want to play anything.'

Martin passes the ball and Dad gets in his usual pickle when it reaches him. Pat Dillon runs over and takes the ball from Dad and shoulders him for good measure. Dad reels like he's sliding back along a capsizing deck. Martin dives in and hits Pat with a crunching tackle. Suddenly, the real game is on.

They're hitting each other for sport out there. Except for Dad, of course. He's standing like a traffic cop in the middle of Mumbai or wherever. Some place anyway where there are no rules of the road or nobody bothers much with them. It's like Martin and all Dad's old pals are working out their feelings about what's happened to Dad the only way they can. Love is weird. Men are weird.

'A marked heightening in tension,' Alan says aloud, but to himself like he's reading a news bulletin or something. 'The situation may get worse before it gets better.'

It's like a game he's playing to distance himself from the physicality that's breaking out big time on the court.

'They'll run out of steam in a few minutes,' I say.

Dad has broken into a run. Not a very quick run and it looks sort of aimless because he keeps changing direction in his efforts to follow the ball. His damp jersey is melded to his skin. Martin gets the ball to him. Dad waits for the tackle to come in, lowers his shoulder and sends the tackler head over heels with an almighty jostle. He finds Martin with a pass and Martin scores. They give one another a high five.

'This is becoming unpleasant,' Alan says. 'I'll wait outside.'

'It's only a game, Alan,' I tell him, but he hurries away as quickly as his stick allows and I know I should get out of this place too.

Dad's flying now, knocking fellows over in his determination to get to the ball first. I look over at Martin. He's making no effort to calm Dad down. He knows what happened at Christmas. He knows what might happen here.

'Jimmy, take it handy,' I shout.

He's knocked Pat Dillon over at least three times. A builder and strong as an ox, Pat's getting fair thick. And

Dad runs into him again. He pushes Dad in the chest. In my head I've jumped to my feet and shouted at them to stop. In reality I'm still sitting here trying to get my motor to start. Not the first time this has happened after I've knocked back some of Dad's tabs.

'What did you say?' Dad demands of Pat Dillon and pushes him roughly.

'Nothing, Jimmy.'

'I'm losing the run of myself, am I?'

I make it on to the court as Martin tries to intervene. Too late. Dad steps up to Pat Dillon and plants him in the chest with a headbutt. I'm rooted to the spot and thinking, *That's the famous Zidane headbutt from the 2006 World Cup Final*, as Dillon goes down and stays down. Dad follows through with his foot and catches him in the stomach. His next kick misses the builder's head by inches. There's one last brutal kick to the shoulder before Martin finally pushes Dad away.

'He started it,' Dad says. 'I didn't mean to . . .'

Martin leads him off, talking quietly to him, calming him down. Pat Dillon gathers himself and climbs to his feet with a little help from the other players. He holds his shoulder and grimaces.

'I'm sorry, Pat,' I say.

'It's not your fault, girl,' he says.

'You won't report him, will you? To the Guards like? Please don't.'

Strong as he is, the pain's so intense he can't answer me. He heads towards the dressing room, helped along by the others.

'The collar bone,' someone says. 'I think it's gone.'

I catch a glimpse of Dad slouching in by the dressing-room door, dragging his foot every few steps. All at once, I remember why that walk seemed familiar from the first off. The Zidane DVD.

It's a documentary film called *Zidane: A 21st Century Portrait* where seventeen cameras follow his every move throughout the course of a game in 2005. He's playing for Real Madrid against Villareal. At the Bernabéu. The cameras often focus on his feet and catch that odd dragging of the toe of his boot along the grass every few steps. I stand in the middle of the court, trying to make sense of all this. I can't breathe in this place for all its high spaces. I head to the main door and get outside. Alan's leaning on his stick over by Martin's car, his back to the school buildings, talking quietly to himself.

The night air is cold. Frost sparkles on the wide grass margins under the avenue lights. Above me, the bare branches of trees finger the sky. We're deep in winter, but a few leaves still rustle up there. I wonder if every leaf has to fall before a tree can begin to bud again. Martin emerges from the assembly hall. He's talking to someone on his mobile. Mam?

Dad is next to step out into the night. His tall man's stoop is more exaggerated than usual. Some of the others follow, downcast as students who've got their exam results and have all failed. When Pat Dillon appears, his arm strung up in a temporary sling made from a towel, I head over to the car.

'Who were you talking to?' I ask as Martin approaches

and beeps open the Mercedes. Dad's standing there, his head lowered, avoiding our eyes.

'A client,' he says warily. I don't believe him.

'Is Pat going to make a complaint to the Guards?'

'I don't think so,' Martin says. 'But you can never be sure. He's going to lose a month's work at least so he'll be out of pocket big time.'

'Which is your stupid fault,' I tell him.

'I know,' he says. 'I thought it'd be good for him to work off all that frustration he must feel, all that pent-up energy that's building up in him.'

He gets in the car. Dad and Alan pile into the back seat and I sit beside Martin. He steers us out by the school avenue. We're on the road out to Alan's house in Borris before anyone speaks.

'Can we have some music?' Alan asks, as though nothing out of the ordinary has happened.

Martin turns on the radio. A Country and Western song. The usual love-gone-wrong crap.

'I'd prefer some real music, if you don't mind,' Alan says.

Martin switches channels, gets two no's from Alan and then a yes. An orchestral piece and even more mournful than the C and W.

'Mahler's *Ninth Symphony*,' Alan informs us. 'Fourth movement – the *Adagio*.'

'And there was me thinking it was the Eighth,' Martin says, smiling at me, which makes my blood run cold.

I don't see the man who used to spoil me rotten in him any more. I see a young man watching jealously as Dad came on the scene to swipe Mam from under his nose. I see a middle-aged, divorced man who reckons Dad's accident has given him a second chance. I'm thinking that he brought Dad to the five-a-side and encouraged Pat Dillon to get him all riled up so he'd flip again. The more often Dad flips, the more likely it is that Mam will give up on him. *Great trick*, Angie says.

'No, the Ninth,' Alan says. 'The Eighth is essentially a choral work. Personally, I prefer Brahms's *German Requiem* on the choral side although the finale of Mahler's *Resurrection Symphony* is stupendous . . .'

Alan rambles on until we mount the steep drive into his parents' house. It's a renovated two-storey farmhouse painted white and it glows in the spotlights scattered about the front lawn. His mother waves at us from the front window when we pull up. I don't wave back. The view of her there, small in the window frame, the room softly lit behind her, is like a painting. I bet she doesn't need tablets to find the serenity I see in her expression. Not now that she's about to dump Alan in the residential house in Limerick.

'Well,' Alan says as he unbuckles his safety belt. 'That was an interesting evening, but I won't be coming next time, thank you.'

'Neither will I,' Dad says.

'See you, Alan,' Martin says, like he wants him out of the car rapid.

The light comes on over the front door. Alan's father is there, pure beaming like his son is six years old and coming back from someone's birthday party. The trembling has started up inside me again. I need one of Dad's tablets. More than one. Martin rolls down his window as Peter Foran approaches. He's wearing a multicoloured woollen sweater that I imagine his wife patiently knitting, a work of meditation.

'Hello, Martin,' he says and leans in towards the open window. 'Eala, how are you?'

'I'm grand.'

He's peering in at me too keenly like he knows I'm far from grand. Or maybe he simply can't see me clearly in the half-light. I remember the French phrase Dad gave me to describe a distinguished and wise older man. An *éminence grise*. And I'm thinking Dad can never be an *éminence grise* now. Peter turns his attention to Martin.

'We can never thank you enough,' he says. 'It might've taken years of fundraising to get what you've given us.'

Martin gives a quick sidelong glance at me, guilt written all over it.

'It's the least I could do,' he shrugs and he's clearly relieved to hear the back door open and Alan getting out.

'How did the game go, Jimmy?' Peter asks, leaning closer in by the side window.

'It was rubbish.'

'Not as bad as all that, I'm sure.'

'Worse,' Dad insists and Peter laughs, thinking it's meant as a joke.

'We should go,' Martin tells Peter. 'We're running late already.'

'Of course. Thanks again, Martin. See you at the next meeting.'

We head back into town. I'm wondering if Martin's given a whack of money to the Head-Up Centre. Make some impression on Mam that would, wouldn't it, Martin? The road glitters with ice. Each time a car or lorry approaches, I'm certain it's going to crash into us. My heart's skipping beats. *Relax*, Angie tells me, *you'll soon be downing some of Jimmy's tabs.* I see the headbutt again and the sickening kicks and I'm thinking, *The Man isn't Dad himself or some imaginary stalker. The Man is Zidane.* I'm sure of this, though I don't know what it means.

'Alan doesn't pull his punches, does he?' Martin says.

'At least with him, you know where you stand,' I answer.

'Eala?' He's acting all, like, shock horror, but I turn to the side window.

Our street, at last. From the good end. The river end. We go by Mrs Casey's. A half-filled plastic message bag hangs on the doorknob. She's in hibernation again. Lucky her. We turn into our drive and I let Dad climb out first.

'It worked out perfectly for you tonight, didn't it?' I tell Martin when the back door slams shut. 'You get everyone fired up and Dad freaks out and he's another step closer to getting locked away.'

'Eala?'

'And your big donation? That'll really go down well with Mam, won't it?' I say. 'You think money can buy everything, don't you?'

'No, I don't. And I didn't give them money. I gave them the house in Friary Street.'

My fingernails feel like cat's claws and I want to tear him to shreds.

'So we get to dump Dad in there and you get another shot at Mam?' I say. 'Well, you can forget it because I'll never let you get your hands on her. I'll do whatever I have to do to stop you. Tell everyone you're a dirty old man if I have to.'

'Eala?' he says. More shock horror. 'Don't be like this. You know me.'

'No one knows anyone.'

'Eala, this isn't you. This talk, these notions of yours . . . Should you maybe have a chat with Fiona?'

I get out of the car and follow Dad up the steps. He's got his green retro Puma kitbag slung over his shoulder, but it could be full of rocks he's so hunched over. When I open the front door, Mam is coming out along the hallway. She's brighter than I've seen her for a long time. Beautiful again.

'So how did you get on, Jimmy?' she asks and I'm about to flam some lies, but Dad cuts across me.

'I'm useless at football,' he says. 'And I'm a nutter.'

He throws the kitbag on the floor. She's stunned. She looks at Martin, who's come in behind me. She shakes her head slowly as if to say, *I told you so*.

'You're not a nutter,' she says.

He tries to get by her, but she pulls him to her and kisses him on the lips. And it's not a little peck. *Some show she's putting on*, Angie says. *Does she think you're birdbrained enough to believe in it?* Mam steps back, but she's still holding him.

'Is your door still locked, Judy?' Dad asks.

'We'll talk about this later, Jimmy, OK?'

'Talk? All you ever want to do is talk,' Dad says.

I'm seeing stars. White noise hisses in my ears.

'Martin,' she says. 'Can you stay with Jimmy for a while? Fiona's here. We need to have a chat.'

'Sure.'

Dad starts to descend the stairs to his room. He's not well pleased to see his old pal follow him down. Martin's aflame with embarrassment at what he's heard. I make for the stairs to my own room.

'Eala, please,' Mam says.

She steps aside and I see Sean and Fiona Sheedy sitting on the bay-window sofa. Sean's been crying. Miss Understanding holds his hand on the coffee tabletop and he doesn't pull it away when he spots me. I need a tab so bad.

'Please,' Mam says. 'I don't want to make any decisions without you.'

28

High tea on a low table. That's how Dad used to describe it when the best china came out and we sat round the coffee table here in the sitting room, entertaining some visitor. Back then, we'd always have a fire going. As a kid, I always wanted to be the one to pour and to deliver the cups and saucers and offer biscuits from the fancy gold-rimmed plate. This evening, Mam does the serving. Sean's sitting back on the sofa, all red-eyed and placid. He won't make eye contact with me and I want to scream at him because I can't tell if he's betrayed me, betrayed Dad. Miss U draws me into the small talk.

'And the show's going well?' she asks.

Soft-focus eyes, that same irritating tilt of the head to the side. But there's something different about her that I can't figure out, my head's in such a spin.

'It's OK. It passes the time.'

'I love that show. A modern version of *Romeo and Juliet*, isn't it? And who's your Romeo?'

'A moron called Derek.'

Mam flashes me a warning glance.

'Fiona has something she'd like us to discuss. Something we need to come to a decision on.'

'We can talk about it among ourselves,' I say. 'We don't need her.'

I watch Miss U and the tender way her gaze falls on Sean.

'Things have . . . things have come to a head tonight, Eala,' Mam says and I'm thinking, *This isn't about Dad's prison stretch. It's about what happened this evening in the assembly hall.* I was right. Martin had rung her. 'We all need to take a step back . . .' Mam's struggling and I'm ready to attack her, but Sean cuts me off.

'Starsky's been here.'

'And?' I'm blushing fiercely, stupidly at the mention of Brian's father and I'm wondering if Martin rang Starsky too, filled him in on the details of Dad's headbutt and the rest.

'I told him I didn't poison the dog and he goes, "Grand, but I'm away to Morocco on holiday and whoever takes over the case will have to interview your dad tomorrow." So I had to admit it.'

My head's all over the place. It's like I'm on some mad carnival ride that's out of my control and keeps changing directions in rough, unpredictable jolts.

'He said he'd try to keep it out of court, but I don't want to get off scot-free,' Sean says. 'I don't deserve to.'

'We're all of us stretched to breaking point, Sean,' Mam says and turns to me. 'All of us.'

There's a biscuit in my hand and it's in bits and I can't remember how it got there or how it got broken. I hold the crumbs tight in my fist so they won't fall and mess up the floor. My head won't let me think. All three of them are staring at me. *Say something*, Angie tells me, *anything*.

'The Man is Zidane.'

'Zidane?' Miss U says.

I explain my theory, but it doesn't sound very convincing because I leave out Dad's headbutt. I rabbit on anyway. Mam and Sean are mesmerized, though I can tell it's not my theory they're mesmerized by, but me.

'You may be reading too much into that dragging action of Jimmy's,' Miss U says. 'He's made terrific progress physically, but hemiplegia is difficult to recover from entirely.'

'Hemi–?' I've heard the word before, but my brain's too addled to dredge up the meaning. It sounds like the name of some planet in one of Sean's sci-fi books.

'The paralysis in his left leg after the accident?' Miss U says.

'Right, yeah, right,' I say.

I hold on to the chair tightly with my free hand to stop from shaking. The crumbs in my fist are getting all damp from my sweat. Mam comes and sits beside me. She slips her arm round my waist. I don't want to be touched, but if I move away from her they'll think I'm even freakier than they already do.

'I thought the Zidane thing might mean something,' I say. 'Sorry.'

'There's nothing to be sorry for,' Mam says. 'We're worn out. We need to . . . to . . .'

She turns to Miss U. It seems like Miss U cops at the same moment I do that Mam's expression isn't exactly friendly. There's irritation in it, maybe even resentment. A nervous, saucer-rattling sip of tea and Miss U switches from being our best pal to being a psychologist on the job.

'First, I want to say that in these situations, no one ever

feels they get it right. It's perfectly normal to think that we've failed, that we haven't proved equal to the task.'

'We?' I say. I can't seem to rein myself in. 'What's this we craic? You're not one of us. You don't know what it's like.'

She keeps her cool, her head moving like one of those nodding toy dogs you put on the back shelf of a car. I feel like I'm one more hysterical kid she has to deal with, one of many.

'You're right, of course,' Miss U says. 'I don't know what it's like. But I can see the toll this is taking on all of you. How impossible it is to keep going. Not without some . . .'

Tablets, yeah, I'm thinking and I don't like the way Miss U is looking at me. It's like she knows I'm up to something weird. I wish I could get my foot to stop tapping, but I can't.

'. . . Without some respite. As you all know, Jimmy's had certain, well, behavioural issues of late that he needs help with. The fact that these behaviours are so out of character with the man you knew as your father, makes them all the more difficult for you to comprehend.'

Sean and me swap looks. His comes with the raised eyebrows of a question; mine with a warning frown.

'Normally, the rehab psychiatrist would see him only on an outpatient basis to reassess his medication and such,' Miss U continues. 'But Dr Reid is anxious to keep Jimmy under observation for a couple of weeks and, fortunately, a bed has become available. Respite care is almost impossible to get these days, what with the cutbacks and all, so –'

'This is how it starts,' I say.

'It's for the best,' Sean says. 'We're totally strung out. You are too.'

'Two weeks at most,' Mam says. 'Dad gets a proper assessment and we get to recharge our batteries.'

'And we get used to not having him around,' I object. 'Next time it'll be four weeks and then six or whatever. That's the plan, right, Mam?'

'There's no plan. We need to do this.'

'You need to,' I say and I punch even lower. 'Have you talked to Martin about this? I bet he thinks it's a great idea too.'

Mam puts her cup and saucer back on the coffee table. I wish I hadn't mentioned Martin. No. I wish I hadn't mentioned Martin in front of Miss U. Mam stands up and brushes the crumbs from the front of her dress to the floor. And it bothers me to see that mess on the carpet. I keep wanting to get down on my knees and pick up every last crumb, add them to the fistful in my hand.

'I've a wash I need to put in the dryer,' Mam says and glides from the sitting room wearing her Judy's *hauteur* mask.

Miss U has me in her sights. No sign of sweet sympathy from her now, only the flush of annoyance as she glares at me. *We can swap glares, stares or whatever else all night, Miss U*, I'm thinking, *and you won't best me.* I feel like laughing at her.

'You're on something, Eala,' Sean says. 'You're pure wasted.'

'You think everyone is as dumb as you are?'

'Did Brian . . .?'

'I'm not with Brian, right? I was with him three or four flipping days or something, I can't remember how long, and that was it, right? I copped on to him, right?'

Miss U won't stop gaping at me and suddenly I cop what's different about her. She's started to care about her appearance. A touch of make-up, a deep green dress that goes well with the mousy hair she's had cut looser so that there's more bounce in it than before.

'Break-ups are never easy,' she says, all sweetness again.

'Leave Brian out of it. This has nothing to do with Brian.' Inside I'm shouting, but it's coming out like a whine and I can't make the whining stop. 'Can't you leave us alone? You're tearing our family apart.'

'We're doing a fair job of that ourselves,' Sean says.

'Sean, Eala.' The sudden firmness in Miss U's voice catches me on the hop. 'Listen, we all have – and I include myself in we this time – we all have idealized notions of family, of how we come together and stick by one another in a crisis. It doesn't always work like that. We quarrel, we blame one another, doubt one another's motives. Everyone gets hurt and if this goes on and on without a break, the hurt will never heal.'

I hear Mam coming back downstairs. I wish I could think of some clever put-down that would pin Miss U to the sofa but, of course, I can't. You never can, can you? Especially not when your brain's gone to jelly. Afterwards, half a dozen smart remarks always come to mind and it's too late. 'L'esprit d'escalier', Dad called it. I need a tablet more than I need a row with Miss U or Mam who's at the doorway now. Tom rescues me. He's started to cry. I'm on my feet and away to the door, but Mam's blocking me off.

'I'll go up to Tom,' I tell her.

'There's nothing between Martin and me but friendship, Eala.'

'I know, I know, I shouldn't have said that.' A lie.

'Are you OK with this respite care?'

'Yeah.' A second lie. 'It's only a few weeks.'

She lets me pass. She touches my arm as I go by and I try not to shrink from her.

'Everything's going to work out OK, Eala.'

'Yeah.' The biggest lie of all. I keep moving and call up to Tom from the foot of the stairs. 'Coming, Tom.'

I sneak by Mam's room. The door's not locked. It's open a few inches and I see Tom staring up at the ceiling and crying away without so much as one tear falling. On the second landing, I slip into my own room and make for the wardrobe. I fish out a tablet from my stash. A downer. And a second. One of those antidepressants that make me scarily high for a bit before they set me floating down gently. In the bathroom, I swallow the tablets with a glass of water from the cold tap. The water is tepid and stale. I go back down to Mam's room.

Tom's sitting up in bed, his green tractor alongside him. He raises his arms towards me and I swoop him up and spin him around until he starts giggling. I get him back under the covers and he leans on the pillow, holding my hand.

'Stowy, Eallie,' he says and I lie down alongside him.

'This one is about the day Terry met the teapots.'

'Book. Wead book. P'ease.'

Why not? And why not a Terry the Tank book? I don't have to explain who wrote it, do I?

'I'll find the book.'

'Wiggie,' he says, chuckling at the very thought of my mad red curly wig.

'If you promise not to laugh at me.' I feel my face thawing out, a smile warming it, a loopy smile.

Tom nods and turns his face into the pillow to hide his giggles. I head over to Dad's workroom. I don't need to turn on the light because the curtains are open as always and I know exactly which shelf the Terry the Tank books are on. In the corner over by the window, the tailor's dummy stands guard over Dad's secrets. It has no eyes, no mouth, no ears. I find the book.

As I head up to my own room for the wig, I hear the murmur of conversation from the sitting room. I bet they're talking about me and my weird performance down there. *You'll have to keep your mouth shut*, Angie says, *not blurt out every daft thing that comes into your head or they'll think you're mad*. From further down in Dad's room, no sound comes at all or none that I can hear. Even if Dad and Martin are talking, I can't imagine for the life of me what they can find to say to one another.

'Eallie?' Tom calls.

'Coming.'

I take the wig from my wardrobe. I think about taking another anxiety tablet, but I talk myself out of it. I put on the wig and check myself in the long mirror on the wardrobe door. I'm Angie, looking at Eala. *Two down and one to go, Eala, because Sean and Judy have given up on Dad and it's all down to you now*. But what can I do? I've tried everything. *You'll think of something, Eala, something to drag Dad back out from that black hole*. In Mam's room, I make a grand entrance, my arms wide and bowing to my audience of one. He laughs himself silly.

'Missy Casey!' he chuckles. 'You Missy Casey.'

I have to smile. *You don't know how right you are, Tom.* I go and sit by him, opening the book. *Terry the Tank Meets the Teapots*. I begin to read and, like Mam and Dad always did when they read to us, I ask Tom to point out the details in the illustrations that appeal to him.

'Gun,' he says, pointing to the gun barrel of the tank. Boys will be boys.

'And what colour is this flower?'

'Wed.'

He points at the red bandana Rosie the Mechanic wears above her psychedelic boiler suit.

'Wed.'

His finger drifts down to Rosie's face, down along her body. She's got my black hair and my slightly upturned nose and a tiny tattoo of a swan on her left arm.

'Eallie,' he says.

I read on, taking my time, drinking in the smell of my little brother, the wonder in his eyes, his sighs of satisfaction, one hand distractedly rubbing along the flesh of my arm, the other holding on to his green plastic tractor.

I remember when he was a baby. I remember lying alongside him on this same bed while his busy fists pummelled the air and his legs pumped like a sprinter's. Such a happy time that was. Everyone wanting a piece of Tom – even Sean. Everyone floating on cloud nine. The house radiating milky warmth and contentment. And Dad, the perfect Dad, changing nappies, testing the milk's heat on the back of his hand, singing Tom to sleep, like he sang me and Sean to sleep. 'Row, row, row your boat gently down the stream.

Merrily, merrily, merrily, merrily, life is but a dream.' Never again. Not unless . . . *Not unless you have your own baby*, Angie laughs, *ha ha ha!*

'Eallie cwy,' Tom whispers.

29

Dad's been gone a week now. We don't visit. It might unsettle him. That's the theory. The truth is he was actually glad to go. He told me so the evening before he left. That and a few other home truths that didn't make the parting any easier. I didn't help matters much. I forced him to watch the Zidane DVD.

These sleepers don't always deliver what they say on the box. Or not for long enough anyway. I blank out quickly when I take one along with the antidepressants. There's a queer chemical taste from them that's disgusting, but you want that taste so badly knowing that sleep will soon follow. A few hours later you wake up. The temptation to take another tab is huge, but I've only given in once. The morning after you've taken one sleeper, you feel groggy. After taking two, you're completely out of it and seem to be living in a weird echo chamber.

I'm telling myself all this tonight so that if I do wake later, I won't give in for a second time. I need to be as normal as possible tomorrow. Act my best, look my best. I was thinking I'd ask Jill for a loan of some of her girlie clothes, but she'll be freaked out enough when she hears what I'm asking her to do for me. If she ever does hear. I keep putting off ringing her and it's close to eleven already. I keep thinking of other stuff so I won't rehearse for the hundredth time what I'll say to her when I get up the courage to ring.

So. Dad. The evening before he left. We were down in his room. A small wheelie suitcase stood at the end of the bed. He and Mam had packed it earlier. He lay on the bed. Happy or sad, it was hard to tell between his drugged-up drawl and his constant yawning. I was doped up too. In the pocket of my denim jacket I had the Zidane DVD I dug up in his workroom. *Cruel to be kind*, I was thinking, *that's how it works, right?* I sat on the armchair beside his bed like a hospital visitor.

'You're all ready so?' I said.

'Yeah. All ready.'

'You don't mind going, do you? I mean it's only a few weeks, right?'

'Naw, I don't mind,' he said, stretching his arms and yawning. 'I need a break from this kip.'

'You could move upstairs, if you liked.'

He turned on his side and leaned on his elbow, his back to me, looking out at the evening rain.

'I mean this house,' he said. 'It's so old. Did you ever listen to it?'

'Listen to the house?'

'In the night. The creaks. The pipes banging and gurgling. One of these days the whole place is going to fall down.'

'This house won't be falling down any time soon.'

He looked around the room. The pictures on the wall, the TV, the shelves of DVDs, looked at everything except me.

'Is Marta coming back at all?'

'When you're home from your break.'

'She comes from a little village in the mountains. She misses it a lot,' Dad told me. 'They've got three streets along this slope. High Street, Middle Street and Low Street. They grow wine there. And up above them, they've got these old ruins called the Three Maidens' Castle.'

'That sounds lovely.' *If it's so wonderful,* I was thinking, *why don't you trot off back there, Marta?*

'People shouldn't have to live where they don't want to live. Animals too. Poor old Argos. I should never have beaten him.'

I got up from beside him and went over to the TV. I took the DVD from my jacket.

'I've something to show you.'

'What is it?'

Deep down I knew that what I was doing was reckless, but every feeling is deep down in me now, deep down beneath the fog in my brain. I stood in front of the screen and slipped in the disc.

'You're a pane, but I can't see through you,' he said, his voice high and nervous.

I flicked on Scene Select and picked one at random. The music is cool. Drum and bass with a kind of bass guitar riff above an electronic crackle and buzz. I stepped away from the screen.

'Is this the Man, Jimmy?'

Dad's eyes widened. His mouth hung open like it was a few seconds away from drooling. Dumbfounded. Dumb. *Please don't look so dumb, Dad.* He began to press the buttons on his watch. He couldn't stop his eyes being drawn to the screen. Zidane's in the all-white Real Madrid gear. It's a floodlit game. The cameras don't follow the play, just him, his every move. The sockets of his eyes are dark pools in the glow of white. He does the foot-drag thing, then breaks into a run. Sometimes you don't see any of the other players nor even the crowd. He's watching. Always watching and it's like he sees things no one else can see.

'Is this him?' I asked.

He looked at me as if to say, *Why are you doing this to me?* Then his expression hardened.

'If he comes around here, I swear, I'll kill him again,' he said.

'Again?' I said when I got my breath back. 'It's all right, Jimmy, you can tell me. It'll be our secret. Tell me what you remember.'

'Flames on the water?'

I went and knelt by him and held on to his arm.

'Try to remember more,' I said. 'What did the Man do to make you kill him?'

'I don't know. I was small, really small,' he said. 'I feel bad, Eala, I feel dizzy. Turn it off, please.'

He grimaced, swallowed back hard. I could see he blamed me for this torment he was going through. I couldn't keep up the questioning.

'Jimmy, this is a film about Zinedine Zidane,' I said. 'He's a famous French footballer. He scored two goals in one World Cup Final and got sent off in another. And he's alive, Jimmy. You never killed him. You never saw him except on television playing football.'

'He makes books too. Upstairs,' Dad whispered, his eyes raised to the ceiling. 'He's bad news, he is.'

'Jimmy . . .'

'I'm not so good myself. I break things and hurt people. What am I like, Eala?'

'You're a good man, a lovely man.'

I'm there on my knees and I can't move because if I do I know I'll fall down into the dark. He'd killed a man when he was a kid? Who can it have been and why? He'd begun to pick at one of the little daisies embroidered into the duvet.

'What happens to me, Eala, when I lose it?'

'We all lose it sometimes.'

'Alan never does,' he said. 'And I never lose it when I'm with him. Or with Marta.'

'That's good,' I said.

'I wish Alan was coming to the rehab with me. I'll miss him,' he said. 'I don't know what I'll do when he goes to live in Limerick.'

He pulled harder at the embroidered daisy and it came away between his fingers. He looked up guiltily at me. He gave me the flower.

'I didn't mean to,' he said.

Weird how, when you're in the middle of these situations, you can hold yourself together, hold back the tears dammed up in you and then completely fold up when you're alone again. But every day since Dad left it's been getting harder. Even with the tabs. And what happens when I start running out of these things? I won't have to worry about that if my plan works out. It has to. I can't think of any other way to bring something of the old Dad to the surface, to rescue him from his nightmare world of broken, jagged memories and give him a life again, a reason to live again.

I take one of the pillows from under my head, lie on my side, close my eyes and hold the pillow like it's my baby wrapped up in a soft blanket. I imagine Mam freaking out when she hears I'm pregnant. I see myself insisting on keeping the baby and her doubts turning to pure delight. I imagine how Dad's fascination with my child will grow into responsibility, into love, into realizing that he has children too and that I'm one of them and that he loves me. And I imagine telling him that his dark secrets will always be safe with me, safely buried away forever.

I'd like to take my sleeper now and stay in this dream, but I have to make it happen first. I have to ring Jill. And then Brian. I scroll up Jill's number and press green to go.

'Eala?'

'Well, how's . . . how's it going?' *Perk up*, Angie tells me, *you're slurring your words*. 'Sorry to ring so late.'

'It's half twelve,' Jill says. There's a sleepy pause. 'Are you all right? Are you drunk, Eala?'

'What?' *Don't get thick, Eala*, Angie tells me. 'No. No, drowsy is all. But I can't sleep and I . . . I didn't think you'd mind if I rang.'

'Course not. I got a fright, like.' She sounds even more doped-up than I feel.

'Things all right there, yeah?' I say.

'Yeah, grand. Quiet.'

'They've gone back up to Dublin, have they?'

'No. Next week.'

'That's a shame,' I say. 'I mean, like, it's a shame they're going, not that they're not gone yet, like.'

'Eala, you don't sound right. Do you want me to come over?'

'No, no. Don't mind me, I'm a bit scattered.' Here goes. 'And excited.'

'Excited? Why?'

'I'm going out with Brian.'

'So I've heard,' she says. 'He'll break your heart, Eala, I'm telling you.'

'You got over him, didn't you?'

'That was different.' This is getting too heavy for my liking. 'Eala, there's something you need to know about Brian. I never wanted to have to tell you this but . . .'

'I know all I need to know about Brian, believe me,' I tell her, but I'm thinking, *How does she know about Brian being in the car that crashed into the riverbank wall?*

'I don't think you do, Eala. Listen, Win told me –'

'I know all this,' I insist. 'Brian told me everything, right? He was stupid, he made a big mistake is all.'

'But how can you go out with someone who's so . . . so irresponsible, so careless?'

'It's what I want.' *Lay it on thicker*, Angie says. 'I'm sick of having nothing, nobody.'

'You don't have to be alone so much. You know that. I'm always asking you to come to the cinema and stuff.'

Being tanked up with prescription drugs slows your brain down. Which is not always a bad thing. When your thoughts are flying about pure rapid, you can't pull them together. You miss the obvious connections, the two plus twos that make up four. One plus one making three, in this case. Win plus Brian equals Little Richard. How could I have been so blind?

'Win told me . . .' Jill's not been talking about the crash on our street, she's been talking about Win's pregnancy. Another memory sweeps back. New Year's Eve and we're sitting on the window sill of Mrs Casey's shop and Brian's telling me not to believe Jill if she's dissing him. 'Or Win either,' he'd said. And his sudden, unexpected break-up with Jill? That was probably Win's doing. Warning him off her little sister.

'Eala? Talk to me, will you?'

Another chunk of time seems to have passed me by. I stand up and walk around to get my head moving again, stop myself from disappearing again.

'I'm back. I thought I heard Tom crying here,' I tell her. 'There's a favour I want to ask you.'

'Yeah?' Not *Sure* or *Anytime*, but *Yeah?* like she's thinking, *What's this nutter going to say next?*

'Tomorrow night . . . will you cover for me? Like, invite me to sleep over in your place?'

No answer. *Keep your cool, Eala*, Angie warns me. *Do your sweetly innocent* West Side Story *Maria thing*.

'This isn't Brian's idea, Jill,' I say. 'And I've no intention of getting myself . . . you know what I mean. I'm thick, but I'm not stupid.'

I laugh and it comes out like a pure girlie giggle. I have to dig deeper.

'Please, Jill? All this time since . . .' *No, Angie, I'm not bringing Dad into this*. 'I never asked anything of you before, Jill. Don't let me down. Every day is a let-down for me.'

'Eala . . .'

'Please?'

'OK,' she says. 'But I don't like it, Eala. I'm worried about you. You're so not yourself these days.'

Not yourself. I hate that phrase. But I let it pass.

'I know, I know. But I'll be all right. I'm getting there. Thanks, Jill.'

I switch the phone off rapid. My heart is skipping beats. My mouth is pure dry. It always is nowadays. I take my sleeper and drink off the half-litre glass of water. I'm swimming with the stars and have to lie down. The bed is a boat come loose of its moorings. I still have most of the texts Brian sent in the days after New Year's Eve. I look through a few of them. His pleas give me the courage to ring him. One beep and he picks up.

'Eala.'

'Brian, just listen and say yes or no, right? Are your folks gone to Morocco?'

'They're going in the morning.'

'Can I stay over in your house tomorrow night?'

'You mean like sleep . . .?'

'Yes or no?'

'Yeah . . . Sure . . . if you . . .'

'I'll be there at nine.'

30

Brian's house is on a quiet cul-de-sac of bungalows at the edge of town. Out behind the back walls lies the golf course. As I turn into the street, I can see right across the wide, contoured expanse in the moonlight. Right across to the river. I don't know why, but it makes me feel so lonely. I have to move on, get myself quickly by Jill's house. She'll be watching from her bedroom window, I bet. I think about stooping low as I go by the front wall, but that'd be pure childish. I can imagine the view from her window if I did. My backpack floating along above the cap of the wall with me hidden away under it. I smile and a chuckle breaks out of me. I go by the house and don't look to see if Jill is there.

Mam wanted to give me a lift. She was so glad to see me in good form today and doing this normal sleepover thing that she didn't mind when I said I'd prefer to walk. Sometimes I wonder how she hasn't copped on to my drowsiness in the mornings and my nervy state before I take my evening tablet. Or why Sean hasn't told her of his suspicions. It feels like he's watching me all the time and I can't trust him not to search my room when I'm not there, so I play safe. I keep the tablets in the knapsack I carry everywhere with me.

Brian's is the last bungalow in the cul-de-sac and the biggest. It has more windows in the front than the others and all of them are lit up as I open the gate. There's a fountain hissing in the middle of the lawn. At first, it looks like the statuette of a young Greek or Roman boy is peeing into the pond around him and it's so mad the chuckles start up again. Closer in along the path, I realize that the water's coming from a long, narrow vase he's holding.

I stand at the front door and suck in a few lungfuls of air. I'm not afraid. During the day, I didn't take any tabs because I'd decided to take two before I came here. A good plan. I'm so in control as I swing off my backpack, brush a hand through my hair, zip open my jacket and open another button on my blouse. It's a relief to get the bag off my back. Weird how heavy a bottle of vodka can be.

The other day in rehearsals I played Maria like she was something out of a Britney Spears video. Throwing slinky shapes and come-on looks. Derek was pure lost for words. He couldn't focus on his lines and couldn't come up with any smart ad-libs of his own. Miss O'Neill had plenty to say. She took me aside after my performance.

'I can appreciate the fact that you're trying to find another side to Maria's character, but I'm afraid you're straying too far for my liking.'

'She's so gullible, it's ridiculous,' I said. 'She's not me.'

'We all have our gullible moments, Eala, believe me,' she said. 'And besides, flagrant is not sexy. It's cheap.'

'I don't know why I'm doing this show anyway,' I said and it came out like I was asking her to tell me why. What is it about her that draws me out like this? She never shows any emotion no matter what the situation. And yet I was this close to breaking down in front of her.

'My grand-aunt was an actress,' Miss O'Neill said. 'Never especially famous or anything, but she spent her life on the professional stage. What she loved best was acting in the Gaiety pantos. All that "Oh, yes I do," and "Oh, no you don't," stuff that kids love. Well, she did her last panto when she was in her eighties and crippled with arthritis. I linked her from the dressing room to the wings. Carried her, is more like it. Then she passed me her walking stick and I held her arm while she waited for her entrance. And bang on cue, out she went on to the stage. Dancing like a young girl. There has to be somewhere we can throw away the stick, Eala. It's as simple as that.'

And this is where I'll throw away mine. I ring the doorbell of Brian's house. A car starts up and pulls out of one of the drives back along the street. I press closer to the door and ring the bell more urgently. Not exactly rushing to let me in, is he? Through the frosted glass side panel, I see a shape moving, hesitating, moving again. The door opens.

'Well, Eala.'

I can't bring myself to say anything. What can you say to someone you hate so much and love so much? Someone who made a zombie of your dad and made a fool of you and –

'You look cold,' he says. 'Come in.'

I do a fake smile that feels creepy as soon as I start it up. I go by him and he closes the door behind me. *How's he going to want you if you keep this silence going, Eala?* Angie asks. The hallway is pure flowery. Big, embossed flowers on the wallpaper. Smaller ones in the pattern of the carpet. Even the hallway mirror has a whopping great tulip etched into it. And Brian, tall behind me, staring into my eyes. Bewildered. Time to start making sense.

'Your mother's into flowers?' I say and a snicker comes out. *Not funny, Eala.*

'Yeah.'

I open the backpack and pull out the vodka bottle.

'Do you have any mixers for this?'

Only now do I notice how bloodshot and puffy his eyes are. There's a tissue in his hand and he rubs his nose with it. How romantic is that?

'Sure,' he says, all nasal and grimacing like his own voice is too loud for him to bear. 'I can't drink, though. I'm on antibiotics. Sinus infection.'

'One drink won't kill you, will it?

'I suppose. Is orange OK as a mixer?'

'I suppose. If you don't have any Red Bull.'

'I don't think that'd be very –'

'Joke, Brian. Relax.'

He sneezes. When he's finished clearing up the damage he looks like Rudolf the Red-nosed Reindeer. The flowers on the walls and floor are doing my head in. They're beginning to stir like there's a light breeze catching them.

'Are we going to stand out here for the night?' I ask.

'Course not,' he says. 'I'm not with it. Come into the sitting room. I've the fire on.'

We head in. More flowers. Walls, carpet, curtains, sofa and armchairs and, on the mantelpiece, a crystal vase full of real ones. Lilies with their white mouths open, the orange stamens removed. No mess in this house. There's music playing. Some tragic, singer-songwriter stuff. Over by the corner beside the widescreen TV, there's an acoustic guitar on a stand.

'You never told me you play the guitar.'

'I don't. My father does.' An embarrassing admission that he regrets because I find it so hilarious. I wish I didn't feel so hyper.

'He's not one of those sad middle-aged guys you see on YouTube doing Elvis songs or something, is he?'

'He is on YouTube, actually,' Brian says and sits on one of the two armchairs and not here beside me on the sofa where he's supposed to sit. 'He does a couple of Johnny Cash songs. It's fair bad. I'll get the orange.'

And he's up and away. Leaving me to sit here, the bottle in one hand, the backpack in the other. *Some host*, Angie says. And I'm some guest, sneering at his folks.

I drop the backpack on the sofa and get a quick swig from the bottle and a second while there's time. It goes down easy. When Brian comes back in, the vodka hits my stomach and I have to swallow hard to keep it from coming straight back up. I sit down before I fall. I rest my head back among the sofa flowers and let the dizzy swirl pass before I open my eyes again.

Brian is sitting opposite me. Two glasses and two bottles have appeared on the coffee table and I don't remember how he got there or how they got there. I sit up and try to act naturally. My foot starts tapping. I have to look down at it to make it stop. Another tablet might help.

'Do you have any crisps or snacky stuff?' I ask.

'Sure,' he says. 'I could do some chips or something if you like.'

'No, crisps are fine.'

He's as relieved as I am when he heads to the kitchen. I fish around in my backpack and get another tablet. I cough to cover the crinkling sound of the foil breaking. I take a swig from the bottle of orange to get the tablet down. It's the kind of orange you're supposed to dilute and is so sweet and concentrated, I gag and almost spray the lot out over the coffee table. I'm pouring us a drink as Brian returns.

'Roast beef flavour is all we have,' he says and I have to work hard not to wobble as I pour, he's watching me so closely.

I lean on the coffee table to make sure I set the bottle straight there.

'I don't know if it's me or the table, but one of us is wobbling,' I say. Another dumb chuckle comes. 'You should take it back to the shop. The table, like.'

'I made it myself,' he says.

He's heading towards the armchair and I make room for him on the sofa in as obvious a way as I can, short of saying, 'Sit here and hold me.' He obeys, but reluctantly. I raise my glass and he takes his.

'Cheers,' I say.

'Eala, can we talk?'

'Sure.' The orange takes the edge off the vodka and the third tablet is calming me down. Or is it four I've taken?

'I mean before you drink any more of that stuff.'

'Look, Brian, there's nothing to say,' I tell him and this bit is easy because I've rehearsed the lines so often. 'It wasn't your fault, the car, the speed bumps, what happened to Dad. There's nothing to forgive, if that's what's on your mind,

OK?' And I throw in the clincher I've prepared. Something to prove I'm not some silly skanger throwing myself at him. 'You're not my *bête noire* or whatever.'

'Your what?'

'*Bête noire*. It's French.'

'I didn't do French in school.'

'I was writing this history essay about the Holocaust.' *Shut it*, Angie says. *He's looking at you like you have two heads*. 'And Dad gave me the, whatever you call it, the phrase. It means black beast, like. Something to fear, something to blame or whatever. The Jews were the *bêtes noires* of the Nazis, like. Or was it the other way round? I can't . . .'

'Eala? You're not yourself.'

'Everyone keeps telling me that. Who do they think I am then?'

The house phone rings out in the hallway. It can't be Mam, can it? Jill wouldn't do that to me, would she? Betray me? Maybe I should've left my phone on so I'd know if Mam was trying to find me.

'That'll be my mother,' Brian says. 'She said she'd ring every evening.'

'Leave it.'

'I can't. She'll ring my mobile anyway until I answer.'

'Switch it off then.'

'I can't. She's a worrier. She'll panic if I don't answer,' he says and he's on his feet before I can hold him back, which was supposed to be my next move except my brain couldn't get the message to my hands quickly enough.

'I won't be long.'

He closes the sitting-room door after him. I don't mind. I pour myself some more vodka. No orange this time. I can't hear what he's saying out there, but I can sense the annoyance in his tone. I gulp back the vodka and pour another neat one and knock that back too. I kick off my shoes and lie out on the sofa. *No more talking*, Angie tells me. *When he gets back there'll be no more talking*. I take one of the flowery cushions and hold it close to me. I sink into a daydream, evening dream, whatever. Holding Brian. Holding my child. Humming 'Tomorrow' and 'Somewhere' and 'Tonight'. Out along a river, floating, flowing . . .

'Eala?'

Brian is kneeling beside me. I try to raise my arms to him, but they won't move. I'm cold. My blouse is open all the way down the front. I can't make his three faces come together as one. The coffee table is empty. How did that happen? My arm comes up and falls on his shoulder. I can't remember telling it to.

'Jeez, Eala, what –'

'Angie,' I say, all slurred and slowed down. 'Call me Angie. I know about Win too and the baby. But don't worry, I won't tell anyone, right? Our secret and this is our secret too, right?'

I can't hold my head up so I take a rest. I look for my cushion, my baby, but it's not there. When I wake up I'll find it. I've taken a sleeper by mistake, that's what's wrong. But I'll be grand once I sleep it off. Grand.

'You bastard, you've spiked her drink, haven't you?'

'No way, man. She's out of it. She was out of it before she got here.'

Out of what, I'm thinking? *And what's all this noise?* I force my eyes open. Sean and Brian are scuffling by the sitting-room door, but their movements are weirdly slow like they're underwater. Sean catches him with a punch to the jaw, but Brian doesn't swing back.

'Jeez, Sean, if I did anything would I ring you?' he pleads. 'I don't know what to do. Should we get a doctor?'

'Look at her blouse, you scumbag,' Sean shouts and takes another swing, but misses.

I look down. I'm all buttoned up again except the buttons are in the wrong holes. I start chuckling. I try to lift my head and I can feel the vodka moving up from my stomach and what if it goes back down the wrong way?

'Help me,' I say, but I can't tell if they hear me.

'Help me.' They're so busy fighting, they've forgotten I'm here. I don't want them to fight over me.

'Help me.' *Why won't they listen? Please, listen to me.*

I'm outside of myself. Looking down at the girl lying on the sofa, at two guys trying to wrestle one another to the ground. Further and further up I float and I'm afraid because I need to get back to my body. Except it's not me down there now. It's Angie. Further and further up and what if I never come back together again?

Who will I be then?

31

When I was seven years old, Mam took me to see my first musical in the school assembly hall. We went with one of her workmates whose daughter was playing the part of Ado Annie in *Oklahoma*. I was beside myself with excitement. High on cola and chocolate and 'I Cain't Say No'. Until the interval came and I threw one of my weird wobblers.

The thing is our assembly hall stage doesn't have curtains. So the lights go up for the interval and I'm there, all confused, looking up at the empty stage while Mam's trying to bring me outside. She was a smoker back then. She was also, more than likely, bored out of her tree. But I'm looking back at the stage and I'm going, 'What if something happens while we're gone?' And she's going, 'Nothing happens in the interval because they're all taking a rest, OK?' I'm not convinced, sniffling and sulking as I follow her out. Long after the show was over – days, weeks later – I still had it in my head that we'd missed some really important twist in the tale.

I keep coming back to that memory these days. Keep thinking that while I've been lying here in my room – what is it? – eight, nine days now, things have changed, things have moved on in the house below me and in our lives.

I spent two nights in hospital. The first was a nightmare. I woke in a snow-blind panic in the brightly painted ward, certain I was in a psychiatric ward and that somewhere else in the building, Dad was locked up too. While Mam and a young doctor and a couple of nurses tried to calm me down, I got this flashback of me standing at Brian's door. I couldn't remember anything of being inside the house, but I went ballistic again imagining the worst. I pleaded with Mam to get me the morning-after pill, but she assured me that nothing had happened. They'd checked me out and the thought of being poked at like that really freaked me. I was going mental until I got this jab that seemed to freeze my veins and then slow my brain to a crawl.

'Don't let them make a zombie of me, Mam,' I cried.

'There's nothing to worry about,' she said from so far away I thought I might never see her again. 'You'll feel much better when you wake and I'll be here every minute, OK?'

'What happened to me? Why did I go so crazy?'

I was getting drowsy then and didn't catch everything the young doctor told me. Stress, fatigue, the cocktail of alcohol and Dad's drugs, she said. But I knew that already. What I didn't know was that the antidepressants Dad has to take are some new type and are not to be messed around with. The doctor thought these SSRIs had ratcheted up the anxiety and panic I'd been feeling. I was lucky I hadn't been taking them longer, she told me. I didn't feel lucky. And how ironic is this? She thought it would be a good idea for me to tease out any 'issues' that might be bothering me. With a psychologist. Fortunately, the jab soon sent me into the deepest, longest sleep I'd had for months. Fourteen hours straight I slept.

And sleep is all I've been good for ever since. That and pretending to sleep. Whenever the front door bell rings, as it does now, I'm convinced it's Miss Understanding. I go under the duvet again. I don't want anyone poking around in my brain, stirring up all the stuff I'm not ready to think about yet.

The voices from downstairs are muffled. I let a minute or two pass and I'm thinking about easing the duvet down when I cop that someone's already in the room. I listen. Weird how you can tell who's out there by the sound of their breathing. It's Mam. I listen closer. She's alone.

She's been in pottering around my room a few times already this morning. Twice she's woken me as she put away some fresh clothes in my dresser and apologized in a fluttery, hyper kind of way that wasn't her at all. I know she's psyching herself up for some major announcement. And what else can it be but that she's decided Dad should live in Martin's house when the Head-Up people have got it ready? There's a space in the pit of my stomach where the panic should flood in, but it doesn't.

'I didn't wake you, did I?'

'No,' I say. 'I was stirring anyway.'

She's standing there with another bundle of my clothes. She must've washed every last blouse and hoodie and pair of jeans of mine. That brisk, fresh tang the steam iron raises from newly dried clothes hangs in the air. I take a few big breaths of it. She places the bundle on top of the dresser and sits on the bed beside me. Some loose strands of hair fall across her eyes and she brushes them back.

'You look so much better,' she says.

'I must've freaked everyone out,' I say.

Fingering one of the crocheted daisies on the duvet cover, she doesn't know how or where to start. Only now do I cop that it's the duvet cover from Dad's bed. I look along the line of daisies. The one Dad pulled out is still missing. I try to recall what I did with the threaded flower when he gave it to me, but I can't.

'Do you remember anything about that first night in hospital?' she asks. 'The things you said?'

'What things?'

'The doctor thought you mightn't. "Retrograde amnesia" they call it.'

'What things, Mam?' I don't really want to hear this, but I know I have to.

'All that stuff you'd bottled up inside for so long,' she says. 'I wasn't watching out for you, Eala. I was tired. And I sent the wrong signals to you. And . . . Eala, we have to learn to keep everything out in the open. Everything. No matter how off-the-wall it seems.'

'The baby thing? Can we not talk about it, please?'

Mam lies against me. I can feel her breath on my cheek and her heartbeat on my spine. I close my eyes. The comforting after-wash of sleep calms me. Deep inside, there's a silence like nothing I've ever known. The arguments raging in my brain ever since Dad's accident have stopped. Something has changed in me and, maybe it's because I'm still too tired to think clearly, but I can't account for it.

'It's OK, Eala. Before I had the miscarriage, I was thinking along the same lines. That our having a baby around might somehow bring him back to himself, bring him back to us.'

I open my eyes and the room is bright with surprise. I know what's changed. Angie is gone. Only now do I realize that I haven't imagined seeing or hearing her since I came back from hospital.

'There was more?' I ask.

'Well . . . this business about Martin and me.'

Mam sits up again. I sneak a look at her. She's smoothing out the duvet cover, fixing her hair, delaying. A cloud has passed across her face, a hint of annoyance

'You won't believe this, Eala,' she says. 'Martin and Fiona have been going out together for the last three months. But neither of them wanted to tell me because I was . . . because *we* were going through such a hard time. If they'd been upfront, you'd have had one less thing to worry about.'

Bitterness narrows her eyes, wrinkles the pout of her lips, ages her. I don't like the way this is going.

'I'm tired of people thinking they know what's best for us,' she says. 'Right from the start, Fiona's been harping on and on. "This won't be easy, Judy. Don't feel you've failed if you can't handle him, Judy. Keep all these 'alternative care options' open, Judy. You have to look to the future, Judy."'

This is what I'd wanted all along. Mam showing Miss U the door, refusing to listen to her advice. But now it feels all wrong. She's up and pacing the room, moving things as she goes like she believes nothing is in its rightful place. A hairbrush, the tartan blanket at the end of my bed, the left shoulder of her cardigan. A kind of wildness in her, but vulnerable too. I'm afraid for her.

'We've been to the bottom, Eala, all of us, and it can't get any worse. I'll be giving up the job. I'll get a Carer's

Allowance. I mean, it's not great money, but we'll manage. And, anyway, you were right about Marta. I don't know why I ever took her on. All this nonsense about being Ballroom Dancing Champion of Moravia. I mean, really. All lies, my guess is, everything she said. All lies.'

She's pulling at the top drawer of my dresser again. It won't yield to her. She's trying so hard that the dresser shakes and the floor shakes and the bed sways beneath me.

'Dad tried it on with Marta, didn't he?' I say and Mam gives up on the drawer and fiddles with the catch of the wardrobe door instead.

'He'll be home next week,' she says, bright and upbeat again, opening the wardrobe, the clothes hanging there like a choice. 'And it'll be better this time, Eala, because we'll know what lies behind all those fears of his.'

My brain blanks. Maybe I've done some permanent damage after all, with the bucketload of tabs I've popped. Mam comes and kneels by the bed.

'In the hospital you told us how he remembered living on a boat and his talk of fire on the water and how he was afraid of killing the Man again,' she says. 'And the tracing agency have been able to piece the story together. We know who he was, Eala. Who he is.'

'We have a name?'

Mam nods. She sits on the bed beside me. I stare up at the ceiling and follow the faint traces of the rivery cracks in the plaster Dad filled in before he painted it a few years ago.

'His name is Georges Dorar.' I haven't heard her do a French accent since the days when she still sang '*Hymne à l'Amour*' in the kitchen.

My body unclenches itself. A hush descends on the room. I should be afraid of what I'm about to ask, but I'm not.

'Did he really kill someone then? This . . . *The Man*?'

'No,' she says. 'He was eight years old and imagined it was his fault. But, no. The inquest report is clear on –'

'Who was the Man?'

Mam pulls up the sleeves of her cardigan. It's like there's some unpleasant job to be done and she's trying to convince herself to go at it.

'The Man was his father.'

It's weird, but I'm more shocked at how stick-thin her arms are than by what she's just said. They're the arms of a size-zero model.

'Jimmy's parents were both, well, junkies, I suppose. They lived in fear of having Jimmy taken from them by Social Services. His mother, Cath Wilkins, she'd been taken into care herself as a child. She was sixteen when Jimmy was born.'

'And his father?'

'Thierry, his name was,' Mam says. 'Always a wild kid, it seems. Lost his mother early on and when he was sixteen his father gave up on him and went back to live in Algeria. A year later, he met Cath and when Jimmy came along they'd move from city to city, from one New Age commune to the next. They changed their names so often that Jimmy didn't even know his real name when it all came to an end.'

I sit up and rub my hand along the pale skin on the underside of her arm. Her wrist is so tiny, I can see the throb of her pulse there. A slow pulse, and watching it slows my pulse down.

'It was a suicide pact,' she says. 'Thierry put it all in a letter to Social Services. They saw no end to their running, no future for their child.'

I rest my head back against the wall above the bed. The cold of the plaster passes down the nape of my neck.

'They were living in a houseboat on the Thames in Hammersmith. A week before Christmas, Thierry broke into a pharmacy and took every tablet he could lay his hands on. He crushed the lot and mixed it with some soft drink or other. Cath took her dose and lay on her bed. Thierry took his and woke Jimmy. We'll never know the precise details, but it seems Jimmy wouldn't drink the mix and tried to run to Cath. The oil lamp they used for light got knocked over somehow and the houseboat caught fire.'

She's lying in my lap now. I can't remember how she got there. I pass my fingers through her hair. It hasn't been washed in days. Maybe not since my night of madness in Brian's house. She shuts the world from sight as though to imagine the scene she describes more vividly. I look inward and I see it too. The flames. The molten gold of their reflection on the water. The face of a child, light and shadow playing for possession of his startled eyes.

'Why did he never confide in me?' she says so distantly I know the question isn't meant for me. 'I mean, I understand why it'd be hard for him to dig all that stuff up. But none of it was his fault. There was nothing there that might have made me think less of him. Nothing.'

She doesn't know about the punk-club incident and its consequences. What do I do now? Do I tell her? Might it help her understand Dad's need for secrecy? But she'll totally lose it with Sean and me for keeping the story to ourselves all these months. Her head is like a dead weight in my lap, but I don't stir. She's dozing off or slipping down to hide a while inside herself. It's hard to tell which. Either way, I can't disturb her now.

Georges Dorar. Georges. I repeat the name to myself again and again – Georges, Georges – until it feels like I'm calling out to the boy silhouetted by the flames. Calling him to me, taking his hand. Walking away from the river of fire.

32

'. . . And Alan Rice played this great through ball. The keeper doesn't know whether to come for it or stay. So the sweeper's shouting at him . . .'

Sean lies crossways at the end of my bed, his hands behind his head as he relives the Tipperary Youth League game they won earlier in the afternoon. His first game for months. They're making up lost ground on the League leaders. Five points behind now with two games in hand. They'd won today's game with the last-minute goal he's describing.

'. . . And Brian nips in, rounds the keeper and the points are ours.'

That's Sean all over. Mr Sensitive.

'Tom's on the sideline, hopping up and down and punching the air. It was so cool to be out there playing again. I didn't realize how much I missed it.'

'This wouldn't be a parable, by any chance, would it?'

Sean drags his sore body up into a sitting position. He looks at his puzzle of a sister. We need to talk about Mam and the secret she doesn't yet know, but I can't get up the courage to start. It's like I'm on a basketball court or whatever, all togged out and I'm so nervous, I don't want the ball to be thrown in yet.

'Do I look like Jesus or what?' he says. 'A parable?'

'Yeah, like, I should get out of bed and stop moping or whatever?'

'Hey, relax. I was talking about the game against Saint Michael's,' he said. 'I wouldn't know a parable if it bit me on the buttocks.'

I feel suddenly skittish. When we were kids, I had this nasty little trick of making a fist of skinny knuckles and catching Sean on the flat of his thigh with it. Fair sore it was. I do the trick now and he yelps.

'Aw, jeez, man. I'm in agony here already.'

He's grimacing and laughing and he comes at me with his old trick. The ear twist. I duck under the duvet. He follows me in. I duck back out. He follows me out. It's pure daft, but we keep going in this crazy loop. Him, letting me catch him on the thigh. Me, letting him grab my ear. And it gets so funny we have to lie back and laugh it off. When I raise my head again, Sean's goes all serious.

'There's something I want to tell you, Eala,' he says. He can't decide whether to stay sitting or go for a walk around the room. 'Something you should know . . . about Win.'

'Leave it, Sean.'

'No, it's important,' he insists. 'See, Win's told the parents who the father of her kid is and it's the guy who runs the nursing home she worked in. He's married with kids. Was married.'

'Who told you all this?'

'Brian,' he says. He inspects a nasty-looking graze along

his shin that makes me wince when he pulls up the leg of his tracksuit. It doesn't seem to bother him too much. 'He told me about the joyriding with Sham Healy too.'

'And you can forgive him for that?'

He shrugs and gets to his feet. On his way to the door, he limps at first, but is moving fine after a few steps.

'I'm telling you the story is all. He's interested if you're interested, like.'

'Nothing Brian says can change what happened to Dad.'

Something keeps him from leaving. He takes a quick look back to the landing, the stairs below. His hands are slung deep in the pockets of his blue tracksuit bottoms. Only now do I cop that it's one of Dad's French national team tracksuits he's wearing.

'I don't call him Dad any more. Not even in my head,' he says. 'I call him Jimmy.'

'Since when?'

'I dropped over to Martin's apartment the other evening. Fiona was there. She's moved in, like. And we had this major chat.'

'And she told you to stop calling him Dad?'

'No, it wasn't like that. She was talking about situations like ours that she's come across and she said something that really hit home. She said that people never get their heads round what their father or whoever has become until they, like, see him differently. See him like he's a long-lost uncle or a cousin you've never met before or –'

'So he's some distant relation to you now?'

'No way. But when I was coming home, I remembered one of those Judge Dredd stories and everything sort of added up.'

'So you found the answer in a comic?'

'Maybe I did,' he says. 'See Judge Dredd has this clone – actually they're both clones, but that's another story. And this clone, Rico, he's called, is one of the bad guys. In the end, there's a showdown and Judge Dredd kills Rico in this apartment building and –'

'Now Dad is one of the bad guys?'

'Course not. But the thing is the paramedics are getting ready to carry Rico's body out to the ambulance and Judge Dredd says, "No, I'll do it," and then he goes . . .' Sean checks himself, swallows hard. 'He goes, "He ain't heavy, he's my brother."'

'That was a song, wasn't it?' I say. 'It's on one of Dad's oldie CDs.'

'Yeah. It's kind of corny I know. But so true, though. I mean, it's not like you'd want to spend your life with your brother, but you'd walk through fire for him, wouldn't you?'

There's a hint of bronze in the late afternoon light. The faintest rhythmic hum of a busy Saturday town square reaches us. My legs and arms ache to be stretched. Over by the door, Sean's still hovering. It's almost like he knows we're not finished here yet.

'Sean, I think we have to tell her about Dad doing time.'

He doesn't seem all that surprised. He nods.

'She was going to find out anyway,' he says, and I'm the one caught by surprise. 'The tracing agency followed through on the name Georges Dorar and they've got the details of the court case. Martin said he'd tell her, but I want to do it. I feel I have to, like.'

'We'll both do it,' I say and he's OK with that, maybe even glad.

It's hard to imagine we'll ever be at one another's throats again like we used to be. But I suppose we'll have our moments. Everyone does. There's a clattering from the hallway, a door banging shut, the bouncing of a football. From below, Tom calls out.

'Sean! P'ay football! P'ease, p'ease, p'ease!'

'Coming.' Sean throws his eyes up to heaven, but he's grinning too. 'You know I was thinking, I qualify to play for three countries now. Ireland, England and Algeria. Maybe even France. That's fair cool, isn't it?' He laughs. 'Have to win the Tipperary Youth League first, though.'

And he's gone, a drum roll descending the stairs that reverberates in me long after he's reached the hallway below. Time to get moving again. Time to ring Jill, see how she's doing now that the Win epic has taken another twist. I've been exchanging texts with her for a few days and, in fairness to her, she's never mentioned her sister. I imagined it would be weeks before I'd work up the energy to actually talk to her. To be honest, there's another reason for this call.

I've been out of school two weeks and knowing how seriously Miss O'Neill takes her shows, I find it hard to believe that she'd have me back. I find it even harder to believe that I actually want to go on stage, but I do. The songs have already started to hum themselves in my head. 'Tonight'. 'Somewhere'. 'I Feel Pretty'. So I scroll up Jill's number and go for it. She can't speak at first. There's a lot of shuffling and sniffling, followed by silence.

'Jill, are you there? Don't be crying.'

'Oh, Eala, I'm so glad you didn't . . .'

More sobs. *Don't drive me back under the duvet, Jill*, I'm thinking.

'Didn't what, Jill?'

'You know . . . didn't, like, OD.'

'I wasn't trying to top myself. Is that what they're saying about me?'

'You were so not yourself, I didn't know what to think.' There's another wistful pause. 'You poor thing, you've been through so much.'

Being pitied like this is fair annoying. Still, I can't be angry with Jill. In spite of all the lousy things I said about Win and her baby, she never gave up on me.

'Jill, you've been good to me but, please, don't feel sorry for me,' I tell her. 'I don't want anyone looking at me and seeing "Victim" tattooed across my forehead, OK?'

'Sure.'

'So, how's Win doing?' I ask because I know she wants me to and it feels like a fair enough trade.

Jill hesitates. It's like she so wants to pour her heart out, but is half afraid I'll throw another wobbler.

'She's gone back to Dublin and Dad is, well, his old self again. Worse even. He won't talk to her because she refuses to chase up this married guy for maintenance. It's a mess.'

To my surprise, she leaves it at that and doesn't trouble the silence with sighs as she usually does.

'How's the show going?' I ask, feeling ridiculously nervous.

'It'll be better when you're back.'

'But I've been out so long. Hasn't Miss O'Neill given my part to someone else?'

'No . . . not yet. She said she'd wait until after the mid-term break.'

'She's feeling sorry for me too, I suppose.'

'Eala, the part is made for you.'

'Yeah, me being the sweet little drama queen and all.'

'Exactly,' she says and I laugh. 'Are you coming back to school on Monday, Eala? Say you are.'

'Yeah,' I said. 'I'm starting to miss accounting.'

I can't remember how long it's been since I had a conversation with Jill that didn't end in a row. It feels good not to be fighting any more. With Jill. With myself.

So I'm still in if I want to be. I slide down under the duvet for a while. I bathe myself in the kind of dreamy warmth I had forgotten existed and I get about sixty seconds of it before I hear Tom charge up the stairs. No one else can make so great a racket with so few limbs. He gets to my door. He's a ball of sweat, his curly hair a wet mop. His eyes are so wide it's like everywhere he looks he sees something amazing.

'P'ay football in Berni? P'ease?'

'Give me five minutes and I'll be there, OK?'

I get out of bed and pull the stale sheets off. I open down the top half of the window. The dust rises as I whip off each sheet. Tiny particles pepper the air and the breeze dances them.

33

Our school is on a height at the edge of town. On evenings like this, the sky above the town glows like the reflection from a golden bowl. It's one of those pure still evenings. Whatever cold there is, is the kind that makes you feel warm inside. I head over the brow of the railway bridge. Below, on the brightly lit platform, people wait to greet someone from the train or to leave. I cross over towards Friary Street. I could take a shorter way home, but I'm killing time. Mam's not talking to me or to Sean.

My first day back at school hasn't been half as cringe-worthy as I imagined it might be. I got the occasional funny look from some people. But only some and they're a waste of space anyway. Having Jill to hang around with helped. Being back at rehearsals did too. Derek or no Derek. I had to kiss him in the scene we rehearsed and it didn't bother me. At least he'd brushed his teeth.

I hung back after rehearsals and helped Miss O'Neill lock up the assembly hall. I had a favour to ask. On the last night of the show every year, a cheque is presented to some charity from the raffle takings. I asked if it could go to Head-Up this year.

'Absolutely,' she said and gave my arm a squeeze. 'You're a trooper, Eala.'

Then she was stuck for words, which is unusual for her. 'I'll get the lights for you,' I said and she nodded.

I flicked the bank of switches, one by one. The lights crackled and faded, the assembly hall growing steadily smaller until it vanished. Weird how the dark can seem so vast sometimes and, at others, small as the dark in a keyhole.

When I left Miss O'Neill, I found I had three missed calls on the mobile. Jill. Brian. Brian. Jill left a message. She'd had a row with Benno. They're meeting after Evening Study. 2 C IF THIS WAS REALLY MEANT TO BE. That's Jill for you. Romance is too bland without the taste of high drama. There was no message from Brian. I didn't know what to make of this. Then I decided not to make too much of it.

At Martin's house on Friary Street, the high timber gates are closed, but I peer in by the gap where the hinges hang. The street lamp on the opposite footpath lights the drive, the front lawn, the house, so big I used to think of it as a castle. Signs of the renovation work are everywhere. A JCB and a cement-mixer on the drive. A trellis of scaffolding on the front wall of the house. I wonder how long all this will take, how long before Mam is forced to make a final decision.

On the gate pier beside me, there's one of those intercoms with a keypad. I know the combination for opening the gate. Martin showed me long before I could even reach up to it. I remember Dad holding me up there too, pretending he didn't know the number as I pressed the keys, telling me I was a magician when the gates began to open in. And I really thought I was. But there's a big padlock on the gate these days and I'm not magician enough to unlock that. My phone rings. I don't even think not to answer it.

'Eala?'

'Well, Brian.'

'Are you all right?'

'I'm grand,' I say and I'm stuck. It's an impossible conversation. Too much to say or avoid saying, more like. I struggle on. 'And you?'

The line breaks up with blustery noises. He's outdoors somewhere, some wild place. His answer is lost. There's a breathy shuffling, a whistling and then a silence that doesn't get time to set in too thickly.

'Eala?'

'I lost you there. Where are you exactly?'

'Down in Cork,' he says. 'Down at that field I told you about. The Wet Field.'

'It sounds like a hurricane down there.'

I'm standing here on a quiet street in the pale orange light, but I'm out in the wilds of Cork too with the dusk descending around me, the wind blowing in my hair and whipping into my ears so loudly that I won't ever have to hear myself think again.

'Eala? Can you hear me? What I said?'

'No.'

'I love you, Eala.'

Until now, I haven't noticed how much my shoulder aches under the strap of this school bag. The wind rises again down in Cork.

'Can we give it another try?' he asks.

'After my big scene in your house? Who'd want to go out with such a weirdo?'

'Another weirdo, maybe?'

'Thanks a lot.'

'No, no, I was messing.'

'Me too,' I say.

The burn on my cheeks is a pleasant glow. I move away from the gates of Martin's house. Weird how the bag on my shoulder feels lighter when I walk.

'What are you doing in Cork anyway?'

'It's a long story. I won't bore you with the details, but I got a lot of stuff sorted. A lot of stuff.'

'The longer the better,' I say. 'I just want to hear you talking.'

'Well, it's kind of down to you, really, Eala. See, Dad went ballistic when he heard about your . . . your visit, like. So he's laying into me and I go ballistic too and I spit out the whole story about being in the car with Sham and all that. Then everything comes out and Mum's there like a referee letting him talk, letting me talk, calming us down when it gets too heavy. It's like this thing's been waiting for years to explode and nothing could get sorted until it did. I know what I'm going to do now.'

I'm heading down the Long Mall. Mrs Casey's shop is on the other side. The front door is bolted, but there's a weak light shining inside. I remember how she stood on our doorstep in that flimsy nightdress and I feel lousy for being so mean to her. She has nothing. I have something.

'Eala?'

'Yeah, I'm here. I'm nearly home.'

'We came down today to have a look round this college where they teach furniture-making. I've to decide between this one and another college up in Galway.'

'That sounds good.'

I'm at the turn into our road. There are no cars at the junction, but the traffic lights don't know that. They keep going green and amber and red until they're needed again.

'And we came out to visit Grandad's grave and called to some of the old neighbours,' Brian says. 'The folks are waiting back there for me. I better head on up.'

'Yeah, I'm home now anyway.'

'Listen, Eala,' he says. 'Have you heard about Trigger Healy?'

'No?'

'They caught him outside Nenagh yesterday with his supplier. Nabbed them doling out a load of cocaine. Plus, he took a swing at Dad and they got him for assault. They reckon he'll get five to seven years.'

I've stopped walking now and I'm at our front gate. Down in Cork, Brian seems to set off at the very moment I stop. I think of Trigger Healy sitting in a cell somewhere. Maybe I should be punching the air with delight, but I couldn't be bothered wasting the energy.

'You won't believe this, Eala,' Brian says. 'They put in a drainage system in the Wet Field last summer and it didn't flood this year. So the swans never came. I wonder where did they go?'

'Where's the nearest river?'

'About half a mile up this road.'

'That's where they'll be.'

'D'you reckon?'

'Somewhere nearby anyway.'

'Kind of sad, though, isn't it?'

'Not for the swans,' I tell him.

'Yeah,' he says and thinks about it, or that's what the quietening storm in the phone sounds like. 'So. We'll give it another shot, yeah?'

'We'll see how it goes, yeah.'

'Catch you later then.'

'Catch you later.'

I go in along our drive, skirt around by the side of the darkened half-basement window and in around to the Bernabéu. In by the kitchen window, I see Mam leaning against the worktop. She's got a plate in one hand, a fork in the other. She never sits at the table to eat these evenings and most of what's on the plate goes in the bin and it's on to the next job and the next. I try to anticipate what the next job might be and get it done in the hope that she'll slow down.

Last evening, she insisted on washing the kitchen floor even as we told her about that long-ago fight at the punk club and the court case and all of that. Sean did most of the talking and it didn't take very long really. We waited for her reaction, which took forever. All the while, we're retreating as she wields the mop and glances threateningly at our feet. In the end, we're stuck in a corner, afraid to step out on to the wet floor tiles. Then she starts on us.

'So he was always some kind of thug,' she said. 'Is that what you're implying here? That he's reverted to type since the accident?'

'We wanted you to understand why he found it so hard

to, you know, bring up his past,' Sean said. 'This has nothing to do with Jimmy. Jimmy can't help it when he flips.'

She tossed the mop into the plastic bucket of water. Filthy suds splashed up on to her skirt. I thought I could hear the sizzle of their popping bubbles, but that can't have been possible.

'I notice it's all Jimmy this and Jimmy that with you two now, isn't it? And not Dad, like it's always been.'

'Jimmy is not Dad,' I said.

I thought my heart would break when I came out with that, but it had to be said. The last leaf has to fall or winter will never end, is how I see it, is how it is. Mam wasn't impressed.

'You,' she said. Spat, more like. 'You frightened me half to death in the hospital. And you.' She rounded on Sean. 'Worrying me sick with your carry-on, hanging around the streets and drinking and God knows what else. And this is the thanks I get for trying to keep the show on the road, for trying to . . . to . . . What do you want? You want me to abandon him, is it?'

'It's not about what we want, Mam. It's about what Jimmy wants,' I said.

'What Jimmy wants? Jimmy wanted to play that stupid Wii game all day. He wanted to go play five-a-side with his old pals. For God's sake, Eala, he wanted to go and live in bloody Moravia. That's the whole point. He knows what he wants, but he doesn't know what's good for him.'

'He knows he's not happy living in this house, living with us,' Sean said. 'It's not his fault and it's not ours.'

She wandered around the kitchen like she'd reached the centre of a maze and couldn't find her way out. She passed by the cooker, talking to herself, not out loud, but you could see this big debate happening in her constantly changing expression. She stopped up, glanced back at the cooker like she'd copped something there. She tried the light switch in the cooker hood. It didn't work. It hadn't worked for years.

'Jesus H. Christ, how many times did I ask him to fix this?' she said. 'How many times? But no, no, of course, he didn't fix it. Tonight, tomorrow, next week. When I finish *The Flutterbyes*, when I finish Terry the Bloody Tank, when I . . .' She punched the underside of the cooker hood and punched it again. 'Bastard. Lying, secretive bastard.'

'He was always so good to us,' I say. 'Nothing can change that.'

She landed one more shot on the cooker hood. The rectangle of plastic covering the light fell on to the ceramic hob. It didn't damage the smooth glass-like surface, but the skin along Mam's knuckles was torn. Stupid things came into my head to say. *Would you like a cup of tea, Mam, a glass of wine? I'll get a bulb for the cooker hood tomorrow, Mam. Why don't we go into the sitting room and light a fire and watch some TV, Mam?* But she'd left us standing there and gone upstairs before I could get a word past the lump in my throat.

Out here in the Bernabéu, I look up at the moon. It's a sliver away from being a full moon. The light from the kitchen window forms a long rectangle on the grass. At its centre a white plastic football lies like something waiting to happen.

34

'Well, Jimmy.'

'Awright?'

'I missed you.'

He's had a haircut, tidy but not too tight. He wears a silvery grey shirt over a Real Madrid T-shirt. I kiss him on the cheek and hold him tight. He doesn't exactly resist, but it's like he's waiting for the embrace to end. He sits down on the sofa and fishes a stringy piece of tissue from his pocket. He's raising it towards his cheek, but hesitates.

'Judy's told me you've had the flu,' he says. 'I hope you haven't passed it on to me now.'

'Course she hasn't,' Mam says. 'She's well over it.'

He changes his mind about wiping my kiss away and puts the tissue back in his pocket. He sighs, distracted by some thought. A wide yawn brings him back to us. To me.

'You've got well skinny, you know that?'

'Thanks, Jimmy, I'll take that as a compliment.'

Sean's laughter is nervous and an octave too high. Tom is laughing at Sean's laugh. Mam and me are smiling hysterically. The TV isn't on, but Jimmy prefers to look at it than at us. There's no fire in the grate, only ashes. We calm down, embarrassed for each other and everyone makes a move at the same time.

'Right then,' Mam says. 'Let's get some dinner going.'

'I've a new DVD for you, Jimmy,' Sean says. '*Avatar*, did you see it yet?'

'No.'

'I'll go get it then.'

'Want a wee-wee! Wee-wee, quick!' Tom pipes up.

'I'll take you,' I say. Unlike the others I didn't have a plan when I started moving. 'Hold on to it, OK?'

I'm halfway up the stairs with Tom in my arms before I realize we've left Jimmy alone in the sitting room. Raised voices suddenly fill up the stairwell. He's turned on the TV. The volume goes down a few notches. The disconnected noises of channel-hopping start up. Fragments of music, talk, cartoon sound effects like broken memories. Nothing he wants to linger on.

'Huwwy, huwwy!' Tom pleads and I quicken my steps.

We make it just in time. There's a long mirror on the airing-cupboard door directly opposite the toilet. It's too weird and always makes me want to hurry when I sit on the pot, but Tom loves to watch himself pee and usually laughs his head off. Today he doesn't look in the mirror.

'Jimmy sad,' he says.

'He's tired is all,' I tell him, but he's not convinced.

We head back down to see if Mam wants some help in the kitchen. In the sitting room, they've started to watch *Avatar*. Tom joins them. I find Mam standing by the worktop near the kitchen sink. She's got a carrot in one hand and a vegetable peeler in the other. Neither hand is moving. There's nothing to stare at along this bare stretch of wall, but she stares anyway. She looks pure weary after the drive down from Dublin.

'Will I wash some potatoes?' I ask and she stirs herself.

'Yeah,' she says. She brushes the fringe from her eyes with the back of her hand. 'He looks lovely, doesn't he? The shirt and all. I can't remember the last time I saw him in a shirt.'

She continues to peel the carrots. She used to have this knack of peeling off long, perfectly unbroken shavings. When I was a kid it drove me crazy when I'd try and fail to do the same. 'Your hands aren't patient enough yet,' she'd tell me. But her hands work erratically now. Short strips are scattered out and beyond the chopping board and half the skin is left on the carrots.

'Insisted on buying a new shirt,' Mam says. 'And when I asked him what colour he wanted, he says he'll know when he sees it. I think it's because of that old black and white newspaper photograph of his father. The shirt he's wearing might be blue or green maybe, but it looks a powdery grey.'

The table is set. She's slicing the carrots now and I wish she'd pay more attention to the knife that strays too close to her fingers as she daydreams.

'He looks . . . What's the word I'm looking for?' she says. 'More mature somehow.'

'Will I finish cutting those carrots for you?' I say because I can't bear to hear the hope in her voice.

'Go on in and watch the film,' she says. 'I'll get the stew going and follow you in.'

'Are you sure?'

She nods and goes back to cutting the carrots, chopping

so hard that the toaster on the granite counter rattles. The metallic shiver grates on my brain as I leave the kitchen. In the sitting room, Jimmy's slouched back in the armchair. He doesn't look up when I come in. His eyes are fixed on the TV, but he's not focused on it. Tom sits on the floor by his feet holding on tight to the kiddie's football we bought for him. I sit on the sofa beside Sean. We glance at one another and the glance holds for a few seconds. I don't know what it is we're saying to each other. Jimmy pulls in a long, tired breath. I wonder if he's back there again in the houseboat, waiting for the madness to start.

Sean called over to Martin's apartment last week to collect the file. There were photocopies of the fake black-market birth cert and the real one, newspaper cuttings of the inquest in 1974 and the trial in 1982. When I first saw the front-page photo of Thierry and Cath, I was perplexed. He didn't look especially like Zidane. Tall, yes, but gaunt and lank-framed with this big, late-sixties Afro hairstyle. The closest resemblance was in the eyes. Something dark and beautiful and inscrutable about them. Alongside him, Cath seemed tiny and you could see that she'd once been very pretty, but the light had already left her downcast eyes and her blonde hair fell in ratty strings.

Jimmy yawns and yawns. I think of the terrors he's endured. The constant fear his paranoid parents instilled in him, the horror of that night when they crashed and burned. I think of the weirdness of having his name changed so often as a kid. The double weirdness of having to take on yet another identity so that his years in prison wouldn't come against him. I think it's a miracle that he held it together all these years and never allowed a trace of bitterness or anger with the world to poison our lives. Who needs superheroes when you've had a man like that for a father?

No one's watching *Avatar* now. Jimmy's eyes have closed. Tom is sleepy too. Sean looks out by the bay window as the daylight fades. There's no sound from the kitchen, but Mam's still out there. Jimmy stirs again. He sits forward abruptly. He fingers his watch in that agitated way of his.

'Are you all right, Jimmy?' Sean asks and looks out the window again like something out there's bothering him.

'I'm fucking not,' he says and Tom points up at him, shaking his head. 'Fuck off, Tom.'

'Fucky, Jimmy,' Tom says and makes a run for the door, but I catch him.

'It's OK, Tom,' I tell him. 'Jimmy's only joking. We won't say that bold word any more, right?'

Suddenly Jimmy's tearful. He's staring at Tom's frightened smile. Mam's at the open doorway. She's got a tea towel wrapped tightly around her fist. The other fist is pressed to her temple.

'Is the film good?' she asks.

'It's rubbish,' Dad says. He stands up too quickly. His eyes do a kind of dizzy swivel. His spread fingers float down on to the arm of the sofa to keep him steady. 'Alan doesn't have to move to Limerick. He'll be living in the new Head-Up house in town, so why can't I?'

'We talked about this on the drive down,' Mam says. She's so pale that the redness about her eyes is like some weird mascara. Tom starts bawling.

'You talked,' Dad says. 'But you didn't listen.'

I try to calm Tom down, but it's Mam he wants. He goes to her. She doesn't sweep him up into her arms. Sean's looking out the window again. Maybe looking at the reflection of this stand-off in the glass makes it seem less real.

'This is your house, Jimmy,' Mam says. 'We're your family. Not Alan.'

'I told you I didn't want to come back here. I get a pain,' he jabs himself so hard in the stomach it hurts me. 'Every time I come into this house, I get a pain in here. And in my head. I don't belong in this house. I don't know why, but it upsets me. It makes me feel . . .' A grimace of desperation collapses his face. 'Like a fool, like I can't do anything right, like I'm . . . trouble. When I'm not here, do you fight and argue all the time? Do you? Do you?'

The front doorbell rings. Sean's off the sofa and tearing past me in an instant and it's like I'm sucked along in his slipstream because I don't know why I'm following him. He snaps the front door open. Clem Healy looks up at us from under his hoodie. He's scared. He keeps glancing back over his shoulder. His lower lip trembles as though he's about to burst out crying.

'What do you want?' Sean asks.

'Can I come in?'

He wipes his runny nose on his sleeve and hops from one foot to the other. I wonder if he's been sniffing some of his father's wares. Maybe not. His eyes aren't wild enough. Pathetically sad, more like. He's got his MP3 player in his fist like it's his only possession in the world.

'Can I talk to Mr Summerton?'

'How did you know he was here? How long have you been watching the house?'

'A few days only. Was he away somewhere?'

Sean's trying hard to keep his fists to himself, but I can see it's tearing him apart. Clem looks beyond us. From the end of the hallway, Mam stares in disbelief at the kid who shattered our lives. Clem's hoodie drops back, exposing his scraggily shaved head and his scrawny neck. It seems like he's decided I'm the only one who'll listen to him. He holds up the MP3 player towards me.

'I couldn't come when my da was around,' he tells me. 'Mr Summerton owns this. I should'a brought it before. I wanted to.'

The cold of the evening has drifted into the hallway. I take the MP3 player from Clem. His head goes down. There's a crack along the screen and one of the earphones looks like it's been stepped on. Sean takes the player from my hand and checks out the damage. He tries switching it on, but nothing happens. It seems almost silly to me now, but I still feel sad that we'll never know the last song he heard.

'Get out of here, Clem,' Sean says.

The kid shrinks away from him. But, no, it's not Sean he's shrinking away from. Jimmy's followed us out from the sitting room. I'm sure he doesn't know who Clem is, but he's wary of him all the same. Mam steps forward to the door, ready to close it.

'You should go,' she tells Clem, but he's watching Jimmy and he's going all weepy again.

'I'm awful sorry, Mr Summerton,' he says.

'Sorry for what?' Jimmy says and comes closer.

'For hurting you.'

'It was you? It was you that messed up my head?'

Mam's trying to ease the door to a close, but Jimmy makes a sudden lunge and slaps Clem across the face. The kid doesn't back off. He waits for the next blow like he's learned not to bother trying to escape punishment. Jimmy throws another swipe, but Sean catches his arm.

'Leave it, Jimmy,' he pleads. 'He's not worth it.'

The tears are flowing down Clem's cheeks now. He makes strange hegging sounds as he struggles to hold in the cries he's bottled up inside maybe all his short, unhappy life. Jimmy tries to break free of Sean. Tom comes running out of the sitting room with his football under his arm and stops dead when he sees them push and shove against one another. He's holding himself like he needs to go to the toilet.

'I'n afwaid,' he cries.

Jimmy gives up the fight. He looks down at Tom and reaches out to touch him. Tom flinches, but he doesn't run to Mam or to me. He doesn't know what to do. His eyes are big with yearning like the eyes of starving children. And I realize Mam has that look too. All of us do. Even this stuttering mess of a kid on our doorstep.

'Do you have anyone at home with you now?' she asks him as she picks up Tom and comforts him.

'No. Sham done a runner after Da got done,' he says. 'Mam might come back, though.'

'Do you have any idea where she lives now?'

He shakes his head. Jimmy has retreated to the stairs leading down to his room.

'We'll find her,' Mam says as she rocks Tom in her arms. 'Go on home now.'

'Thanks, missus.'

'I shouldn't have hit him,' Jimmy says and Sean goes back along the hallway to him.

'It's OK, Jimmy,' he says. 'You didn't hurt him. He didn't hurt you, did he, Clem?'

'No, I'm fine, not a bother on me.'

'I should've removed myself from the situation,' Jimmy says. The words, rolling off his tongue like he's practised them over and again, catch all of us by surprise. 'That's what I've got to learn, Dr Reid said. When under stress, remove yourself from the situation, find a quiet place to sit and . . . and . . . something else . . .'

He's ringing beeps on his watch and the sound doesn't freak me, only makes me grieve. He turns away and disappears from view down the stairs to his room. Clem should disappear too, but he doesn't have the sense to.

'I done good, didn't I?' he asks of Mam.

She doesn't answer him. From the rest of us, he chooses me again.

'Didn't I?'

'Yeah,' I say. 'Yeah, you did.'

Clem heads down the granite steps. As he reaches the bottom and I'm about to close the door, he stoops down and gathers up Tom's green tractor. He flicks the front wheels and watches them spin. He flicks them again. He looks up at me and smiles sheepishly. We meet halfway on the steps and he hands over the tractor.

'Eala?' Sean calls from above. 'Everything OK, Eala?'

'Yeah, no sweat.'

Clem's staring at me, wide-eyed with puzzlement.

'I didn't know your name was Eala,' he says. 'I didn't even know Eala was a name.' He looks away to his left. You can't see the junction where the accident happened from here and yet, somehow, I sense he's picturing it in his mind. I've no idea where this is going, but I know it's going somewhere that matters.

'Eala is the Irish for swan,' I tell him.

'He was trying to get up off the ground and I was holding his head together and telling him, "Don't move; don't be moving." But he kept trying and he kept saying, "Eala's singing tonight, Eala's singing tonight." I didn't know what he meant. Then he passed out and a woman came along and she was shouting, "It was your fault, I seen you!" and I done a runner.'

I can't speak and Clem thinks I'm blanking him out of contempt.

'It wasn't my fault, Eala,' he says. 'Sham was following me cos I sold some gear too cheap. I got the prices mixed up, like. "Fifteen," I said. Fifty it was.'

Still I can't speak and Clem turns away. When he reaches the street, he glances back. I raise a hand and get back a tentative wave. I climb the steps to the front door in a pure daze. With each upward step, I'm telling myself that I was the last thought on Dad's mind and it's the kind of little girl's secret I never imagined I'd have again, the kind I'll always keep.

Mam and Sean haven't moved from the hallway. Now all three of us stand here. Me by the front door, Sean at the sitting-room door, Mam at the head of the half-basement stairs. Tom's head rests on her shoulder, his eyes closed. He's taking deep breaths of Mam's aroma and carrying it into sleep with him.

I want to go down to Jimmy. Sean glances worriedly towards the stairs and I know he does too. But all of us know it's Mam who needs to go down there and know how she must decide. The haunting, almost human wail of a cat reaches us from the dark outside. I go to Mam and raise my arms to take Tom from her. Time falls on to my hands, each second heavier than the one before. She lays Tom on my shoulder and heads downstairs. I hear the door open below, her soft call.

'Jimmy?' There's no answer. 'Jimmy? Where –'

I hear her footsteps cross the room, the catch of the toilet door, a punched-breath shout.

'Lads! He's gone! He's gone!'

35

The kitchen is less crowded, quieter. It's quarter to five in the morning and we're waiting for first light so we can go searching again. Mam sits at the head of the table and I sit beside her. She's got the cordless house phone in her hand. We both stare at the tablecloth like we're expecting some kind of map to appear on the blank white linen. There are four other chairs at the table, but no one else sits. Keeping their distance from Mam, I suppose, but she hasn't erupted for a good half-hour now. We've all been at the receiving end. Starsky too when he was here earlier. In fairness, he took it well. Brian was standing over by the sink with Sean, not knowing where to look. He's still there.

'I've got every squad car I could muster out on the roads,' he told her. 'And we're going through every lane, every vacant house in the town, the industrial estates and –'

'So what are you doing sitting here?' Mam said. 'What are we doing sitting here?'

'We can't organize search parties until morning, Judy.'

'But it's so cold out there,' she cried. 'Don't you realize how bloody cold it is out there?'

And it is cold. Minus two, the temperature indicator showed

when I was out in the Mercedes earlier with Martin. We drove over to the house on Friary Street. Martin used a wrench to break the padlock on the gate. No, *demolish* the padlock. He kicked in the front door when he realized his key didn't fit any more and we listened to one another's bellowing echoes in the empty rooms long after there was any point to it.

Then we went out to the golf club because the River Walk ends there. He swept the velvety green course with his headlights from the car park. He swept it again from a gate at the other end of the course. I should have known it was a pure waste of time, but I suppose you do these things because you can't think of what else to do and you have to keep on the move.

Sean and Brian met up with Starsky at the Head-Up Centre prefab, but had no luck there or in the old dance hall alongside. They drove slowly along the road that leads out to Alan's house in Borris, talked to Peter Foran and searched the fields around the house with him. Nothing. It was getting harder to believe that Mam was wrong about the river. She'd spent the last few hours going up and down both banks with Fiona and a couple of Guards until, eventually, they persuaded her to come home.

Back at the house, we'd all carried the cold inside with us on our breaths. The heating wasn't on and none of us thought to go to the switch in the utility room. Fiona made coffee and no one drank it.

Since Starsky and the other Guards left, barely a word has been spoken except in brief, whispered conversations. We all manage to contain our unease somehow or other until Martin blurts out,

'Is there somewhere we haven't thought of?'

Mam rounds on him. I don't want to look at him suffering her wrath, but I can't help it. I hadn't realized until now that he's been wearing a short-sleeved summer shirt all this time and is shaking uncontrollably. He's a pure wreck. I ask myself why I'm not in the same state. I ask, but I don't have an answer.

'Haven't you done enough damage already, Martin?' Mam says.

'Judy,' Fiona Sheedy says. 'That isn't fair. I know you're –'

'And you too. None of this would've happened if he hadn't set his heart on that house, that ridiculous fantasy.'

'It's not fantasy, Judy,' Fiona insists. 'It's independent living, a chance to regain a sense of self-worth, to relearn boundaries, all of that. And hope too.'

Mam's not having any of it.

'You and your bloody psychobabble. Boundaries, self-worth, independent living. I'm sick of hearing all that crap. I've been using the same stupid psychobabble with my clients all these years. And where has it got any of them? What kind of lives have they got? What kind of life can Jimmy ever have outside these four walls?'

Fiona sets down the coffee mug she's been nursing at the worktop and approaches the table. Mam's hostile look doesn't work on her and she sits down. I suppose she's seen a thousand looks like that. Including mine. But I'm with her this time, hoping she'll find the right things to say.

'Jimmy's already living his own life, Judy. He has been for months now. The Head-Up Centre, new friends, new interests, new hopes. You've seen him up there, how relaxed he can be, how helpful he is to everyone, how popular he is.'

'And this is where it's led,' Mam says. 'The river.'

'He's not in the river,' Martin puts in. He comes halfway across from the breakfast counter and stops like he's forgotten where he's going. His trousers sag from his thin frame, his black shoes are covered in mud. *Poor little rich man*, I'm thinking. 'No way. No way is he in the river . . . because . . . because he can't be.'

It's a pretty lousy effort at reassurance and he knows it and Mam does too. She turns towards him. This is Judy's *hauteur*, but infinitely more poisonous.

'Are you getting some kind of tax break for giving the house to Head-Up?' she asks him. 'Is that your game?'

'Ah, jeez, Mam,' Sean says, but Martin raises his hand. 'Let her beat me up,' he seems to be saying.

'Well, after all,' Mam goes on, 'you couldn't sell that house now if you wanted to, could you, Martin? Nobody's buying with this recession going on, right? So you might as well cut your losses, get a tax break for handing it over to a charity. Plus you get the bonus of acting like your only concern all your miserable little life hasn't been money, money, money, yeah?'

Grief makes wounded animals of us. I already knew that in spades. But wounded animals can cut you to pieces. Especially if you stand there and take it, which is what Martin does. Fiona is smarting too and though she holds back, the effort shows. She's not the psychologist now. She's a woman watching her partner get a hammering he doesn't deserve.

'If it wasn't for the likes of you and all the other greedy little bastards wanting more and more, this country, this whole bloody world, wouldn't be in –' Mam's running out of steam, losing track of whatever argument she had in mind. 'We wouldn't be in this awful, this impossible mess . . . we'd have a decent society, a decent health service . . . we'd have kids like Clem Healy off the streets and getting the chances they deserve . . . We wouldn't have to depend on the charity of rich little shits to take care of our . . . our . . .'

Martin waits until the silence belongs to him and then he speaks very quietly.

'Judy, listen. The Head-Up people were fundraising for a house here long before I got involved, long before Jimmy had the accident. I was able to make it happen more quickly and I was glad to. That's all. And yeah, maybe money was my god for too long, but at least I have something to give.' He falters. 'Something to give the best friend I ever had and that I miss like . . . like I miss Angie . . . More even. More than I miss my own child, Judy.'

There's maybe ten feet between Mam and Martin, but it's like they're looking at one another across all the years, all the way back to when they were teenagers in love and all the way forward through the good times and the bad times and the worst times that have brought them to this exhausted early morning. Mam lowers her elbows on to the table and holds her head in her hands.

'Eala,' she says. 'Find a sweater for Martin. He's freezing. And turn on the heating.'

I'm glad to have something to do. Fiona gets up from the table too and goes to Martin. She wraps her arms round him and his head dips on to her shoulder and stays there. Brian glances at me as I go by. Worried for me, but trying to make a smile of it and I return the favour. I wish I could hold him now, but that will have to wait. I head into the utility room and flick the heating switch. The burner kicks into action and settles into a steady roar like a far storm. I head upstairs.

The darkness is a relief from the scrape of raw light on my eyes this past hour. I stop halfway up the stairs, press my fingers into my closed eyelids until the stars come. I go on. Sean's room is in its usual chaotic state. Half of his clothes are on the floor, which in a weird way makes it easier to find a sweater for Martin. I take a peek in at my own bed where Tom sleeps with the fingers of one hand tangled in Jill's hair and the fingers of the other resting on his little football. Jill doesn't stir. I don't know how she got him to sleep with all the panic earlier on. I owe her big time.

At the door of Dad's workroom, I hesitate. It's slightly ajar, which is unusual. Then I remember that we checked all the rooms earlier and probably left it open in our hurry. At least, whoever checked it, Mam or Sean, did. I looked through the first-floor rooms, not the ones on this landing. This would be too weird, Dad hiding in there all this time. My heart thumps as I push on the door. I turn on the light. It blinds me for a few seconds.

The workroom is perfectly tidy again. Books on their shelves, the drawing blocks stacked away, a new sheet pinned to the drawing board, the Timberland peaked cap straightened on the mannequin's head. Everything awaits his return. And, of course, there's nowhere to hide in this room. You're either here or you're not and he isn't and never will be again.

I go and sit on the revolving high chair. *Give me a spin, Daddy, I promise I won't get dizzy.* I close my eyes and set myself in motion. Round and round I go, swirling onwards and upwards into a darkness that's not fearful because, out at its far edge, I sense his calm presence and know that I'll never fall as long as I never forget he's there, always there. Round and round I go. *Dad, don't let Jimmy do anything foolish; don't let him be cold or afraid out there; don't let him be hurt or broken any more than he already is; don't let him hide himself from us.* I slow down to a stop and wait for my whirling brain to catch up with me.

Something has changed. The air feels vivid and, outside, the dawn chorus has started up. The birds are going crazy with excitement and it's like they're these beautiful creatures with no memory and every new day is such a blast for them and every new sky such a vastness of light, they can't help singing. When I turn off the drawing-board lamp in Dad's workroom and look out the window, night has begun to give way to day.

I head back down to the kitchen. Everyone's in exactly the same position as when I left, which seems impossible because it feels like I've been gone for ages. Not everyone. Brian's gone. Sean sees my disappointment. He makes a cigarette-smoking gesture and nods at the back door. I wish Brian didn't smoke, but you can't have everything, I suppose. Martin and Fiona let go of one another. I give him the sweater and he pulls it on. It's a few sizes too big for him and he gives Fiona a wry smile.

'I'll do some breakfast,' she says and reaches for the kettle on the worktop.

'Let me,' he says. 'You shouldn't be on your feet so much.'

Some instinct draws my eyes to her stomach. No major bulge or anything, but I give her a questioning look anyway and she nods. I'm glad for them.

'Is there a toaster?' Martin asks me. He's got some colour back on his cheeks. Quite a lot, actually. 'We should eat.'

I fish out the toaster from the press by the cooker, the bread from the silver bin. *No matter what kind of day it's going to be*, I'm thinking, *you have to get ready for it*. I wash the coffee mugs. The hot water stings the chill pleasantly from my hands. It's all so weirdly ordinary, this busy but hushed beginning to a new day.

The back door creaks inward. The shock of cold lingers on Brian's face like stunned surprise. No, it is stunned surprise. I smell the smoke and realize the cigarette is still between his fingers though he's stepped inside.

'What?' I say.

'Jimmy's next door. I saw him passing by one of the upstairs windows.' He cops on to the cigarette in his hand and looks at me apologetically. 'The back door is open out there. I saw it from the wall.'

Chairs scrape back. Mam and Sean and me are on the same wavelength, but it doesn't help us move any more quickly. Each of us sick to the stomach, knowing how Jimmy had come to loathe Mrs Casey. Each of us petrified.

'Do you want me to go?' Martin asks.

'No,' Mam says too sharply and softens her refusal. 'No, I'll go. It's OK. Everything will be OK.'

'I'll get in by the back door,' Sean tells her. 'And let you in the front.'

She nods and we unfreeze ourselves. I follow as she heads out to the hallway. I feel Brian's hand on my shoulder as Mam reaches the front door.

'Do you want me to come with you?' he whispers.

'Better not,' I say. 'Ring your dad. Tell him . . . tell him he should come over.'

'Are you all right?'

'I've no choice, Brian. I have to be.'

I run to catch up with Mam. She's already climbing the steps up to Mrs Casey's door when I get outside. There's a plastic message bag hanging from the doorknob. From the pebbles of our drive to the roof of Mrs Casey's house, the waking world is frosted over, but I hurry through it without slipping or sliding. Sean lets Mam inside as I reach the foot of the steps. I hear her calling. Her voice is coaxing, forgiving.

'Jimmy?'

I walk into the answering silence. I've never been inside Mrs Casey's house before. It's a mirror image of ours, but feels older, much older. Dark brown with age it is. The doors, the wallpaper, the carpet on the stairs. And the smell is ancient too. Not unclean, but stale, heavy with dust. Sean is treading softly from door to door along the hall. He turns to Mam and shakes his head. She begins to mount the stairs. We hear the click of a light switch from the room straight ahead of us on the first landing. I'm a few steps behind Mam. I can see the clench of her calf muscles as she climbs, though she moves as gracefully as ever.

'It's all right, Jimmy,' Mam says, her voice firm but gentle. 'It's me. Judy.'

On the landing we gather. There's not a sound from inside the room. Mam tries the doorhandle. I expect it to be locked or blocked in some way, but it's not. I can't look and Sean can't either.

'What are you doing here, Jimmy?' Mam whispers and his answer's a whisper I don't catch.

Mam goes inside and, at first, I don't see him, I see Mrs Casey. Her head tiny on the pillow. Her eyes closed, her mouth open, no rise and fall of breath in her. Dolls never grow old, but if they did, they'd look like this. Mam moves closer to the bed and now I see him. Sitting on the side of the bed, his shoulders hunched, holding Mrs Casey's hand.

'What's the story, Jimmy?' Sean asks, too much anxiety in his voice to keep it at a whisper.

Mrs Casey stirs, makes troubled dream noises. As her face moves on the pillow, I see the bruise on her right cheekbone, a purple blush. She settles again. Jimmy stretches his neck and rubs it with his free hand. He's pure jaded, slow lids battle the tiredness in his eyes.

'Every time I let go of her hand, she bloody wakes up,' he says. 'She won't let me get the doctor.'

Mam releases his hand and takes his place. She's checking Mrs Casey's pulse.

'Why does she need the doctor, Jimmy?' she asks.

He's sidling away further along the bed, trying to squeeze the life back into his hand.

'She's had a fall,' he says. 'I found her at the back door and I had to carry her up here. She wouldn't let me call the doctor. She wanted to put on her face, but she was crying so much, the make-up got washed away every time she tried. The police aren't going to nab me, are they?'

'Why would they want to nab you?' Mam says. 'You haven't done anything wrong, have you?'

'No,' he says. 'I don't think so.'

'What brought you out here, Jimmy?' I ask.

'When I went out in the garden, I heard her crying. Didn't you?'

Across from the end of the bed stands a tall chest of drawers. Along the top, there's nine or ten framed photos. Old sepias of a wedding day, a young couple sitting on a tartan blanket at a beach, a night of formal dress, him in his dickie bow, her in her tiara. All the other photos are of him. Getting a few years older before the photos stop.

'Sean,' Mam says. 'Go and ring the hospital.'

'But she's not ready,' Jimmy says. 'She'll get well thick with you, Judy.'

'We'll get her ready,' Mam says.

She takes her hand from Mrs Casey's, feels the old woman's forehead, lifts the blanket a little to look along those frail bones for further damage. There's a small patch of blood on the nightdress near the hip. From outside on the landing comes Sean's voice, low and urgent. Mrs Casey wakes. She looks at Mam, confused at first, then frightened. Her gaze flits by me like I don't exist and fixes on Jimmy. Her eyes light up.

'Raymond,' she says.

'Oh, bloody 'ell,' Jimmy groans softly. 'She's off again.'

He doesn't look at all like the fair-haired man in the

photos. He's uncomfortable now because Mam's gazing at him too. Love looks the same on every face, no matter how young or old that face is. Pain too.

'Raymond asked me to fix you up for the doctor,' Mam says. 'We want you looking your best, all right?'

She cleans Mrs Casey's face with the moist tissues and finds some eye shadow on the bedside table. I can't believe how steady her hands are, how composed she is. When Mrs Casey closes her eyelids for the eye shadow, they stay closed, and before very long we hear footsteps on the stairs and we have to leave her to the ambulance crew in their yellow Day-Glo jackets and the nurse with her blue cardigan pulled tightly about her against the cold.

From the top of Mrs Casey's steps we see a squad car parked behind the ambulance. Brian leans in by the side window talking to Starsky.

'You told me I wasn't going to get nicked, Judy,' Jimmy says accusingly, but she links his arm, gets him moving again.

'They've come to help Mrs Casey,' she says.

'She needs help an' all,' he says. 'I told her who I was, but she wouldn't believe me. Who's Raymond anyway?'

'Someone she used to know,' I tell him.

On the footpath, they walk ahead of Sean and me. Mam's trying to fall into step with him, but it's not easy with that foot of his dragging every few paces, and it almost looks like he's yanking her along, though not roughly. Brian and Starsky greet him, but he just nods and gets by as quickly as he can.

Sean hangs back, talking to Brian and to Starsky, explaining what's happened, I suppose. I catch up with Mam and Jimmy on our drive. Martin's Mercedes is still parked there and they've stopped alongside it. They look beyond me to Mrs Casey's house. The ambulance crew carries the metal stretcher down the steps over there. The cold creeps in around us. Wedding-day cold.

'Do you really mean it when you say I can move into the Head-Up house?' he asks her. 'Say you do. Please, Judy.'

'I do.'

36

I don't know what this mad rush is about; maybe it's the adrenalin still pumping through me, but I'm in such a hurry to get out of the dressing room, I don't bother to wipe off the heavy gunge of stage make-up. I've wasted enough time already changing from my costume. Jill grabs me in one of her dramatic hugs. There are tears and whispers, but I can't hear her words among the shrieks and the squeals. I break away from her, all smiles and see you tomorrow but, of course, she can't hear me either so we laugh instead and I head through the crowd and it's more smiles and more words I can't hear, but I answer anyway. 'Yeah.' 'Brilliant.' 'Sorry.' 'Gas, wasn't it?' 'Sorry.' 'Thanks.' 'Can I squeeze by?' 'Thanks.' 'Thanks.'

Outside the door, some of the younger guys are doing high fives and shoulder slams and trying to push one another into our dressing room. I make it down the stairs to the assembly hall corridor and it's jam-packed with people. I can't see Mam and Jimmy among the first-night throng. *They'll have gone outside to wait*, I'm thinking, *because all this noise will have freaked Jimmy out.*

There's no short cut to the exit so I have to plough on through. Faces I know and faces I don't know pop up before me and I try to be polite and swap a word or two, but it's all starting to feel a bit weird. The make-up feels like it's congealed in the shape of a mad, laughing mask that I can't undo. I don't like the way my heart is racing because I don't want my brain to go racing after it. I'm still less than halfway along the corridor. I think. Everyone in the corridor seems to be at least a foot taller than me and it's so hot in here, I can hardly catch a breath.

Someone takes my arm and we start to shoot forward. Brian. Sean's with him. They're not as polite as I am as they push through, but I keep the head down and pretend I don't notice. We get to the exit and Brian swings the door open for me. The breeze touches my cheeks and I can breathe again.

'They're waiting for you over at the front gate,' he says. 'You were class, man.'

Sean lays his arm across my shoulder and gives me a squeeze.

'Great stuff, Eala,' he says and releases me.

Brian touches my arm. I wish I didn't have to go, but I do. I nod towards the front gate.

'They'll be getting cold. I'll ring you later, OK, Brian?'

He gives me a quick, half-embarrassed kiss on the cheek as the crowd mills past us.

'Yeah, no sweat,' he says.

I can't stop myself from breaking into a half-trot as I go out along the school avenue. I've never felt so happy nor ever felt so sad. Running helps me keep some kind of balance between the two. The ground lamps lighting up the trees on either side of the avenue make it seem like I'm still on stage. I glide by a few groups of slow-walking smokers and, at last, the front gate is in sight. Mam's there under the light globe of the high pier. I get a quick glimpse of Jimmy before he ducks into the shadows. Mam's arms open even as I falter, my legs gone to jelly. She holds me and I bury my face in her coat collar.

'You were so good, Eala. I'm so proud of you.'

'It was the hardest thing I ever had to do, Mam, the hardest thing,' I tell her and the pain of kneeling centre stage and singing that last chorus of 'Somewhere' sweeps across me. It didn't matter that it was Derek's head in my lap. It wasn't him I was singing for anyway.

'I know, love, I know,' she says. 'But you did it and you did it in style.'

'Will you be OK when he's gone, Mam?'

'I'll be fine, Eala,' she says. 'We'll all be fine. Jimmy too.'

The avenue is filling up with people. We let one another go and Jimmy's appeared again. He looks so nice in the grey shirt and new tweed jacket Mam bought for him. He's staring at me like he can't remember who I am.

'Well, Jimmy,' I say.

An uncertain smile flickers across his face as he studies me. He looks away, looks at me again. And suddenly I cop what it is that makes him so hesitant. I must seem pure weird out here in the night with this stage make-up plastered all over my face.

'You look different,' he says. 'Older.' His gaze drifts upwards towards the tops of the budding trees that line the school avenue and then comes back to me. 'You've got the loveliest voice, Eala.'

He just wanted a decent book to read ...

Not too much to ask, is it? It was in 1935 when Allen Lane, Managing Director of Bodley Head Publishers, stood on a platform at Exeter railway station looking for something good to read on his journey back to London. His choice was limited to popular magazines and poor-quality paperbacks – the same choice faced every day by the vast majority of readers, few of whom could afford hardbacks. Lane's disappointment and subsequent anger at the range of books generally available led him to found a company – and change the world.

'We believed in the existence in this country of a vast reading public for intelligent books at a low price, and staked everything on it'
Sir Allen Lane, 1902–1970, founder of Penguin Books

The quality paperback had arrived – and not just in bookshops. Lane was adamant that his Penguins should appear in chain stores and tobacconists, and should cost no more than a packet of cigarettes.

Reading habits (and cigarette prices) have changed since 1935, but Penguin still believes in publishing the best books for everybody to enjoy. We still believe that good design costs no more than bad design, and we still believe that quality books published passionately and responsibly make the world a better place.

So wherever you see the little bird – whether it's on a piece of prize-winning literary fiction or a celebrity autobiography, political tour de force or historical masterpiece, a serial-killer thriller, reference book, world classic or a piece of pure escapism – you can bet that it represents the very best that the genre has to offer.

Whatever you like to read – trust Penguin.